Covens and Curses

K. Malady

To water, for keeping me hydrated, and to sleep, for being that elusive friend who never returns my calls. May this book serve as a reminder to drink more, stress less, and maybe—just maybe—catch a nap once in a while. (Written on behalf of Emily and the author, who are both running on caffeine and sheer willpower.)

Also By

THE ASCEND TRIALS
YA fantasy romance adventure
IF THE WALLS FALL (Book 1)
WHEN WALLS RISE (Book 2)
WHILE STONES TURN (Book 3, upcoming)

THE HARMONY CHRONICLES
NA paranormal romance/contemporary fantasy
A STAR'S HIDDEN FIRE (Book 1)
A BONE INTERRED (Book 2, upcoming)

THREADS OF FATE
NA/Adult romantic fantasy retellings
THREADED SECRETS (Book 1)THREADED DES-
TINY (Book 2, upcoming)

KNEELING KINGDOMS
Adult interconnected standalone romantasy
A KINGDOM TO REMEMBER (Book 1)
A KINGDOM TO PROTECT (Book 2, upcoming)

<u>WELCOME TO THE TROPE-ICS</u>
Sweet and spicy standalone romantasy novellas in an interconnected world
Coming Jan. 2025

Chapter 1

The polished brass nameplate on the door to my corner office gleams as I flick off the lights—'Emily Lane, Partner.' It's a title that came with enough blood, sweat, and billable hours to fill a vampire's wine cellar. If vampires drank *sweat*, that is. Not that any of the vampires I know do.

"Leaving already, Emily?" Paige, our after-hours receptionist, raises an impeccably shaped eyebrow as she catches sight of me slinging my dingy messenger bag over my shoulder and heading to the elevator.

"Self-defense class," I say with a shrug that doesn't quite shake off the weight of last month's paranormal entanglements.

Punching things has become my latest pastime since I can no longer donate blood. No matter that donating blood to vampires—fang to skin—is akin to the high you get from drugs. Not that I've ever done drugs, but others described that way. For me, it finally lets my mind quiet, lets me de-stress and get a good night's sleep. But ever since Tina's demise, ever since I realized how I'd behaved after, there's been no one else I wanted to get close to on that level. I'm still dipping my toe into the friendship pool—relationships, too—and the intimacy of a vampire/donor match-up is too much at once. I hadn't realized just how intimate it was before Tina died, and I won't be making that mistake again. Lucian, the vampire coven leader, might be up for a connection, but that would only complicate an already convoluted pseudo-relationship. The 'high' isn't worth that. Hence hitting things, the next in a long line of habits to replace donating with something less... fraught. It isn't working so far.

"Then drinks with the gang," I finish.

"Ah, keeping those werewolves at bay, huh?" Paige's laugh twinkles like the chandelier above us, unaware of how close her joke hits to home.

Chicago is a sanctuary city for the paranormal—werewolves, vampires, ghouls, and more—who were revealed to humans during the Prohibition era. 'Sanctuary city' might be sugar-coating it, considering most of the designated areas for them are basically slums. And don't even get me started on the restrictions placed on them after Lucian was wrongfully charged with murdering a mayoral candidate. If this is how Chicago treats its "friends" in the supernatural world, I'd hate to be their enemy.

The goodwill the public briefly extended after Lucian's exoneration, a byproduct of their guilt, has gradually reverted to the norm. Meaning, being pro-paranormal is still an unpopular stance.

Which is exactly why the firm stays split on my paranormal connections. When I made partner, the higher-ups practically held their noses over anyone dealing with the supernatural community (translation: me). But, of course, they're more than happy to cash in on the deep pockets of those "paranormal sympathizers," as long as they don't have to hear the details. My involvement in clearing Lucian's name—with a little help from a conveniently timed hobgoblin ally—is still splashed across the headlines, but the firm just pretended not to notice. It's tough, walking that fine line between two worlds and trying to keep my reputation intact in both.

But after Lucian was cleared of the murder charges, everything went quiet. No supernatural incidents, no drama—for an entire month. But I can't shake the feeling that there's a storm brewing. Maybe it's wishful thinking; I promised to be an ally to my paranormal friends, and here I am, with Lucian's case behind me and nothing to show for it. It feels like I'm waiting for the otherworldly shoe to drop.

I shake off the worry and return my attention to Paige. "Something like that," I reply.

Stepping outside, the city wraps around me, skyscrapers reaching up like guardians of the mundane, a world that willfully ignores the creatures lurking in their shadows. I weave through the bustling sidewalk, dodging power walkers and distracted texters, until I reach the coffee shop squished between a yoga studio and the gym hosting my self-defense class. The smell of roasted coffee beans hits me first, battling with the faint tang of gym sweat and coconut-scented yoga mats. My insomnia's been playing a greatest-hits tour lately, and if sleep isn't on the setlist, I might as well lean into it with a top-tier espresso. I step inside, already picturing the first blissful sip.

"Are you Emily Lane?" The voice comes from a guy slouched in a corner booth, his hood pulled low over his eyes, which are fixed on me with an intensity that suggests he's not here for the free Wi-Fi.

"Depends who's asking," I say with a biting smile. I meander beside his booth, my professional curiosity piqued despite the alarm bells chiming in my brain. At least this might give me a chance to test out my newly earned self-defense moves.

He pulls down his hood, revealing tan skin and chiseled features capped by wavy brown hair. He's built like an unsinkable battleship, with broad shoulders and a powerful frame. A faint scar cuts across his left cheek, while a dark tattoo peeks from beneath his collar.

"Rhett Baxter," he says, thrusting out a hand that looks strong enough to crush walnuts... or skulls. "Dani—Danielle Greene sent me. She said you might be able to help... someone like me."

I take a bracing sip of my latte. "Officer Greene?"

My ally who hides her lupine identity from most, but cheers loudest for my advocacy in the paranormal world.

The surprise must be written all over my face because he nods, a hint of a smile dancing across his rugged features. "Yes, she believed you could help with a... situation."

I swiftly fish out the rose-tinted glasses from my bag, a gift from a vampire to pierce through certain glamours and unearth the secrets paranormals wish to keep hidden. Think 3D glasses, but instead of another dimension, they reveal another layer of our own. Through the lenses, I don't just see Rhett Baxter, I see him in his paranormal form. His appearance morphs and twists into something primal and fierce—a creature with the body of a wolf but the visage of a half-human beast, sporting an elongated snout and baring gleaming teeth. Thick fur blankets his form, a tapestry of grays and blacks. His once-piercing blue eyes now glow a fiery yellow. The glasses reveal his true form: a werewolf.

Behind him, a hobgoblin smirks and waves at me from within the coffee shop walls. One of those quirky things about old buildings is that you might find a few invisible friends hiding there.

I settle into the booth, stashing away the glasses. "Alright, you've got my attention."

"My family home, Oakheart Estate, is haunted," he says, diving right in as though he's got a fire under him. Or, apparently, a ghost after him. His hands tremble as he reaches for his coffee, a faint whiff of dust lingering in the air.

"Haunted, huh?" I lean back, crossing my arms. Even in a world where paranormals *sort of* coexist with humans, ghosts are always just campfire tales. "Last I checked, my law degree didn't come with a certificate in ghostbusting."

"I know it sounds unbelievable," Rhett says, desperation creeping into his voice, "but we're at our wits' end, and Dani said you've dealt with... our kind before."

"Dealt with" is one way to put it. Out loud, I just say, "One murder case doesn't make me a ghost whisperer." But I can't deny the rush of excitement and satisfaction that came with solving the murder and clearing Lucian's name.

"It's urgent," Rhett insists.

"Urgent" always seems to be the go-to descriptor for anything that can't be solved with a silver bullet or a court order. But this time, he might be right. Rhett's eyes are wild, like the full moon's got nothing on the chaos at his family home. I drum my fingers on the tabletop, the sticky varnish of the coffee shop booth clinging slightly to my skin.

"Listen, Mr. Baxter, haunted houses are more in the wheelhouse of reality TV ghost hunters, not lawyers." I take a sip of my now lukewarm latte, raising an eyebrow. "Unless the ghosts are planning to sue for unlawful eviction?"

He doesn't crack a smile. Instead, he leans forward, his voice dropping to a conspiratorial whisper. "It's not just bumps in the night, Ms. Lane. We're talking a full-fledged curse with objects moving, strange voices... My family is terrified."

Curses? Now that's a twist. Paranormals are cagey enough, but witches and magic? They're a whole different ball game, one that isn't broadcast to anyone not already 'in the know.' Even after a century of cohabitation, humans remain clueless about magic's workings. The witches aren't telling, and those aware of their existence guard their secrets like dragons hoarding gold.

Despite my skepticism, a spark of curiosity flickers down my spine. "And you're certain it's not just faulty plumbing?" I ask.

"Ms. Lane... Emily," he pleads, "I wouldn't be here if I wasn't desperate."

A tiny part of me buzzes with excitement at the thought of delving into another unknown crevice of the supernatural world. But the rational lawyer in me slams on the brakes. Ghosts? Curses? Might as well add a dragon to the mix and call it a fairytale.

"Mr. Baxter, I'll be frank—I'm a lawyer, not a paranormal investigator." My tone is firm, yet I catch myself fidgeting with the ever-present recorder in my pocket, a habit when my mind races through the facts of a case. It's like my fingers have already decided and are waiting for my brain to catch up.

"I know," he admits. "But you're not just any lawyer. You've seen things, been involved with creatures like me. If anyone can figure it out, it's you."

"Flattery will only get you so far," I quip, though a knot forms in my gut. His earnestness tells me this is no joke. The

Baxters are in deep trouble, and somehow, they've pegged me as their savior.

He leans forward, his voice low. "Hell, I'll take out an ad in the newspaper singing your praises if that would work."

"Why not go to the paranormal police?" I ask.

I'm assuming they exist. Fae laws exist, I learned that from that irritating favor I did for a hobgoblin named Wilkin. Which means there must be some enforcement arm... maybe even a court system.

I frown internally. That's probably something I should confirm before I get myself into trouble. I've already stolen from a pixie. For all I know, there's a paranormal warrant out for my arrest already.

Rhett's heavy scoff pulls me from the bunny trail that was about to breed into panic. "There are things you can do that they can't," he says simply.

Like what? Charm their way out of a parking ticket with a smile and a blink of my over-tired eyes? Order cheap takeout from joints the health department wouldn't even risk entering?

"Please, Emily," Rhett says, interrupting another runaway train of thought. "I'd do anything for my family. Wouldn't you?"

He looks at me with this ridiculous level of sincerity, like I'm the magical glue that can hold his life together. It's almost funny, except it's not, because the guy is so serious I half expect him to break into a soliloquy about family, loyalty, and saving the day. Finish the look off with the vibe of desperation rolling off him, the kind that says, *Hey, I'm barely holding it together here, so maybe you could throw me a bone?*

But here's the problem. Rhett's playing the "family is everything" card, and I'm standing here with a deck full of nothing. I don't have a family. No sprawling family tree stretching back generations, no storied estates layered with memories and the whispers of the past. More like a shrub. And it's not even well-watered. My roots are shallow, barely planted. *Recent*, even, since I'd only realized I had friends six weeks ago. Family has always been just a word to me, some abstract, fleeting idea I've never fully understood.

Except... the look in his eyes tugs at something within me. It's not that I believe in all this family drama of his—Oakheart Estate and its supernatural soap opera can stay right where it is, thank you very much. But for a second, there's this weird ache, like maybe I want to understand what it's like to have something worth clenching your fists over. Or maybe I just need a snack. Hard to say.

"Fine," I say, sighing. "Give me the details and I'll *think* about it. What exactly is going on at Oakheart?"

His relief is palpable as he recounts eerie events that sound ripped from the pages of a Gothic novel. An entire room off limits from objects levitating, whispers echoing through empty halls, and a sense that something malevolent lurks within those stone walls.

"Sounds like a regular Tuesday," I deadpan, but inside, my head's spinning. This isn't my realm. I argue cases, dissect statutes, occasionally get paranormal clients off the hook, not exorcise spirits.

"Please, think about it?" Rhett's hand lands on mine, his grip pleading. "We live in a human neighborhood and if the hauntings continue, our existence will be revealed."

"Okay, okay," I relent, pulling my hand back gently. "I'll mull it over."

As I leave the coffee shop and head towards the gym, my brain churns with legal strategies and potential loopholes, none of which applies to the supernatural. The firm's been on me to get new cases. My stint as a local celebrity means they're not handfeeding me clients like they are other partners, punishment for my 'unbecoming' affiliations. So, I'm climbing the ladder one case at a time.

And here I am, knee-deep in discussions about ancestral curses and haunted estates. The Baxters *would* pay, Rhett said, even if the work is more legal-adjacent. My biggest client, Frances Montgomery, is the same—demanding I show up to dinners and political events, not writing motions or appearing in court. Would it be that different?

"Get it together, Lane," I mutter under my breath. "You're supposed to be a pillar of reason, not chasing after apparitions."

But as the city lights twinkle to life around me, mimicking the stars above, I can't shake Rhett's desperate expression. He believes in me, even if I'm still skeptical about ghosts.

"Ah, what the heck," I sigh, knowing my curiosity likely won't let this go. "Looks like I might be brushing up on my detective skills after all."

The clink of glasses and the low hum of conversation envelop me as I slide into our usual booth at O'Malley's, the bar that's become a Tuesday night staple for my law school crew. I'd skipped out on most of them earlier this year, but after my brush with mortality, Megan made it her mission to keep the Tuesday night gatherings going strong. Last month, when I tried to bail again, Megan staged a protest in my office until I caved.

Megan, Brian, and Matty are already there, nursing their drinks with the casual ease of people who've weathered torts and trials side by side.

"Guess who might be playing Nancy Drew in the Werewolf Chronicles?" I announce as I flag down the server for whatever drink is on special.

Megan leans her elbow on the table, resting her chin in her hand. "Please tell me this isn't another one of your 'paranormal pro bono' cases," she groans, her brown eyes wide behind fashionable frames.

It's not like I've had a *plethora* of paranormal cases. Just two, and one barely counts. But I let that slide.

"Definitely not pro bono," I say with a smirk. "But let's just say my clientele is expanding beyond the realm of the living."

"Okay, spill it," Brian urges, setting down his beer. He looks more amused than concerned, which isn't surprising considering he's been attempting to befriend the hobgoblin living in the walls of his place.

"Haunted mansion, family curse, desperate werewolves. The works," I say with a shrug, trying to sound nonchalant despite the butterfly circus in my stomach.

"Wait, you're serious? Ghosts now?" Matty asks, raising an eyebrow. His tousled brown hair falls effortlessly over his forehead as he leans close, his honey-brown eyes crinkling in concern.

"Apparently so. And I used to think hobgoblins were a stretch," I muse aloud, still coming to terms with the day's bombshells.

"Speaking of," Brian interjects, "have you heard from your wall dweller recently?"

"Please, Herle is the silent type," I retort with a playful glare. I'm still not convinced the Chicago hobgoblins didn't get together and create 'Herle' as an elaborate prank. "Does yours actually talk back?"

"Of course, but the conversations with Pietre are private," Brian teases with a wink. His pale skin goes ruddy, from embarrassment or the heat of the room. "Attorney-client confidentiality."

My brows raise. "Uh-huh, sure," I say, taking a sip of my freshly arrived drink.

"Ghosts *and* werewolves, Emmy? You're really throwing yourself *deep* into the supernatural this time," Megan quips, but there's a flicker of concern in her eyes that she quickly masks with a bright smile. "Just be sure not to get lost in all of that... paranormal drama again. We need you grounded here with us mere mortals," Megan says.

"They're no different from us," I say with a shrug.

"Except they have fangs," Brian jokes.

"So do I," I reply, baring my teeth, which sends laughter rippling across the table.

"I hope this isn't like last time." Matty finally speaks up, his tone gentle but firm. "Things got pretty... intense with the Belmont case."

Intense meaning the true perpetrator—former and now disgraced Mayor Peterson—tried to choke the life out of me, *after* taking out his chief competition for reelection. Using his slight resemblance to Lucian, based on their shared lineage, and planting a family heirloom, he'd thought he'd wrapped up Lucian's conviction with a bow. Until I started digging.

"It shouldn't have," I counter. "That's the point. Everyone treated Lucian differently just because he's a vampire when it should've been a run-of-the-mill case. There should have been an actual investigation, but everyone was so happy to catch one of the 'bloodsuckers' that the truth didn't matter."

"If you say so," Megan says, adjusting her glasses. She purses purple painted lips and exchanges a glance with the other two that says they might be humoring me.

I force a smile and raise my glass in a mock toast. "To the living and the creatures of the night. May they one day find common ground."

They gamely clink glasses and the night goes on, all talk of the paranormal left behind. Dinner passes in a blur of half-eaten burgers and shared laughter, but my thoughts keep drifting back to Rhett Baxter's haunted plea. As we stand to leave, Matty lingers close, his hand brushing mine.

"When are we doing this again, just us?" he asks, a hopeful note in his voice.

"I'll check my calendar," I murmur.

Assistant District Attorney Matthew "Matty" Barnes, with his irritatingly handsome face and newly acquired sense of humor that pushes past his more staid personality, has been chasing me like a man on a mission for almost two months. We've been on a few dates—nothing serious, of course—and somewhere along the way, he's mastered the art of making my heart do backflips. It's maddening, really. I've always been great at compartmentalizing—emotions shoved neatly into a box labeled "Do Not Open," buried under piles of logic, career goals, and a dash of cynicism. But with Matty, the box isn't just cracking open; it's practically bursting at the seams. He makes me want to let my guard down, to show him something more than Emily Lane, lawyer extra-ordinaire.

And that would be *fine* if it weren't for the fact that a certain vampire has taken up prime real estate in my head. Not that I asked him to. But here I am, burning through my already scarce supply of sleep, replaying the stolen kiss that was probably just a stress-induced blip in the middle of a murder investigation. At least, that's what logical me keeps insisting.

To make things messier, I almost lost both of them—Matty *and* Lucian. A misunderstanding here, a bruised ego there, and suddenly the fragile thing we created felt like it was crumbling. It's only recently we managed to scrape things back together as sometime-friends, and even then, the cracks still show if you squint hard enough.

"Emily, if you need some time..." Matty starts, but I cut him off with a reassuring smile.

"Don't worry about me. I've got everything under control." At least, that's what I'll keep telling myself.

"It's only been six weeks since..." He gestures vaguely to my neck. Not to any vampire bite marks, I hadn't indulged in those lately, but to the spots where Mayor Peterson's violent grip had left a necklace of bruises. They've healed, but the memory lingers.

Still, I wave off Matty's concern with a dismissive flick of my hand, trying to mask the slight discomfort that still echoes in my bones.

"That's old news, Matty. Water under the bridge," I reassure him, plastering a smile on my face that doesn't quite reach my eyes.

The memory of Mayor Peterson's violent outburst is a stark reminder of the dangers lurking beneath the surface of our seemingly mundane world. Except there, it wasn't the paranormal out to harm me, but a charismatic man.

Stepping out into the cool night air, I let out a long breath, the weight of the world—or maybe just Oakheart Estate—on my shoulders. The moon hangs high in the sky, projecting an ethereal glow over the deserted streets as I make my way to the vampire quarter. It's not full yet, that's in another two weeks. Which makes me wonder: how would a cursed house handle a haunting during a full moon? Would it turn into a supernatural circus with spirits flying around like its open mic night? Or would they just hunker down while the werewolves took center stage?

Chapter 2

I stalk down the streets of Old Town, the night air thick with the promise of rain and something more, a metallic tang that beckons me deeper into the realm of the supernatural. It's a scent I've grown accustomed to since delving into the world of the paranormal—a blend of blood and magic that saturates the vampire quarter of Chicago. The vamps who aren't idling inside the old brick buildings spend most of their time at the local park, dilapidated, but still theirs. Come sundown, it transforms into a perpetual party for the undead and the human donors Lucian graciously permits to visit. Considering the (il)legality of donating to vampires, Lucian's leniency is nothing short of remarkable.

"Emily Lane, as I neither live nor breathe," a voice calls out, tinged with amusement and a British accent that never fails to sound theatrically put-on.

"Stardust, you need a new catchphrase," I say, turning to see the vampire emerging from the shadows, his arm entwined with that of a young man sporting a shaggy mop of dark hair and an easy smile gracing his tan face.

Ray, Stardust's donor and lover, nods at me in recognition. His life's taken quite the upturn since I nudged him toward that job opportunity after closing Lucian's case. That and getting out of his difficult living situation.

"Quite the night for a stroll, isn't it?" Stardust drawls, sweeping a hand through his wild blonde mane that makes him look like he's just stepped off a glam rock album cover. He's all sparkle and starlight, even in the dim glow of the streetlights. His real name is Richard, but everyone calls him Stardust because of his resemblance to a certain rockstar, mismatched pupils, sharp cheekbones, and all.

"A night like this was practically made for strolling," I reply, giving Stardust a playful grin. "And I see the two of you are out for your own evening constitutional."

Stardust chuckles. "You know me, darling. I can never resist a chance to strut my stuff under the moonlight. Besides, Ray here was in *desperate* need of some fresh air after being cooped up all day."

"Still at the jeweler's, Ray?" I ask, reaching up to adjust the messy bun that's become my trademark.

Ray nods in agreement, his smile widening. "Five a.m. to noon every day. Lets me sleep when Star does every afternoon so we can spend the whole night together."

"Even though he refuses to move in with me," Stardust says, mock pouting.

Ray rolls his eyes and ducks his head against Stardust's leather-clad shoulder, not responding to the teasing argument. Both turn their attention back to me.

"You looking to donate, Emily girl?" Stardust asks, his mismatched eyes twinkling.

"As tempting as it is to be a walking blood bank for you, I think I'll pass tonight," I reply with a soft chuckle.

The mention of donation always brings to mind the bloodeez packs stashed in my apartment—leftovers from my not-so-distant past of dealing with vampires. Those packs were supposed to keep me safe, boosting my blood reserves for hungry fangs. But I haven't touched them in months. Not after Tina. And definitely not after Lucian. I'm trying to put all that behind me—no more blood donations, no more one-night flings to shake off stress. I still haven't figured out how to replace the relief those things used to bring me. Punching things helps, but only so much. Anything that doesn't come with emotional baggage—or fangs—would be a step in the right direction.

"Besides," I quip, "Ray would probably disembowel me if I bared my neck to you."

Ray chuckles while Stardust raises an exaggerated eyebrow, his lips curling into a mischievous grin. "Not donating to *me*, my dear Emily. But Lucian would certainly welcome your generous donation."

The mere mention of Lucian's name sends a jolt through me—part thrill, part dread. We've been stuck in this awkward limbo ever since I cleared his name. It's like we're trying to find a new normal: me, grappling with the magnetic pull I feel toward him, and him... well, being Lucian—calm, enigmatic, and maddeningly unreadable. We're *something* now, though I'm not sure what. Not quite strangers, not quite friends, but definitely not just coven leader and random donor anymore.

And yeah, I'd flirted with him back then. Hard. How could I not? He ticked every box I had: dangerous vibe, murky past, smoldering looks, and an aura that practically screamed "commitment-phobic."

But everything changed after we kissed—just once—and then fought like it was the end of the world. That kiss had been electric, a fleeting moment where all the tension between us boiled over, but it was followed by a blowout that left us both raw and defensive. Afterward, I pulled back, retreating into safer territory, untangling myself from the knot of complications we'd created.

Lucian, though, wasn't having it. While I scrambled to re-build my walls, he seemed determined to pull me closer, like he could somehow convince me that we could make sense of the mess. But it was too much—too layered with unre-solved feelings, too risky with his world and mine already a powder keg of secrets. And then there's Matty—steadfast, infuriatingly sweet Matty—quietly working his way into my life with every coffee date and crooked smile.

Now I'm stuck in a tug-of-war with my own desires. Do I want to offer Lucian my neck, kick him in the shins, or lose myself in another kiss until we're both breathless? Throw in Matty's steady presence, and it's like I'm watching my life barrel toward the Niagara of bad decisions.

Thankfully, Lucian's busy helping Severin at Moonlit Haven tonight, sparing me from making any questionable choices. For now, anyway.

I shoot Stardust a warning glance, placing a finger to my lips in a hushing gesture. "Let's keep Lucian out of this conversation, shall we?"

Stardust raises his hands in surrender, a dramatic pout on his lips. "As you wish. The mention of Lucian is banned from our delightful banter."

"Anyway," I steer the conversation away from dangerous territory, but I'm not sure how to start. "You have a minute? I could use your thoughts on something."

He presses his hand against his chest in mock-alarm. "Ask-ing us for help? Ray, love, go down into the tunnels and check if hell has frozen over."

"You're hilarious," I reply dryly. Although, he's not wrong that this is an unusual request from me. I half want to take it back. "I'm weighing the pros and cons of taking on a new case. A werewolf family drama that could use a human touch. Not exactly legal work, but more of my snooping around."

"A werewolf sought you out for that?" Stardust raises an eyebrow, but doesn't seem surprised. "Makes sense. You're not bound by moon phases or and only susceptible to sunburn in the traditional sense."

"You should do standup with all these jokes," I mutter, though I can't deny the truth in his words. Being human does have its perks in the supernatural world. "But seriously, I need to keep the specifics under wraps. Especially from Lucian."

"Your secret's safe with me," Stardust promises, crossing his heart with a flourish that only a glam vampire could pull off. "What's wrong, love?"

I let out a sigh, half-relief, half-resignation. "I came into law to do good work, wear sharp suits, and make partner by thirty-five. Now I'm more focused on this paranormal consultant thing I've got going on. The universe has quite the sense of humor."

"Darling, the universe isn't as funny as we are," Stardust quips, linking his free arm with mine as we leave the area beside the park and continue down the cobblestone path. "Now tell us everything about the awaiting werewolf."

I launch into the details as Stardust leads me and Ray to another house. Not the majestic mini-mansion of Lucian's, but a small townhouse down the street from the park. Its brick exterior is worn and faded, vines crawling up the sides and around the windows.

Stardust ushers us through the black front door. The foyer is bathed in fluorescent light, the walls covered with abstract artwork and painted in deep burgundy hues.

"Is this your place?" I ask, my brows raised.

Stardust and Ray shed their coats, hanging them on sleek silver hooks.

"You didn't think I slept in the tunnels, did you?" Stardust asks.

The tunnels are actual, winding passageways beneath the city. Some are old sewer systems, others are maintenance channels, and a few are even older, half-forgotten pathways leading to the Underground. It's a hidden supernatural settlement, equal parts marketplace, meeting space, and urban haven for the paranormal crowd. When vampires—and other species—need to move around freely, they can slip through these tunnels, traveling from point A to point B without worrying about sunlight or nosy neighbors.

I offer Stardust a noncommittal murmur in response. Better than admitting I'd never thought about it. If pressed, I'd probably have said they either shared space in Lucian's mansion, slept outside in the park, or, yes, stayed in the tunnels and Underground.

With an exaggerated roll of his eyes, Stardust nudges us toward the compact kitchenette as Ray sets about brewing tea.

Once we're served and perched in Stardust's living room, I can't help but marvel at the oddity of my surroundings. The walls shimmer with a subtle iridescence, like the inside of an abalone shell, and every marbled surface seems to be carved from moonlight itself. It's like stepping into someone's psychedelic dream, yet here I am, sipping on chamomile tea as Stardust lounges across from me, his lean frame draped over a chaise that's outrageous enough to belong in Liberace's living room.

"Magic," Stardust muses, twirling a lock of his wild blonde hair around one glitter-encrusted finger, "is all about balance. For every spell cast, there's a price to pay, a condition to meet."

Ray nods, his expression earnest as he leans forward, elbows on the coffee table. "Like those old fairy tales where the witch grants you three wishes, but you lose your soul or your firstborn gets gobbled up."

"*Exactly* like the fairy tales," Stardust agrees. "With magic beans, poisoned apples, and all. Where do you think the stories got it?" He frowns, his sparkling eyes serious for once. "To curse a family home... it would've taken some serious mojo. And a terrible price. That's not something you do on a whim."

A chill skitters down my spine. *Someone out there is twisted enough to hurt themselves just to drag someone else down with them?* That's next-level disturbing.

"I'm guessing finding and asking the witch who did it to *undo* it is... probably not going to be easy," I say.

Stardust chuckles, the sound ringing like wind chimes in a summer breeze. "Darling, you've hit the nail on the head. Witches are a crafty lot, you see. Elusive creatures, hidden in plain sight among us. They don't leave breadcrumbs for us to follow. It's not like there's a neon sign saying 'Cursed by Madam Ashwick.'" He leans in closer, his eyes gleaming with mischief. "You gotta dig deeper, love. Find the root of their ire and hope it leads you down the right rabbit hole."

I take a deep breath, trying to absorb this newfound information. The possible task ahead settles on my shoulders like a heavy cloak. "So, I'd need to uncover why the Baxters were cursed. Which means," I add, trying to keep the unease out of my voice and the memory of Peterson's thick hands out of my head, "this will probably be dangerous."

Stardust chuckles. "Dangerous, yes, but thrilling, wouldn't you agree, my dear Emily?" His eyes hold a glint of mischief as he takes a sip of the blood bag he emptied into a coffee mug, the plain white porcelain out of place against his flamboyant persona.

"Could be both," I muse aloud. And I've not been one to back away because of something as trivial as 'danger.'

"Isn't helping out sort your thing now?" Ray asks. "Making friends across the paranormal divide, and all."

I nod. That was the promise I made, to help however I could. *But does that mean hunting for cursed ghosts?*

We lapse into silence, each lost in thought about the implications.

Six weeks ago, I wouldn't have bothered with getting their advice. Who needs cheerleaders when you're a one-woman cavalry charge? But things are different now. My lone wolf act wore thin, the edges fraying like the cuffs on my favorite blazer. Danielle, Lucian, Sara, Stardust, Megan, Matty, Brian, even *Liz*—they all started breaking through that wall I put around myself.

"Anyway," I say, breaking the silence with a forced chuckle, "enough about curses and imminent doom. What's new in the world of bloodsucking and moonlit escapades?"

Stardust perks up immediately, the gravity of our prior conversation sloughing off him like a discarded cape. "The usual, of course. Dodging wooden stakes, seducing innocent bystanders, advocating for vampiric rights at the local supermarket."

"Sounds exhausting," I deadpan, though I'm secretly impressed by how effortlessly he navigates his life.

"Tell me about it," Ray chimes in, rolling his eyes dramatically. "He had to attend two different undead fashion shows last week. You should've seen the glitter fallout. We're still finding sparkles in the sofa cushions."

"Those were very important social engagements in the Underground," Stardust says with mock indignation.

"Of course," I reply, smirking even as the weight of my decision hangs over me like a storm cloud. "How could I forget the paramount importance of vampire haute couture?"

As the laughter fades, a cozy sense of camaraderie settles over us, like a favorite old blanket. Hanging out with Stardust—who's as authentic as they come—reminds me exactly why I wanted to dive into this paranormal thing in the first place. It wasn't just about the intrigue or the mysteries. It was about being an ally, about making sure that those who live in the shadows have someone watching their back. Someone who knows the law and can wield it to protect them when no one else will.

I might not have fully decided about the Baxter case, but here I am, cracking jokes with a vampire and his donor, and it hits me—being a good advocate isn't always about courtrooms and fancy suits. Sometimes, it's just about showing up, listening, and standing by the people who need someone in their corner.

And if I can get *paid* to do that? Be the lawyer I've worked so hard to become, while actually making a difference? Well, that's the kind of win I can get behind.

The floorboards groan beneath my restless steps, the rhythmic thud of my pacing the only sound in the otherwise dead-silent apartment, amplifying the tension twisting inside me.

"Okay, Herle," I call out to the alleged resident hobgoblin, who's been as chatty as a mime at a funeral. "I could use some supernatural wisdom here." Silence greets me, as usual. I snort. "What's the matter? Cat *still* got your tongue?" My attempt at humor falls flat in the empty space.

I release my hair from its bun prison, running my fingers through the long strands as the knots of tension slowly unravel while I weigh the pros and cons. The partners at Johnson & Marcus would probably have a collective aneurysm if they knew I was considering a haunted house case. I can already see Lawrence's face, eyebrows poised to launch into orbit.

I stop mid-stride and glance around the dimly lit room. I have to remind myself that this isn't just about proving I can handle the bizarre and the paranormal. It's about doing what's right, even if it means veering off the well-trodden path of legal work. Like Ray said, that's what I promised I'd do after the Peterson debacle. And if that means using whatever skills I have to do some more... non-traditional work, so be it.

With a steadying breath, I fish my phone from my pocket and punch in Rhett Baxter's number. He picks up after one ring, sounding like he's about to pop a blood vessel.

"It's Emily Lane," I begin, the decision solidifying with each word. "I've thought about your situation, and I'll look into the haunting at Oakheart Estate."

"Thank you," Rhett exhales, relief palpable over the line. "We need to meet—"

"First thing tomorrow evening, after my office closes," I interrupt, already picturing my calendar's objections. "Send me the details, and we'll get started."

"Absolutely. And thanks again. Y—"

"Goodnight, Rhett." I hang up before I second guess my choice.

As I slip under the covers later that night, the faces of those I'm fighting for flicker behind my closed eyelids. There's more at stake than just restless spirits. I'm risking my firm's ire, my limited free time, possibly my sanity.

"Bring it on," I murmur, the words somewhere between a dare and a plea. Whatever's coming—challenges, obstacles, total disaster—let it. Because when Emily Lane commits, she's all in, whether she's a lawyer or a half-baked investigator.

At least until everything goes sideways, which, let's face it, it probably will. Hopefully, this time, it won't end with me fending off a murderer.

CHAPTER 3

The next evening, I navigate my car up the narrow road, a winding path that slithers through a hamlet outside one of Chicago's poshest suburbs.

"Of *course*, you'd live in a neighborhood where the houses have more turrets than a medieval castle," I mutter under my breath as I approach the wrought-iron gates, the gravel crunching beneath my tires like brittle bones.

Oakheart Estate rises ahead, a gothic monstrosity amidst the manicured lawns and perfect hedges of this affluent neighborhood. The manor itself looks like something out of a Brontë novel; all sharp angles and towering spires that claw at the moonlit sky. It's impressive, in a pretentious, 'look-at-me' kind of way.

I step out of my clunker, straightening my blazer and trying to muster some semblance of professionalism for what awaits beyond. This whole place *reeks* of money, the kind that's passed down through generations so long they're practically mythological. The kind I'll never see in my lifetime.

The neighboring estates stand as opulent giants, their bright facades shielded by ancient trees and carefully sculpted hedges. They're not just homes; they're fortresses against the common plebeians like me. I can imagine the locals, with their pressed suits and designer dogs, trading gossip about the mysterious mansion that doesn't quite fit their swanky aesthetic.

I pull my tape recorder from my purse as I start down the path, ready to start talking to myself in the form of notes and observations. You'd think now that my social life has exploded, the running commentary would stop, but nope. I'm still my best listener.

Except tonight, my monologue's got an audience.

Lucian leans casually against one of the stone gargoyles just inside the gates, his black hair tied back revealing the sharp contours of his pale face that could make statues envious. As usual, he's draped in a tailored black suit that molds to his muscular frame, his signature silver cufflinks flickering in the dim light against his pale skin. The clothing manages to scream 'I own the night' without uttering a single word, an impressive feat for anyone who's *not* a centuries-old vampire.

"Lucian," I say, raising an eyebrow as I imagine yanking out every jewel in Stardust's favorite coat for tattling on this job to Lucian. Meanwhile, my traitorous heart does a little pitter-patter routine at seeing him. "I didn't expect to see you here."

He meets my gaze with a hint of a smirk. "I've been told by my fledglings that I have a knack for showing up where I shouldn't," he replies.

"Sure, like dad crashing the party," I say, my brow furrowing. "But this feels more than coincidental. Did Stardust spill the beans?"

He frowns, his gray eyes darkening. "Not Stardust, but I will have a chat with him once we're finished here."

"*We're* not *anything* here, Lucian. This is my job," I say, tiredly. "If not Stardust, then who? Do you have some kind of supernatural tracking device on me or something? Or maybe there's a weekly newsletter for all paranormals in Chicago, keeping tabs on my whereabouts?"

"You have quite the imagination, Emily," he says. "It was Officer Greene who thought it prudent to inform me of your planned appearance here," he says, with that smooth, infuriating confidence that makes it clear he's used to being ahead of the game. It had us butting heads when we first met, when he tried to run the investigation and have me sit on my hands waiting for him. That dynamic didn't last long.

I bite back a sigh from the memories and retreat to my usual humor. "So, not a newsletter, but a paranormal hotline. Or do you guys have weekly monster mash meetings?"

Lucian chuckles softly. "It's less of a hotline, more of a finely tuned network."

"Right, because nothing says 'covert operation' like a gossip chain rivaling high school cliques," I retort, unable to keep the grin from tugging at the corners of my mouth. Despite everything, the banter is easy. Natural, even.

But the back-and-forth is cut short by the not-so-subtle stares of the non-paranormal residents out for their evening strolls down the long lane. They grip their pearls and leashes tighter, eyes flitting between Lucian and their smartphones—debating, no doubt, whether to summon authorities or their book club buddies first.

"Seems like you're causing quite the stir," I observe, nudging Lucian with my elbow.

"A hazard of my existence," he replies, his gray eyes flashing with a mix of amusement and resignation. "Blending in has never been my specialty in human areas."

I eye him again. Actually, he fits into this gothic tableau perfectly. With his looks and energy, it was as if he was a living embodiment of wealth and mystery, a creature of the night who had staked his claim on this realm of money and supernatural intrigue. "Do you suppose it's the brooding," I ask, "the failed murder frame-up, or the fact that you're, you know, dead?"

"All the above, I suppose." He smirks at me. "You'll get used to it."

If this ends up on the news again, he's not wrong. I plaster on my best grin and give a wave that's so enthusiastic it could double as a parade flag, hoping it'll get the looky-loos to move along. Eventually, they shuffle off, mumbling to each other like they're about to write me into their gossip column.

Once we're alone again, I step closer. "Now, you showing up here does wonders for my ego but you know I'm meeting with Stardust at the park tomorrow night. Your standing invitation and all. Couldn't wait that long to see me again?"

"I've been counting the seconds," he says, deadpan. But there's a glint in his eye that gives away the joke.

"And the *real* reason?"

He glances up at Oakheart Estate, his gaze lingering on its looming, spooky exterior. There's something in his expression—maybe a flicker of concern? It can't be fear I'm clocking. "There's more to this haunting than just ghosts, Emily. As far as I know, there's no such thing as ghosts."

"And you're old enough to know," I murmur. To Lucian, I add, "Since when did you become my personal bodyguard? I thought vampires were more of the 'bite first, ask questions never' persuasion."

"I worry for your safety," he admits, his gaze intense. "Given your... eclectic clientele, caution is advisable."

"Is this a werewolf-vampire rivalry thing?" I ask, arms crossed. "Because if I need to start wearing team colors, I'd like to be informed ahead of time."

"Emily, this isn't a joke." The corners of Lucian's mouth twitch, betraying his attempt at sternness. "If there are werewolves involved—"

"I see. So, werewolves bad, vampires... less bad?" I inquire, meeting his gaze head-on.

"Something like that," he murmurs, not quite meeting my eye.

"What about Danielle?" I ask. "She's part of the furry club, after all."

A smirk dances on Lucian's lips. "Danielle is a... special case," he confides, his tone laced with cryptic implications.

Danielle, Sara, who isn't a 'special' case to Lucian? I suppress the inappropriate—and frankly, unnecessary and pointless—jealousy bubbling in my chest and opt for another joke instead. "Does she enforce a no-bite policy?"

"Let's just say she's earned my trust," he says, leaving it at that.

"Must be nice," I quip, my heart thrumming in my chest as I turn to the yawning darkness of the grounds. Trust is a currency I'm still trying to accumulate from the paranormal set. Bringing a vampire to a werewolf gathering might tank my credit rating. But with mortality knocking louder than ever, an immortal guardian at my side could prove invaluable. Even against spectral foes.

Turning back to Lucian, I raise my brows. "But back to 'why you're really here.' Ghosts got your goat?"

"No," his voice low enough that I have to lean in to catch his words. "Werewolves. They are supposed to claim territories in their designated areas, much like vampires do."

"Like a supernatural suburbia?" I ask. Truth be told, I'd never checked out the werewolf quarter that's supposed to be near South side. Werewolf teeth don't hold the same physical allure as vampire fangs, so there's been little incentive to explore.

"Something like that." A fleeting smile crosses his lips. "But many choose to live among humans, hiding in plain sight rather than segregate themselves."

"Sounds cozy. Do they get a newsletter too?"

"Only during full moons," he retorts, and I'm reminded again why I like him. "The family here, they must be one of those who've decided to blend in. I don't recognize them from any coven leader meetings."

"Wait, you actually have meetings?"

"Occasionally," he confirms. "It helps maintain peace between the clans—or at least gives the illusion of it."

"Handy," I muse, considering the implications. A family of werewolves living undetected in a neighborhood where the biggest concern is probably which vintage pairs best with foie gras—it's intriguing, to say the least.

"Indeed," Lucian agrees, his focus unwavering on the house. "But it also renders them vulnerable. If their secret's out, if the curse reveals them, there's no predicting the consequences."

He knows firsthand what that extra attention does. In his case, increased restrictions against paranormals and a looming murder trial.

"Which is where I come in," I add, that familiar spark of ambition kindling within me. This isn't just another case;

it's a puzzle waiting to be solved, a mystery begging to be unraveled. And I'd like to think I have a knack for finding the missing pieces.

Lucian's eyes soften with a glint of understanding as he nods. "Exactly, Emily. Your investigative skills and tenacity are invaluable in situations like this. But I can offer something more. My knowledge surpasses others in magic, I'm stronger than your average human, and I could be your extra set of eyes and ears in places you might not easily venture." He holds out his hand. "I'm not here to hinder you; I want to help. And besides, isn't it nice to have a partner in this endeavor?"

I raise an eyebrow, considering his offer. It's still hard not to scoff at the idea of needing anyone. Ties were something I shed along with my small-town past, something I thought I could compensate for with sheer ambition and a string of successful verdicts. But these days, there's a little hum of warmth when I get a text from Megan asking if I'm up for a late-night burger run or a knowing nod from Stardust after a tricky day at work. Those connections matter now.

And having a partner in this dangerous dance could be more than just convenient—it could be life-saving. The problem is, the more time I spend with Lucian, the more complicated things get. It's hard enough navigating the supernatural world without the added distraction of his unreadable expressions, his maddening mix of charm and mystery, or the memory of that kiss still lingering in the back of my mind. And now, with him bantering like we're a seasoned improv duo? Letting him get closer might keep me alive, but it might also be my undoing.

With a sigh, I relent, shaking his hand firmly. "Fine, but stay close and don't draw unnecessary attention. We're here to solve the curse mystery, not start a paranormal war in the suburbs."

A smile sneaks onto Lucian's face as he gives a quick nod.

We move towards the looming Oakheart Estate together, a fusion of human determination and immortal grace. Up close, it's an eerie silhouette against the night sky. The grand double doors before us are ornately carved with ancient symbols, and the windows are covered in brocade that looks dusty even from the outside.

"Quite the place for a haunting," I remark as we approach the entrance, my heels making that annoying gravel crunching sound. "I know it's a cliched choice, but you'd think spirits would prefer somewhere less... drafty."

Lucian lets out a chuckle, smooth as silk against the night sky. "Ghosts aren't known for their preference in real estate, Emily."

"Too bad. A seaside cottage might lift their eternal woes."

"You can suggest it," he says dryly. Then he gives a half-hearted bow, more sarcastic than gallant. Classic Lucian—smooth talker with a side of mystery, all wrapped up in a fancy suit. "Shall we?"

Together, we head for the giant oak doors, the beginning of a mystery that's just begging to be solved.

The doors swing open and we're greeted by a scene straight out of a billionaire's mansion. Or something from the Munsters. Out strides a man who's clearly the head honcho around here, his Armani suit so sharp it could cut glass, and his hair perfectly styled like he just stepped off a magazine cover.

"State your names and purpose," the man booms, his voice a rumble akin to distant thunder, his stance as imposing as a fortress wall. This must be Rhett's father, Alex, the leader of this covert coven. His eyes, storm cloud gray, fix on Lucian like he's a rabid raccoon.

"We're here to see Rhett," I say, not keen on witnessing the clash of werewolf and vampire dynamics firsthand. "He hired me to investigate your... problem."

Alex's lip curls like he just smelled something rotten. "We don't have problems," he snarls, staring down his nose at us. "And we certainly don't need vampires poking their noses where they don't belong."

A lady dressed in pink Chanel, who I figure must be Rhett's mom, Sylvia, peeks from behind him. Her expression is wary, as if she expects us to sprout fangs or claws at any moment. Ironic, given they're the werewolves. She nods along with Alex's tirade.

"We're not here to cause trouble," Lucian says, trying to play peacemaker. He steps forward like he's about to waltz, all graceful and unbothered by the tension. "I'm Lucian Belmont, and this is Emily Lane. Mr. Baxter hired—"

"Dad," Rhett's voice cuts through from within the house. "We've discussed this. I found Emily through Officer Greene. She's trustworthy."

Alex's steely gaze softens the slightest bit as he turns to regard his son, Rhett, standing confidently at the top of the staircase. The family resemblance is impossible to miss: matching sharp jawlines, piercing eyes, and that "my way or the highway" vibe they're both wearing. It's like looking at a before-and-after ad for alpha males.

"I trust your judgment, Rhett," Alex concedes, the words dragged out like he's tasting something bitter but with a faint glimmer of pride underneath. "But that doesn't mean we should let our guard down. Not with outsiders involved."

"The neighbors are *already* talking," adds Sylvia, her fingers nervously playing with the expensive lace at her neckline. "Exposure would be disastrous for us."

"I understand your concerns, Mr. Baxter," I interject, trying to sound both polite and assertive. It's a delicate balance when dealing with these snobby werewolves who seem to ooze privilege underneath their simmering power. "Although I'm not a specialized paranormal investigator, I am an attorney, and discretion is my professional creed."

Alex eyes me warily, his judgmental gaze scrutinizing me as if trying to determine my worth. "And what can an attorney do about this curse, Ms...?"

"Lane," I reply. "And I plan to get to the bottom of it," I add, staring him down. "I'm good at uncovering secrets and finding solutions. So if there's a curse hanging over your family's heads, I'm your gal to help break it. If that's what you want."

Rhett descends the staircase, each step deliberate and sure. "We want this curse lifted," he confirms, his voice filled with a quiet determination that tells us all he means business. "It's been tearing our family apart."

"And causing chaos in your lives, I imagine," Lucian adds, his tone sympathetic. "Curses have a way of lingering, inflicting their brand of suffering until they're put to rest."

Alex's jaw clenches at Lucian's words, a silent admission that it's the truth. It's clear they'd prefer to keep this in-house, but with a curse hanging over their heads like a storm cloud, pride's a luxury they can't afford.

Chapter 4

Alex ultimately relents, motioning for us to enter the spacious foyer. The place is a stark contrast to the Baxters' outfits, a time capsule of tackiness. The foyer is a burst of colors, with gilded walls and heavy velvet curtains in black and gold, just dripping with drama. Dusty chandeliers hang overhead, casting a harsh light over the white marble floors, and a staircase that looks like it belongs in a soap opera. And the whole place is packed with furniture, a parade of gaudy, over-the-top pieces, each one fighting to be the flashiest thing in the room. I try not to stare, but it's like the house is daring me not to look away.

Worse is the smell. The air is heavy with the sickly sweet scent of perfumes and air fresheners, likely trying to mask a musty and damp odor that seeps from the walls. Beneath it all, there is a hint of something decaying.

Emerging from the shadows are more characters—a teenage girl with hair like spun silver, a kid barely into double-digits clutching a teddy bear for dear life, a young redheaded guy with a permanent scowl etched on his face, and an older couple whose faces are a roadmap of every worry they've ever carried.

Alex gives a stiff introduction with a sweep of his hand. "And don't take too long," he warns.

"Of course," Lucian assures him. "We wouldn't dream of overstaying our welcome."

"Too late for that," mutters the hard-faced redhead—Trenton. I'm guessing he's Rhett's younger brother, or maybe a cousin. Alex wasn't exactly thorough with introductions. But the family resemblance is there in the stubborn jawline and the way he squares his shoulders like he's ready for a fight. His blue eyes lock onto mine, and there's a challenge simmering just beneath the surface.

"Pleasure to meet you," I say, with a hint of sarcasm I can't quite hold back.

"Likewise," Trenton replies, but his smirk tells me he's heard the bite in my tone and matches it with interest. Beneath the attitude, those blue eyes hold a flicker of something... intense. Maybe anger. Maybe hurt. Whatever it is, it's the kind of thing that'll either make him an ally or a pain in my neck. I'll put money on the latter.

"Right then," I say, clipping my words with a briskness that hides my curiosity. "Tell us about the haunting." I whip out my tape recorder, poised to capture every detail.

The room falls silent, the collective hesitance of the Baxter family wrapping around us like a thick fog. They shuffle uneasily, exchanging guarded looks that say a lot about the weight they're carrying.

"Six months," Alex begins, his voice a low growl, "that's how long we've been dealing with... incidents." He hesitates, as if the word 'incidents' is too mild to describe whatever they're facing.

"Objects moving on their own, shadows where there shouldn't be any, and the sounds..." Sylvia chimes in, her gaze distant as she wraps her arms around herself, "whispers that turn into howls when the moon *isn't* full."

"Classic haunted house," I mutter, but Lucian gives me a look that says, "Shh, serious business."

"Any idea what might have triggered it?" Lucian asks.

"None," Rhett interjects, his eyes dark with something more than just the frustration of the unknown. "It's as though we woke up one day cursed, without rhyme or reason."

"Sure, because curses just drop out of the sky like hail," I say, unable to help myself, but the room stays as silent as a crypt.

Okay, no weather jokes. Noted.

While the Baxters keep spilling their ghostly tales, I'm watching them like a hawk. The glances they share, the silent communication—it's like they're tiptoeing through a minefield of secrets. They're a pack, and we're the outsiders crashing through their den.

Trenton and the other kids keep trading these heavy looks that seem way too intense for teenagers, and Rhett looks like he's about one sigh away from blowing up at his parents. I mentally file that for later—there's definitely more family drama here than they're letting on.

Lucian catches my eye, his gaze sharp as a tack, reminding me to keep my head in the game. His presence is like an anchor in this supernatural mess, grounding me so I don't get swept away by all the Baxter theatrics.

"Have you tried reaching out to other werewolves?" I suggest, doing my best to sound helpful and not too nosy. "Maybe someone else has experienced something similar."

"That's not an option," Rhett says quickly, too quickly. His mother places a hand on his shoulder, a silent plea for him to hold back. It's obvious they're balancing on a tightrope, caught between two worlds—trying to blend into their affluent, human neighborhood while wrestling with a curse that threatens to blow their cover sky-high.

"Fair enough," I say, clicking off my tape recorder. I'm not going to second guess how they interact with other covens, not without good cause.

"Let's start with the basics then," Lucian offers diplomatically. "We'll need to do a walk-through of the house, see if we can sense anything out of the ordinary."

The Baxters exchange glances, talking without words. Finally, with a nod from Alex, we're good to go.

"Lead the way," I say, pocketing the tape recorder and squaring my shoulders.

"Thank you," Lucian adds, his gratitude genuine but filled with that vampire charisma that no doubt keeps his coven in line. I roll my eyes, though he can't see it.

I trail behind Rhett as he guides us through the grand foyer of the mansion, with Lucian keeping pace as my silent shadow on the right. The place is a maze of dark wood and serious-looking portraits, each hallway carrying the weight of ages and the faint smell of a rainy day. It's the kind of house that whispers secrets in your ear when you lean too close to the walls.

"Built by my great-great-great, add another seven greats, grandfather," Rhett says with a sweep of his arm, pride and reluctance mingling in his voice. "The man had more money than sense, and a knack for drama." He grins at me over his shoulder, teeth flashing white against his tanned skin.

"Sounds like someone else I know," I quip, earning a raised eyebrow from Lucian. I shrug. "What? If the cufflink fits..."

We pass through a dining hall that could double as a ballroom, and a library that I swear is just showing off with its two-story ceilings and ladders that slide along endless shelves.

As we ascend a staircase that curls upward like a question mark, Sylvia Baxter falls into step beside me. Her eyes are the color of storms on the horizon and just as foreboding. "Rhett didn't tell you about the house's dignified history?" she asks.

"Ah, no," I reply, glancing at Lucian who gives nothing away. "We just met, and I only got a quick rundown of the problem."

"I see," Sylvia says. "I simply wondered if he—"

"If he what?" I prod gently. Rhett's shoulders stiffen in front of us.

"He's never valued our family's legacy. Or how we've preserved it," she discloses. "He was always more interested in tearing down the history than building it up."

I eye Sylvia closely, trying to peel back the layers behind her fancy facade. There's a bitterness in her tone, a resentment simmering beneath the surface.

Before I can say anything, Lucian jumps in like the smooth operator he is. "Legacy can be a heavy burden to bear, especially when it comes with expectations," he says, his gaze flickering between Sylvia and Rhett.

Sylvia's eyes narrow just a fraction before her face slides into that perfect, practiced mask of calm indifference. "Yes, well, not everyone appreciates the sacrifices we make," she says coolly, her words dripping with unspoken accusations. The tension in the air is thick enough to slice with a butter knife and I half expect someone to flinch. Probably me.

Lucian pauses beside me, his posture relaxed but alert. I can tell he's itching to take control, to defuse the tension, but this isn't his coven. It's a den of werewolves with more secrets than a politician, and our job is to uncover them without getting bitten. Literally.

"Why don't you ask Rhett to show you where the hauntings appear to originate?" I suggest.

He nods and glides towards Rhett and the others.

I pivot back to Sylvia. "Looks like you all are pretty close-knit now," I observe, my curiosity piqued and my instincts tingling. "Did something change?"

"Rhett left us," she says, and there's a world of hurt in those three words. "After his brother Roger, Trenton and Amy's father, passed away. A difficult time for our family. He thought we weren't being true to ourselves, hiding who we are. He said we swept his death under the rug like it was just another inconvenient truth."

I know a family secret when I see one, and the tension in this house is thicker than the legal jargon in a contract. The haunted house isn't just haunted by ghosts; it's plagued by the unresolved issues festering from within.

"Maybe he just needed some space..." I venture, hoping to pry more from her.

"Perhaps." She pauses at the top of the stairs, her gaze distant. "He finally saw reason and returned. He's even taken on the leadership role... Some might say he returned with his tail between his legs, but I see it as him trying to make up for past mistakes. For once, he cares about our illustrious reputation."

"What does Trenton think?" I ask, watching Rhett from afar. He's pointing out an antique vase to Lucian, but his attention seems half-hearted. Trenton is skulking behind him, looking more moody preteen than young adult. Sylvia had directed the other kids and the older couple back to their rooms before the tour began, but Trenton refused.

"Trenton idolized Rhett as a child," Sylvia admits, her voice softening, though not entirely. "But he's not as forgiving of the abandonment. He's angry, and his resentment festers. If it were up to him, we wouldn't bother with secrecy at all. He's always talking about modernization, exposure... so long as his cell phone has service." She tightens her lips into a line sharp enough to draw blood. "But they're family. They'll find their way."

"Family often does," I murmur, though I'm speaking metaphorically rather than aspirationally. If my dad suddenly waltzed back into my life acting like everything's peachy keen, I'd be leerier than a cat in a room full of vacuums.

As we follow Rhett through another set of rooms, my mind buzzes with questions. *Could Trenton's father be the restless spirit here? Why hide a death in a family that surely has seen its share of the otherworldly? What* exactly *are they hiding?* And something about what Sylvia revealed presses even more of my buttons. Maybe Trenton's resentment goes deeper than frustration with secrecy. Maybe his bitterness isn't just anger—it's action. In a family steeped in tradition, what better way to force change than to curse the very legacy you feel trapped by?

As we trail Rhett through another set of lavish, dust-laden rooms, my mind spins with questions. Maybe Trenton's resentment goes deeper than a grudge over secrecy. Maybe it's not just anger—it's action. In a family shackled by tradition, what better way to rebel, to force change, than by cursing the very legacy you feel imprisoned by? Or could Trenton's *father* be the restless spirit haunting this place? Why would they hide a death in a family that's no stranger to the otherworldly? What exactly are they so desperate to keep buried?

"Are there any family customs regarding death?" I ask casually, trying to weave another thread into the tangled web of secrets without setting off any alarms.

"Traditions, yes. But none that would be relevant here, I think." Sylvia's gaze meets mine, sharp and assessing. "Why do you ask?"

"Curiosity," I say, flashing my most innocent smile. "Comes with the job."

"Of course," she replies, though I'm pretty sure she doesn't buy it for a second.

We round another corner. But it's clear these walls hold more than just family portraits.

The antique grandfather clock in the hall strikes eleven, the chime filling the house like the opening credits to a scary movie. Rhett leads us to a bedroom on the first floor that looks like it's been collecting dust since the days of whale oil lamps. If I thought the rest of the house was a museum to bad taste and antiques, this room is a mausoleum. The immediate family takes their places, with Sylvia perched primly on an embroidered settee, her hands folded neatly in her lap.

"Looks like someone's idea of Victorian chic met a garage sale," I mutter to myself, eyeing an ominous painting of some dour ancestor on the wall behind the bed. Its eyes seem to follow me, judging from beyond the grave. Likely critiquing my choice of outfit.

"Every night at midnight," Sylvia begins, her voice steady but holding a weariness that seems to seep from the very walls, "the curse takes hold."

"Sounds punctual," I quip, trying to lighten the mood. Nobody laughs.

Note to self—they do not find me funny. At all.

"This is the epicenter," she says, continuing to ignore my witticisms.

I study the room, taking in the furniture that looks like it's one sneeze away from total collapse and wallpaper so faded it might as well be a distant memory. The moonlight filters through the dusty curtains, creating eerie shadows that dance across the warped floorboards. Rhett stands by the window, staring out at the crescent moon with a look that screams brooding protagonist. Whatever he's thinking, it's probably as complicated as the vibe in this house.

"Why here?" I ask.

Sylvia's gaze darts towards the window as if expecting a ghostly apparition to materialize at any moment. "We have no idea. There is nothing special about it. It's not a room with *any* magical significance."

"But it is closest to the street," Alex says, leaning against the doorframe.

Meaning it's prime real estate for any supernatural antics to catch the neighbors' attention.

"Ever thought about just... boarding up the windows and locking the door?" I ask.

Lucian's sharp gaze flickers towards me, a silent warning not to push Sylvia too far. But it wasn't a joke, it was a legitimate suggestion.

Clearing my throat, I lean forward and try again. "Is there a reason this room isn't as... well put-together as the rest of the house? Could that be why the haunting is focused in this room?"

Sylvia's eyes flicker with something—a flash of guilt—before she quickly masks it. "It was my grandfather's room, but after he passed... Roger used it as a playroom and then as his study," she admits, her voice barely above a whisper. "He was attached to the history of this room, wouldn't let us change a thing. Not even the dingy dust cover. After he died, no one had the heart to touch it."

My brows raise and I exchange a weighted glance with Lucian. Saying this room isn't significant, but was Roger's hangout before his death? Something is rotten in the estate of Oakheart.

"Have you tried communicating with the ghosts? Asking what he—they—want?" I ask, my mind already ticking off potential negotiation tactics with what is likely Roger's ghost.

"Communicating?" Sylvia scoffs. "This isn't a wayward spirit searching for closure, Ms. Lane. This is something... else."

"Something more vindictive?" I suggest.

Sylvia nods, her gaze distant. "Exactly," she whispers, her fingers twisting together nervously in her lap. "And I fear its vindication will mean our downfall."

Rhett makes a rough noise in his throat but doesn't turn around.

I glance over at Trenton sitting on the dusty bed; his jaw is clenched tight enough to crack walnuts. He's watching me like I might sprout horns any minute. I pull out my rose-colored glasses—my only trick for seeing the unseen—and slip them on, peering around the room.

"Still the same old—ahem—expensive decor," I mutter, more to myself than anyone else. Nothing reveals itself beyond the ordinary, no hidden energies or spectral glimmers.

"Those won't help you here," Trenton snaps, rolling his eyes. "We're all paranormal, remember? If there was something to see, don't you think we'd have seen it by now?"

"Not everyone is blessed with your supernatural vision," I say lightly, tucking the glasses back into my pocket. "Some of us have to rely on cheap parlor tricks to keep up."

"Actual talent would be better," he retorts, but his tone's softer now.

"Touché." I give him a mock salute, holding back a joke about one of them biting me. And for a split second, I think I see the ghost of a smile on his face.

"Midnight approaches," Sylvia says, drawing our attention back to the curse. "You'll want to be prepared. Whatever this is… it's relentless."

"Then let's not keep our supernatural host waiting," I reply with a defiant lift of my chin. I've faced down courtroom ghouls far scarier than whatever haunts these halls—or so I tell myself. When it comes to ambition, I'm still all about fighting for the win, whether it's against the living or the dead.

Chapter 5

My cell phone tells me we have fifteen minutes until our haunted house comes alive. Err, starts haunting, that is. The rest of the Baxter family, except Rhett, vanishes elsewhere into the house, hiding from the spooky shenanigans.

I quickly turn on my tape recorder and open my phone's camera, tossing the latter to Lucian. "For posterity or evidence. Whichever comes first."

"Should we seek out our strategic positions?" Lucian suggests, scanning the room with a practiced eye.

"Bedside for me," I decide, slipping into the role of observer with ease. "You take the armoire. If anything jumps out, I want you to have a clear shot for the camera—and me to have an exit strategy."

"Always the pragmatist," he comments.

"Hey, you're the immortal here," I reply.

"I'll remain here," Rhett says from the window. He leans against the wall, crossing his arms almost idly, as though staking out a haunting is a regular occurrence. Although for him, I guess it is.

We settle in, the waiting game now at play. I opt for the floor rather than the dusty bed but still must hold back a few sneezes. My tape recorder rests beside me, silent for now, but ready to catch any confession, spectral or otherwise.

"Ghost hunting with a vampire and a werewolf," I chuckle, shaking my head as I adjust the settings on my recorder. "Sounds like the start of a bad joke, doesn't it?"

"Or an excellent one, depending on the punchline," Lucian retorts from his watchful post near the armoire. "Something to do with a clove of garlic and a silver knife. I'll let you know when I've come to it."

"I don't remember you being this... funny," I say, eying him. I'd clocked the banter outside but wasn't going to look a gift horse in the mouth. Even annoyed—and, fine, romantically off balance—by his intrusion, it's fun to spar.

"You haven't known me all that long," he says mildly.

I won't remind him that that's *somewhat* of a lie. Technically, I've known him for years, while I was proving myself trustworthy and reliable—and discreet—to the coven, particularly Tina, so the vamps would let me donate blood. But Mr. Tall, Dark, and Handsome coven leader was more like Mr. Tall, Aloof, and Intense, never chummy like Tina and Stardust. But a staid coven leader protecting his 'troops' from those things and people that could harm them probably didn't have the time, or interest, in laughing it up with the walking blood-bags he barely tolerated.

"Besides," he continues softly, "it's only recently we've become... companions."

A flush threatens to overtake my entire face. Damn my stupid emotions that being reminded I have friends makes me all warm inside. I touch my cheeks with the back of my hands. "I suppose sharing a toothbrush will heighten any relationship," I tease, throwing out an innocent callback to when we became more than acquaintances. Better that than bringing up the kiss. Definitely safer.

"We did not share a toothbrush," he says, sounding slightly affronted. But the ticking at the corner of his mouth tells me he understood the reference.

"Alright, let's focus," I say, more to myself than to him. "Any expectations for tonight, my aged comedian friend?"

"Uncertainty," Lucian states simply, crossing his arms. "Ghosts should not be real. Thus, these events are unpredictable. They defy logic, which will likely irk you."

"Sounds like it's irking *you* more than me," I counter, clicking on the tape recorder. "But unpredictability is just unsolved patterns. Everything has an explanation."

"Even ghosts?"

"I suppose," I say, my voice steady even as a whisper of doubt creeps in. "If pixies and unicorns are real, why not ghosts?"

"You believe ghosts would not have been seen before now?"

I shrug. "I think even paranormals have blinders on sometimes. What if there's another type of glass, lilac-colored maybe, that shows ghosts, like my rose-colored shows you all? And no one has found it."

"It means tonight will be less productive than we planned," Lucian responds dryly.

I ignore his skepticism. "Honestly, it's the magic part that gets me. If you're going to curse someone—a family, even—in a way that *costs* you, why not curse *them*? With bad breath, or misfortune, or, hell, violent injury—"

"Emily," Lucian warns, watching as Rhett tenses.

I wince. "Sorry. I'm not *asking* for it. Just... why curse someone to be *haunted*?"

"Perhaps you'll get your chance to ask the ghost," Lucian murmurs as the tick of the grandfather clock in the hall marks the seconds down.

I shift on the dusty coverlet, trying to get comfortable without making too much noise. The old house groans around us, a soundtrack of unsettling creaks and groans. My tape recorder sits idle in my lap, ready to capture any anomalies.

The clock ticks past midnight, and it feels like we're in some clichéd horror flick. The air is thick with tension, as if the house itself is holding its breath, waiting for something—or someone—to shatter the silence. My heart thrums a staccato rhythm against my ribs, anticipation sharpening my senses.

"Did you hear that?" Lucian suddenly tenses, his entire body going predator-still.

My heart leaps into my throat as I strain to listen. There it is—a faint scuttle, like claws scraping wood. "Rats," I offer, hoping to convince myself more than anyone else.

"There are no rats here," Rhett grunts as he moves closer towards the door.

"Perhaps the beginning of our cursed evening," Lucian counters, and there's a thread of excitement in his tone.

"Astute as always," I whisper sarcastically, hoping the bite in my tone hides the slight tremble in my voice.

The air thickens, heavy with anticipation, and the hairs on my arms lift with a strange static. There's a faint metallic tang in the air—supernatural energy, or maybe just the dust. Old houses really could use better ventilation.

But instead of some grand spectral reveal, it's just me, staring into the anticlimax. The silence stretches out, tense as a violin string, primed to snap with the slightest sound.

"Any minute now," I say, not sure if I'm taunting the curse or bolstering my courage. "This ghostly gala better be worth the invite."

"Patience, Emily," Lucian chides softly, though his expression tells me he's enjoying this just as much as I am—if 'enjoying' is the right word for this macabre stakeout.

Then it happens. An *actual* shift in the atmosphere, a flicker of movement in my peripheral vision. I twist my neck to check, but there's nothing there—just the pressing darkness. I stand, my heart thumping against my ribs like a gavel demanding order in the court of my chest.

"Did you see that?" I ask, my voice barely above a whisper, half expecting the shadows themselves to answer.

"See what?" Lucian rumbles, his body coiled, ready to pounce.

"Something... I don't know, it was like—" I cut off as the temperature plummets, a cold so bitter I can see my breath misting before me in ghostly exhalations. Lights flicker overhead, creating eerie shadows that dance along the walls in a spectral waltz.

"Definitely not part of the normal power grid issues," I note, my attempt at humor hollow in the face of the unfolding enigma.

"Indeed," Lucian agrees, stepping closer to me, and I'm oddly grateful for the solid presence of someone who doesn't have a heartbeat. Go figure.

We're about to speak again when a sudden, penetrating shriek slices through the room, emanating from nowhere and everywhere all at once. It's a sound that scrapes against my skull, primal and chilling—and decidedly humanoid.

Rhett sucks in a sharp breath, looking like he wants to bolt.

And then it truly begins—the subtle shift from mundane to mayhem. A book thuds to the ground from a shelf across the room, pages fluttering like the wings of a trapped bird. We both whip our heads toward the sound, eyes wide.

I flinch, despite myself. This is the stuff of campfire stories and late-night horror flicks, not the courtroom dramas I'm used to.

"Did you see—" I start, but Lucian holds up a hand to silence me.

"Watch," he commands softly, and I do.

I can hardly believe my eyes as the room comes alive around us. A vase teeters precariously on its pedestal, threatening to shatter at any moment. A painting on the wall tilts askew, its frame groaning as if it's protesting the disturbance. Overhead, the chandelier sways ominously, its dusty crystals catching the flickering light in a way that makes them glint like shards of ice. It's as if the house itself is waking up—and it's not in a good mood.

Then more sounds come—a chorus of whispers that swirl around us, the words indistinct. Goosebumps prickle over my skin, a visceral reaction to the disembodied voices that seem to taunt us from the shadows. The chandelier's bulbs start flickering erratically, but in a discordant pattern.

"Magic or not, it's got style," I manage to say, though my voice is barely above a gasp. I'm recording, documenting, witnessing—but a part of me, that lawyer always searching for the truth, wonders what tricks are at play in the darkness.

"Stay sharp," Lucian reminds me, his protective nature slipping through the cracks of his collected exterior. "We don't know what else may come."

"Right," I agree, gripping my tape recorder like a lifeline. "Sharp as a stake through the heart."

"Let's hope it doesn't come to that," he quips, but the humor falls flat as we brace ourselves for whatever comes with the next flicker of light or wisp of shadow. The repartee between us is forgotten as we stand united against the unknown—hunters of the night, even if one of us is armed with a law degree rather than fangs.

And then, it's the climax. All those things teasing us with movement suddenly come alive. Objects levitate, swirling in a maelstrom of poltergeist fury, and I duck as a lamp whizzes past my head, missing by inches.

"Emily!" Lucian grabs my arm, pulling me away from the bed as the room seems to spin around us, the laws of physics taking a nosedive into chaos. He retrieved me just in time, as the bed starts spinning upward, higher and higher towards the vaulted ceiling.

Dust swirls around us, kicked up by the movement and I sneeze, coughing out the taste of thick talcum.

"How subtle," I shout over the chaos, my sarcasm still intact even when faced with apparent wrathful spirits. I grab my glasses from my pocket and jam them onto my face as another book hurtles towards us.

"Focus, Emily!" He's scanning the room, every inch the predator, except this time, his prey is something even he doesn't understand.

"Right, because focusing is easy when furniture is auditioning for Cirque du Soleil!" I retort, but my eyes are darting around, trying to find patterns, explanations, anything that could ground this in reality. The glasses show me nothing, no ghostly apparitions, no spectral trails. Just the rose-colored image of a violent room.

But then, a creak—a mundane, everyday sound—pulls me back from the brink of belief. I frown, focusing on the noise as I put away the glasses. "You hear that?" I nudge Lucian, trying to focus my ears on that piece of normalcy fighting its way through the eerie spectacle.

"Footsteps on floorboards," he says, his eyes narrowing. "Or something pretending to be."

"If it is," I muse, clinging to rationality like a life raft in stormy seas, "we know ghosts don't have feet."

"Let's not jump to conclusions, any of the family may be inspecting the curse," Lucian cautions, though I catch a glint of agreement in his gaze. Our skepticism syncs up, a strange partnership between the supernatural and the legal-minded.

"No jumping here, feet firmly planted on the ground," I retort, but my mind is already cataloging every abnormality, searching for the man behind the curtain, so to speak. The curse may be terrifying, magical even, but I've cross-examined enough liars to know when something doesn't add up. *Because* where *were the ghosts?*

And then, as quickly as it started, it stops. The items drop, the sound fades, and the chill dissipates. The room reverts to its usual, albeit slightly less dusty, condition. The books float back to their shelves one by one, the vase slides back to the center of its pedestal as if guided by invisible hands, and the tilted paintings straighten themselves like obedient soldiers falling into line. We're left standing in the sudden stillness, panting, staring at each other with wide eyes.

"Do you really think—?" I begin, but Lucian shakes his head, cutting me off.

"Too early to tell." His voice is steady, but there's a flicker of something in his eyes—doubt, wonder, fear?

I scan the room. The dust had been blown away, so how was it present when we were entered the room? *Could it be...* ghost *dust?*

I stalk over to the formerly teetering vase. I examine it carefully, half expecting to find wires or some elaborate string setup. But there's nothing—no trickery, no hidden mechanism. Just an ordinary vase, perfectly intact and sitting innocently on its pedestal, as if it hadn't been part of a supernatural whirlwind moments ago. I move to one of the paintings next, running my fingers along its edges and checking the frame. It's solid, normal, just like the vase. No sign of tampering. I take a step back, frowning.

"Emily..." Lucian's tone shifts, drawing my attention to the window where a single red rose lies on the inner sill, petals perfectly intact despite the earlier turmoil, window still shut and locked from the inside.

"Okay, that's new," I say, stepping cautiously toward it. No card, no note, just a rose—a symbol, a message? My fingers hover above it, hesitant to disturb the enigma.

"An offering, perhaps?" Lucian suggests, equally wary.

"Or a clue," I counter, my inner lawyer is doing somersaults, piecing together a case with incomplete evidence. I peer out the window, searching for something, *anything*—footprints in the grass, movement in the periphery from someone running off. But there's nothing, just a silent night.

"Emily, look at this," Lucian calls out, and I turn to see him holding a small, intricately carved box. "It was hidden beneath the settee."

"Because of course it was," I mutter, crossing the room to join him. He flips the latch, and the box creaks open to reveal—

"Empty," we say in unison, staring at the velvet-lined nothingness.

"Or is it?" I probe, my curiosity piqued despite myself. "Can we take it and check?"

"This is your case," he says, closing the box with a soft click. "And we have more questions than answers."

"Story of my life," I reply, but there's a thrill in my voice that betrays my true feelings. There's something here, something more than just tricks and illusions, and I'm going to uncover it.

I shove the box into my bag with my tape recorder, tucking the rose into my pocket for good measure. With one last glance around, we tiptoe out of the room. The floorboards creak underfoot, louder than the sound we heard during the haunting, betraying our presence in the otherwise silent house.

"Speaking of my *many* questions after that performance," I whisper, scanning the shadowy corridor, "where did Rhett go? I assumed he'd be front and center for the ghostly grand finale."

The wheels in my brain are turning, cranking out theories faster than a jury reaches a verdict on a parking ticket. I've always had a knack for reading people, a skill that pays dividends in the courtroom. And right now, Rhett's no-show feels like a deliberate act—a sleight of hand to distract the audience while the magician prepares the real trick.

Lucian nods, his face set in thoughtful lines. "Although if he fears the curse as much as his mother appeared to, perhaps he hid away until it ended," he says.

"I guess," I say, my nose wrinkling. "Although that wasn't all that scary."

"I seem to recall you shaking when the entire room began to thrash."

"Sure," I reply. "I was surprised. But it was just some screams and floating objects. Nothing to panic over."

"As the Baxters advised, the panic," Lucian says dryly, "is from the potential exposure. You certainly recall what happens when extra attention is given to the paranormal set."

"True. Scary or not," I muse aloud, "I prefer my mysteries served with a side of incontrovertible proof, not paranormal pageantry and nonsensical clues."

"Then let's find your proof," he challenges, the glint in his eye speaking volumes. Whether our answers will come from beyond the veil or from someone hiding in plain sight, only time will tell. But one thing's for sure—Emily Lane doesn't lose—not to the living, and certainly not to the dead.

Cut to black.

Chapter 6

The phone buzzes against my desk, breaking the monotony of legal paperwork. I snatch it up, thumb pressing the screen to life, and Sara's words blink back at me in blue and white bubbles.

"Emily, I'm a mortician, not a mad scientist with a subterranean lab." Her text drips with the dry humor that's become a staple in our exchanges. At Lucian's suggestion—and confirmation I wasn't overstepping by asking—I left the box with Sara before work this morning, hoping her keen eyes and scientific expertise could shed some light on the discovery.

"Understood, but you're the closest thing I've got to a Scooby-Doo detective agency," I type back, adding a winking emoji for good measure. It's funny how Sara and I have gone from adversaries to texting buddies in just a few weeks—thanks, primarily, to a certain vampire acquaintance. Somewhere in the chaos of our initial interactions, a strange bond formed between us. But despite my best efforts, jealousy still flares up whenever Sara's connection with Lucian surfaces. They share a history that seems to defy time itself, often leaving me like an outsider peeking into a world I can't fully grasp.

"Being the last resort isn't all that complimentary," she fires back.

*"Not last, *best*,"* I reply. *"I sent the other thing to a real lab, if that helps?"*

The rose is being dissected and analyzed as we speak, just in case. I'll figure out how to handle the fallout if it turns out to be a ghost rose when the time comes. That's Future-Emily's problem.

Sara sends a handful of skull emojis, a reminder of her expertise in all things dead, and adds, *"That does help. I'll let you know if anything interesting turns up."*

"And don't accidentally cremate it, okay?" I send back, a grin sneaking onto my face despite the seriousness of our task.

"Wouldn't dream of it," comes her swift retort.

Before I can type another response, the door to my office bursts open, and Liz Thompson—assistant extraordinaire and fashion maven—blazes through like a comet with auburn hair. She's all bright-eyed urgency in her designer ensemble, a stark contrast to my own tried-and-true business attire.

"Em, you need to jet. According to your calendar, Rhett Baxter's expecting you at his work, like, yesterday."

"Already?" I feign surprise, even though I've been watching the clock like a hawk.

"Yup, and considering he's one of the few clients still keen on your... supernaturally friendly... services, I'd say don't keep the man waiting." Her grin is impish, unaware of the full extent of Rhett's heritage.

"Thanks, Liz. You're a lifesaver." I slip my phone into my purse and grab the tape recorder, ever ready to catch stray thoughts and whispered secrets.

Liz hands me a scrap of paper with an address scribbled on it. "It's an electrician's shop on the south side. How can an electrician afford such a big retainer?" she muses. "Like, that was down payment on a mega-yacht sized."

"Careful budgeting," I reply dryly, tucking the note in my pocket.

"Oh, Em," Liz says as I make my way towards the elevator. "I was looking over your hours sheet from yesterday. You billed six hours after work for a consultation with this guy?" Her perfectly sculpted eyebrows raise in surprise. "What kind of work does he have you doing?"

"I'll fill you in later, Liz," I say with a smile as I sidestep her question. Once I figure out how to bill 'ghost hunter' without giving the accounting department a heart attack.

"Go get 'em, tiger!" Liz cheers, her enthusiasm infectious as I stride out of the office and leave behind the mundane world for the promise of the paranormal.

The clang of metal and the buzz of electricity greet me as I push through the heavy door marked "Doyle Electrical Solutions." The warehouse is vast, humming with activity, a far cry from Rhett Baxter's opulent family manor in the burbs. Clad in overalls, grease smudging his brawny fore-arms, Rhett looks more at home among spools of wire than silver, err, golden spoons.

"Ms. Lane," he calls out, voice ringing clear above the din, "We didn't scare you off last night?" His grin is wolfish, and not just metaphorically.

I return his smile, my own sly one mirroring his. "Not eas-ily scared, Mr. Baxter. Besides, I've wrangled scarier creatures than your lot in the courtroom," I quip, my tone light as I approach him amidst the maze of machinery and tools.

Rhett's laughter cuts through the chaos of the workshop like a knife through butter. "I guess we can't be too intimidating if we're footing the bill for your legal prowess," he jokes, leading me to a quieter corner where we can talk.

My eyes land on a contraption that looks like it could power a small city, its wires intricately woven like a spider's web.

Rhett notices my interest and beams proudly at it. "This is my current pet project," he explains, his eyes alight. "It's a Tesla coil designed to transmit power wirelessly. Imagine a world where electricity flows freely without cables or constraints."

"It's quite a marvel. But why electricity?" I prod, genuinely curious now.

"It's shocking how much power a simple spark can have," he quips with a wink, clearly enjoying his own pun. "I've been fascinated by electricity since I was young, the way it connects everything and everyone in ways we can't even comprehend. But I didn't start playing with wires until I lived in St. Louis, working on the riverboats."

"A *boat* electrician? That's not something you hear every day."

"Like being a ghost hunting lawyer," he jokes with a playful smirk.

I chuckle. "Touche, Mr. Baxter. We're both navigating uncharted waters, it seems." Werewolves on a boat. Sounds as implausible as vampires on a spaceship.

Rhett gives me a once-over with his eyes. "No questions about why I'm here tinkering with circuits instead of sipping champagne and counting my money with the other Baxters?"

"Sure, a little extra-professional curiosity," I admit, pulling out the tape recorder. "So why the interest in the blue-collar life?"

His answer is simple yet revealing—"Proving ground." He leans against the workbench, looking every bit the rugged laborer with calloused hands and determined eyes. "If I can't build something with these two hands, then what good is a name or a bank account?"

"Or a pedigree," I add, teasingly, but there's truth in jest.

"Especially a pedigree," Rhett agrees. "We're the sum of our parts. And I want to be proud of each part, not sit back and let my so-called legacy become my identity."

He gazes into the middle distance, his smile fading. "You know, my brother never got that chance. We kept our werewolf secret hidden, and he paid the ultimate price. Shot in the woods like an animal by some trigger-happy hunter. If folks knew werewolves were real, if they knew we lived among them..."

"Your brother might still be here," I finish softly, his grief like a shroud over the conversation.

"Exactly." Rhett's eyes meet mine, fierce and resolute. "Ignorance breeds fear, and fear... well, it kills."

"Knowledge could save lives," I muse aloud, the wheels in my brain turning. "Or it could ignite a witch hunt."

"Which is why we tread carefully," Rhett affirms. "And why I need your help, Emily."

"But why me, just a regular ol' lawyer? Instead of going straight to a witch for help?"

"Most witches?" Rhett scoffs, wiping his hands on a rag. "They're more shadow than substance these days. They don't want be found. And the last thing I need is to accidentally hire the hexer who cursed us."

I nod, considering. It makes a twisted kind of sense in our upside-down world where vampires own bars and werewolves wire boats.

"Fair point," I concede, leaning against a cluttered workbench. "Except that still doesn't explain me. I may have gotten Lucian off the hook, but curses? Not exactly my forte."

"But Emily," Rhett says, leaning closer, the intensity in his eyes igniting a spark of competition within me, "you're a wildcard. You've proven you can navigate our world and yours. Witches might be adept at spells, but you... you're not one of us, which means you can see things we might miss. You look at the world differently, and that's what we need. And you know when to push, even if it means breaking a few rules."

"Alright," I say, determination settling in my chest like a gavel ready to strike. "Then here's my first look—Last night, you left that room in quite a hurry."

He glances up at me, his brow furrowing. "It was... unsettling. It always is. I thought I could handle it, but..." Rhett shakes his head, a gesture that doesn't shake off the concern etched into his face. "That was Roger's voice. That... that scream."

My brows raise. My hunch that this involves Roger grows roots.

And speaking of roots, Rhett continues, "And then seeing that flower appear? I needed to get out of there."

"Why? It's just a rose," I push, hoping my tone comes off as curious rather than demanding. While the entire haunting is strange, hearing your deceased brother's scream seems like the straw that would break Rhett's back. In comparison, the appearance of a rose didn't seem particularly terrifying.

Rhett's gaze locks onto mine, and I can tell there's a whole greenhouse of information he's holding back. "A rose. Right." He frowns. "Let's just say that roses are more than just flowers for werewolves. They're... symbols."

"Like, what—red for love, yellow for friendship?" I suggest, raising an eyebrow. The idea of a ghost using flower language—one I only vaguely remember from regency PBS specials I watch when insomnia hits—seems far-fetched even in this scenario.

He shakes his head, his jaw tense. "No. They're not about human sentiment. For us, they're more... they're omens."

"Omens of what?" I press, my curiosity piqued as much by the mystery as by the sudden intensity in his eyes.

"Loss," he says after a beat, almost whispering, as if the word itself might summon whatever forces it signifies. "Betrayal. A relationship sundered."

"Cheery options," I quip, trying to mask the shiver his words send down my spine with a grin. "Any thought as to which applies to your ghost?"

"None whatsoever," he admits, and the vulnerability in his admission tightens something in my chest. "But I intend to find out."

"Me too," I nod. "I mean, that is what you're paying for."

Before our conversation can continue, the sharp ring of my phone cuts through the air, startling us both. I glance at the caller ID and my heart skips a beat. Moonlit Haven.

Moonlit Haven is the bar owned by Lucian's second-in-command, Severin. Those not 'in the know' think it's just a fun and quirky bar set up like a speakeasy, with theme nights and costumes galore. But it's really a place for those paranormals who come above ground to gather, play, and meet their human snacks. Succubae find lovers there, fairies do back-alley deals, the works.

"Excuse me," I say to Rhett, answering the call with a sense of foreboding. "Emily Lane speaking."

"Ms. Lane, this is Noah from Moonlit Haven. I received your information from a patron," comes a clipped male voice. "We need you here, now."

A cold knot forms in the pit of my stomach. For them to call me with such urgency means something big must have happened.

"I'm on my way." I end the call and look up to Rhett, who's watching me with an expectant tension. "Duty calls," I announce, regret lacing my words. "Something's come up at Moonlit Haven. Can we pick this up later?"

"Of course," he replies, though his eyes narrow with concern. "Is everything okay?"

"We'll see," I say as I gather my things with haste. "I'll be in touch, Rhett. Thanks for the crash course in eerie floral arrangements."

With a quick nod, I spin on my heel and stride toward the door, the urgency of the call propelling me forward. As I weave through the maze of Rhett's workspace, I feel like I'm leaving one enigma only to tumble headfirst into another. But hey, that's just a day in the life of Emily Lane—paranormal lawyer extraordinaire, solver of supernatural snafus, and apparently, now a fledgling floriculturist.

Panting slightly, I push through the heavy door of Moonlit Haven, the familiar mix of incense and whiskey hitting me like a wall. A woman is at the bar, pouring a drink for a guy who looks like he stepped straight out of a 1920s speakeasy. The background chatter and clinking glasses fade into white noise as I scan the room for any sign of who called me and why. My fingers brush against the recorder in my pocket, a habit when I'm on edge.

"Ms. Lane!" A voice cuts through the murmur of the crowd. It must be Noah. He's standing beside the bar, tall and lean with blond hair falling just above his dark brown eyes. His black shirt, sleeves rolled up to his elbows, show-cases his muscular forearms and the tattoo of a beckoning moon against his umber skin. He also wears a concerned frown. "Thank goodness you're here."

"Noah, I presume?" I quirk an eyebrow, propping my-self up against the counter. "I rarely come running when strangers call, but something tells me this isn't about mixing a killer cocktail."

Noah nods, his expression grave. "It's about Rebecca," he says grimly.

Rebecca. The succubus with a heart of gold, or at least, as golden as a heart can be when you're part of the super-natural underworld. She'd been nursing a broken heart since Frank Mitchell got himself six feet under. She also gave me a talking-to that helped me with Lucian's case, without even smearing her mascara.

Noah guides me through the sea of creatures and wannabe creatures in the bar. I finally reach the booth where Rebecca sits, her voluptuous form draped across the seat, a real damsel in distress—if said damsel wore leather and could charm the pants off anyone with a single look.

"Emily, thank god." Relief and desperation tangle in her voice. "I didn't know who else to call."

"Frank Mitchell's ghost making a comeback?" I joke, sliding into the booth across from her, who manages a weak smile.

"Wouldn't that be something?" she says with a soft smile. Her eyes shift—blue, green, brown—as grief skitters across her expression. But soon enough, she wipes the pain away. "No, it's not Frank. But speaking of which, did you hear Mayor Peterson is finally behind bars? I guess some justice gets served."

"Only if you order it with a side of legal gridlock," I reply, my lips twitching.

Peterson ended up copping a plea just before Halloween. His "I'm innocent" costume fooled no one, not with my trusty tape recorder tearing off the mask. He, obviously, dropped out of the race, leading us to the current political predicament. Stephanie Evans, the self-interested but pro-paranormal candidate, had already withdrawn and couldn't cash in on that short-lived paranormal positivity stint. Tom Turner, with his whole anti-paranormal platform blowing up in his face, quickly followed suit as *that* cockroach knows how to avoid any fallout. The laws are weird enough about write-in candidates in Illinois, leaving us with an election last week and no potential mayor. Emergency rules kicked in and the city manager stepped in as Interim Mayor until the special election in the spring. It's a mess I'm glad I'm not cleaning up.

I turn my attention back to Rebecca and the mess that brought me to Moonlit Haven on a Thursday afternoon. "What's up? You're not about to tell me you've been sued by a disgruntled ghost, are you?"

"Nothing so spectral," Rebecca answers with a forced chuckle. "But it's serious, Emily."

I lean back, my brain already shifting gears from mystic roses to whatever fresh hell awaits, tape recorder already in hand. "Alright, Rebecca. Let's see what we're up against."

She leans forward, her silky white-blond hair pooling on the table. "I've been sued for intentional infliction of emotional distress," she admits, her usually confident demeanor faltering for a moment. "And I need your help to fight this."

My eyebrows shoot up in surprise. "Who would have the audacity to sue you for emotional distress?" I ask, scanning the room discreetly to see if anyone is eavesdropping on our conversation.

Rebecca bites her plump lip, a gesture that may have entranced others but not me. "It's Jenna, the ex-partner of a former lover, Miranda. We weren't even together when they broke up but Jenna is claiming I was the reason for their split."

This is the last thing I need—a case that reeks of supernatural scandal and personal vendettas. "And let me guess, Jenna's story isn't quite... accurate?"

"Spot on," Rebecca says. "She's telling everyone I bewitched Miranda into leaving her, which is ridiculous. I don't use magic!"

I pat her hand. "Not of the witchy variety, sure, but you're a sorceress of sin for the right prey."

Rebecca shrugs. "I can't help it. But it gets worse: Jenna's outed my paranormal status—and Miranda's connection to me—and Miranda's been fired."

And having a relationship with a paranormal isn't a protected class. Miranda's job loss is exactly what I'd feared when I took on Lucian's case. My stomach churns at the revelation, my mind racing through all the potential implications.

"Talk about being stuck between a rock and a hard place—or should I say, between a succubus and a lawsuit." I crack a smile at my joke, though the situation is far from humorous. "What a nightmare for Miranda."

"Jenna is out for blood, and she's using Miranda's pain as ammunition," Rebecca continues bitterly, her gaze hardening.

"Doesn't Jenna realize this could backfire on her?"

She scowls. "She doesn't care who she hurts, even herself, if she gets what she wants."

My mind is already in overdrive, calculating strategies, defenses, and the potential fallout of diving into yet another supernatural debacle that could either make or break my already shaky career.

"Emily, please," Rebecca implores, leaning forward. There's desperation in the lines of her face, a plea in her eyes. "I need your help. I'll pay whatever it takes."

"Money's not an issue, then?" I probe, already knowing there's more to this than meets the eye. My clients need to have resources, but desperation often comes with strings attached.

"Let's just say I have a benefactor," Rebecca murmurs, casting a glance over her shoulder as if worried the walls might be listening.

"Who is it?" I ask, tapping my finger against the table, a rhythm to jog her honesty. The question is straightforward, but her hesitation speaks volumes.

"Someone from my... community. They want to help me through this." She fiddles with a silver ring on her finger, avoiding eye contact. "It's complicated."

I watch Rebecca closely, her evasiveness setting off a warning bell in my mind. But, no matter how interested I am, it isn't my business. "Complicated seems to be the theme of the day," I mutter.

"Will you take the case?" she urges.

"Well, Rebecca," I begin, my tone measured, "I can't guarantee a victory, but I'll do everything in my power to defend you against these baseless accusations. Just remember, honesty is crucial."

"Thank you, Emily. I knew I could count on you." Relief washes over Rebecca's gorgeous features.

"Don't thank me yet. You know how these things go—twists, turns, and the occasional supernatural curveball." But as I say it, I'm already mentally preparing for battle. Still, I can't deny the spark of excitement flickering under the surface. Another case, especially one with a paranormal twist, feels like a win in my book. Sure, my firm would probably blow a gasket if they knew I was taking on yet another job that doesn't fit their cookie-cutter mold, but I can't bring myself to care.

As we wrap up our meeting, Rebecca thanks me again, but I can sense her worry and fear behind the gratitude.

"Take care, Rebecca," I say, standing to leave. "And keep an eye out for anything unusual. Anything at all."

Exiting Moonlit Haven, I know I've got a packed evening ahead, with plans to rendezvous with Stardust for board games. But as I stroll home, my mind is fixated on this case—and the other one too.

"Tomorrow, you and me, we're going to have a little chat," I tell the tape recorder, thinking of the box Sara's examining. "And maybe then, some of these secrets will start to spill."

Chapter 7

Friday afternoon finds me gleefully exploiting company resources for my paranormal investigation instead of gearing up for a weekend of leisure. I spent the morning delving deeper into the history of the neighborhood surrounding Oakheart Estate and scouring the dark web for information on curses. I have to smirk at the delightful irony—here I am, employing the skills polished for cutthroat litigation, approved by the firm, to navigate the ethereal intricacies of the supernatural. And the cherry on top? The billable meter keeps ticking, and the firm can't utter a word of complaint.

"Emily, what's this entry from this morning about 'historical property research?'" Liz's voice cuts through my amusement, her green eyes squinting at the billing sheet. She stands by my desk, impeccably dressed, every auburn curl in place. Meanwhile, I'm rocking my usual *functional lawyer chic* look, accessorized with dark circles under my eyes from another sleepless night.

"Ah, that," I say, deflecting with ease. "It's just some outside general counsel work for the Baxters."

"An electrician needs general counsel?" Her eyebrow arches, skepticism painting her freckled face.

"Technically, it's for his entire family. They've got quite the place out in the suburbs." I shoot her an eye roll that's more sincere than anything I've shown in the past hour.

"Sounds... fancy." She tilts her head, not quite convinced but letting the topic slide off her tailored blazer like water off a duck's back.

"Trust me, it's all very dull legal stuff," I assure her, hoping my nonchalance sells the story. "Now, if you could fetch me the Henderson file, I need to cross-reference something before I head out for my meeting at the Baxters."

"Sure thing, boss." Liz turns with a flourish, her curiosity shelved for now.

"Actually, Liz, on second thought, I might—" My sentence is interrupted by the shrill ring of my cell phone. "Would you mind giving me a moment?"

"Of course," Liz responds with a swift nod, the click of her high heels echoing as she exits, leaving behind a lingering trace of expensive perfume.

It's Sara and I eagerly answer. "Velma, tell me what you've got."

Her chuckle is warm on the line. "Is that a Scooby-Doo reference?"

"Yes, and I'm hoping whatever you're calling about will end with me saying 'jinkies,'" I reply, swiveling in my chair to face the window, the outside world blissfully unaware of the supernatural scavenger hunt consuming my attention.

"Well, about that box Lucian found," Sara starts, and I can almost hear the frown in her voice, "It's just some fancy wood veneer and velvet lining. But there's iron underneath."

"Iron... like the nemesis of fairies?"

"You certainly know your paranormals," Sara responds, and is that a hint of admiration in her voice?

"Only enough to get myself into trouble," I say dryly. I thought it prudent to study up after becoming persona non grata with a pixie.

"Also," Sara continues, pulling me back from my fey-focused musings, "there's a tiny screw stuck in one corner. I pried it out, but nothing it's special. Just dusty, and stripped."

"Random hardware does not a curse make," I say, frowning as I mentally catalog the box as a dead end. While iron hidden beneath its elegant exterior suggests a protective measure against supernatural beings, particularly the Fae, an empty box means there's nothing to safeguard now. Yet, the detail nags at me—why an iron box in that room? Is it a crucial piece of the puzzle or just a red herring?

"Thanks, Sara. Even if it's not the smoking gun, it's one more piece off the board." I try to infuse my voice with optimism, but it rings hollow even to my own ears.

"Anytime, Emily." There's a soft click as we end the call, and I'm left staring at the legal briefs scattered across my desk. They seem laughably mundane compared to the otherworldly investigation I've been sucked into.

With a sigh, I hang up the phone and glance at the clock. Another mystery awaits, but for now, back to the thrilling world of land disputes and liability waivers. At least until mid-afternoon.

I shove the last of the paperwork into my drawer and glance at the clock. *Who schedules a city council meeting at 2 p.m. on a Friday?* Oh right, the kind of people who have more money than sense and less work than a government office on a holiday. I grab my coat and make a beeline for the door.

"Please tell me you'll at least do *something* fun tonight," Liz calls out as I make my way towards the exit.

"Good billables are fun," I call back, flashing her a grin that probably looks more forced than friendly. It's a creed I've repeated so often it might as well be tattooed on my soul—or at least scrawled on my office wall. But that was back when I had my clandestine (and definitely not HR-approved) stress reliever to take the edge off the grind of firm life.

I had to skip the last self-defense class and I can feel my shoulders creep closer to my ears with every passing stress-filled day. If I don't find a healthier outlet soon, I'll end up either cracking or passing out at my desk.

As I slip into the back of the tiny council chamber, I'm thankful for the oversized sunglasses and scarf that obscure my face, along with the high-quality wig. I'd retired the blonde monstrosity and picked up a cute redheaded number. Call it post-partnership splurge. Or call it what it really was—an after Halloween sale in a year when no one was dressing up as Jessica Rabbit.

But the ensemble works, hiding my identity. No need for anyone to know Emily Lane, cutthroat lawyer extraordinaire, is slumming it in upper-class suburbia. I find a spot behind a potted fern that's clearly getting better care than I am these days and settle in.

The gavel hits the block with a pompous finality that's meant to command respect, but all I can think is 'judge wannabe'. The room falls into a silence thick enough to slice through—clearly, these council meetings are the Oscars of this tiny town. I stifle a yawn as the first speaker approaches the podium, droning on about fence heights with the zeal of a televangelist during pledge week.

"Thrilling," I mutter under my breath.

As each speaker takes their turn at the podium, I lean in, pretending to be fascinated. In reality, I'm doing reconnaissance, identifying the influencers, the pushovers, and the mavericks—all potential chess pieces in my grand plan to infiltrate the inner workings of Oakheart Estate's mysteries. But this isn't just a meeting; it's a petri dish for power plays and stifled creativity, a microcosm of everything that's hilariously wrong with bureaucratic micromanagement.

"Thank you, Sean. We will be sure to drop off our donations to the Thanksgiving food drive by next Friday. Now," a councilor announces, his voice dripping with the self-importance only a small-town politician can muster, "next on the agenda is the designation of historical homes." He peers over his reading glasses like he's about to impart some great wisdom, but all I hear is the prelude to a nap. "We'll begin with the oldest of our edifices, Oakheart."

"The *Baxters*," another councilor interjects with a snort, "They've never even attended a single meeting. Why should we extend them any courtesies?"

There's a murmur of agreement that has my eyes rolling back into my head. You'd think they were discussing rogue nations, not the reclusive residents of some dusty old house.

"Furthermore," a woman clad in pearls and a scowl chimes in, "the Baxters' children are at it again with their light shows. It's simply unacceptable."

The room buzzes with discontent, and I'm scribbling down mental notes faster than a courtroom stenographer. Light shows? *Again*? If that's not a neon sign flashing 'mystery', I don't know what is.

The meeting drones on, but my mind is racing. Something's up at Oakheart Estate, something these polo-shirted pencil pushers aren't saying and the Baxters are hiding. And you can bet your last billable hour I'm going to find out what it is.

I squint at the sunlight bouncing off the immaculate lawns, each blade of grass standing to attention like it's part of the neighborhood watch. Clipboard in hand, I approach my first target—the neighbor to the east, a distinguished gentleman pruning his roses with the precision of a brain surgeon. Not red roses, pink. Still, they're roses.

"Excuse me, sir," I chime, summoning my best charming reporter energy. "I'm gathering some local history for an article I'm writing. I couldn't help but notice your impressive garden."

He pauses, peering over his bifocals with a skepticism that could probably curdle milk. "Local history, you say?" His voice is as crisp as his collar, and just as starched.

"Absolutely," I beam, trying to keep my enthusiasm as high as the irises at my feet. "The architecture, the families, anything really. Do you happen to know anything about Oakheart Estate?"

"Oakheart?" he repeats, his gaze flicking to my scuffed shoes and slightly wrinkled blazer. He sniffs, turning back to his roses with a dismissive wave. "I do not gossip about my neighbors, Mrs...?"

"Miss Smith," I lie smoothly, tucking an escaped strand of hair behind my ear. "Miss Emily Smith."

"*Mrs.* Smith," he corrects, clearly more interested in his roses than in maintaining societal niceties—or aiding my quest, for that matter.

"Right," I reply, though there's no ring on my finger. "Well, thank you for your time."

I jot down 'Roses, evasive' next to his house number and move on.

"Hello!" I call out to a woman walking her Pomeranian, who looks at me like I just insulted her choice of leash. "I'm doing a little historical research on the area. Do you have a moment?"

"Research?" She looks me up and down, taking in my sensible blazer—not designer, but not bargain-bin either—and gives me a thin-lipped smile. "What is this regarding?"

"It's about the neighborhood, but primarily Oakheart Estate," I reply, nodding towards the looming structure in the distance. "Any intriguing tales or unusual happenings you've noticed?"

Her gaze sharpens, and her Pomeranian emits a low growl that seems weirdly personal. "Weren't you the one there with that... man the other night? He bore quite the resemblance to the dreadful vampire making headlines."

My stomach does a little flip, but I keep my expression neutral. Lucky for me, *my* weeks on the news cycle weren't important enough for her to remember. "Oh, goodness, no. That must've been someone else. People look alike sometimes, don't they?"

She doesn't seem convinced, and I can tell by the way she scrutinizes my slightly worn heels that she's mentally relegating me to some lower social echelon. It's nothing new—I've never had the luxury to splurge on appearances, and old habits cling like cobwebs.

"Indeed," she says, drawing out the word as though tasting something sour. "Well, I haven't seen anything. This is a respectable neighborhood, after all." Her tone suggests that by respectable, she means *exclusive,* and that I'm not included.

"Of course," I concede with a nod. "Thank you for your time." I retreat, tucking away my tape recorder. She watches me leave, suspicion still etched in the creases around her perfectly made-up eyes.

By the fourth similar encounter, my list is less historical treasure trove and more registry of who's who in the garden club. Half the inhabitants were at the council meeting, turning their nose up at their own neighbors and taking advantage of the free canapes. But my attempts at neighborly banter are met with polite nods and tight-lipped smiles, as if the community has taken a collective vow of silence when it comes to the Baxters and their house.

"History is written by the victors," I mutter under my breath, "but apparently redacted by the residents."

Undeterred, I march up the cobblestone path leading to the next grandiose estate, the click of my modest heels drown out by the hum of expensive car engines and the whispers of silk blouses. I'm an imposter in a land of affluence, armed only with my wits and an unquenchable thirst for the truth—or at least a juicy tidbit I can sink my teeth into.

"Good afternoon!" I call out to another man pruning *his* roses—pink again. What's with this neighborhood and roses? "Beautiful garden you've got there. I'm gathering some details for an article on the area's historic homes. Oakheart Estate has quite the presence, doesn't it?"

He casts a frosty glance over his shoulder, his expression colder than the marble statues decorating his lawn. "Oakheart does not concern us," he says, voice clipped like the thorny stems falling to the ground. "And neither do nosy reporters."

"But it's for posterity," I reply, plastering a grin that feels more desperate than charming. "To honor the stories woven into the very *fabric* of this community."

"Fabric that's none of your business," he retorts before turning back to his roses with all the finality of a judge slamming a gavel.

Deflated but not defeated, I move on, crossing off another name from my mental tally. They say curiosity killed the cat, but in this neighborhood, it seems curiosity gets you the cold shoulder and a view of someone's back. Still, I'm not giving up. This is the tenacity Rhett wanted. There's a thread of a lead here somewhere, and all I have to do is find the right one to pull.

It isn't until I reach a grand Victorian mansion, ivy trailing up its walls, that someone deigns to speak with me.

The door swings open, and I'm greeted by a woman who looks like she just stepped out of a country club catalog. Her tailored navy suit screams expensive, and her silver hair is swept into one of those perfect updos that probably takes three hairstylists and a can of industrial-strength hairspray. A string of pearls rests on her neck like she was born wearing them. Her expression is all business at first, but it softens slightly when she sees me—though her sharp eyes tell me she's already sizing me up and filing the info away for later.

"Good evening," I chirp, turning on the charm. "I'm conducting some research on the history of the neighborhood, particularly the Oakheart Estate. Do you have a moment to chat?"

Her eyes dart towards the distant silhouette of the house before fixing back on me. "Oakheart Estate, you say?"

I launch into my well-practiced spiel about researching the history of the neighborhood, emphasizing the quaint charm of the area. She's all ears, nodding along as I mention what I've learned of the history from my morning browsing the web.

"Not many folks venture there these days," she chuckles, a twinkle in her eye. "I don't know much of the history, we only bought this house in the 90s, but I know a tale or two about that family."

"Oh, do tell," I urge, leaning in. "Emily Smith" might be batting zero, but Emily Lane? She's still got an inning or two left in her.

Before I know it, Mrs. Abigail Jennings has me tucked in at her teak dining table inside her parlor. The room itself is warm and inviting, with a plush rug spread over the polished hardwood floors. It's a room of secrets and indulgences, where tea and gossip were traded with equal measure.

"Tea?" she offers, pouring without awaiting my consent.

"Thank you," I say, taking the delicate China cup. I've never been one for the dainty, but when in Rome—or rather, when in the company of informative antiquarians.

"Now, you were telling me about the Baxters," I prompt when she settles in the upholstered chair beside me.

"The Baxters. Well," she begins, setting her cup down with a clink. "One of the sons, Roger, was always causing trouble for his parents," she spills, her eyes lighting up. "He nearly burned the building down once, doing some recording project, apparently. It was like a fireworks show but not your usual Fourth of July fare."

"Illegal?" I tease, lowering my voice.

She leans in, and I catch a whiff of her pricey perfume mingled with the faint aroma of old books. "Magic, some thought. But that's just silly talk. No magic would ever be around here."

I arch an eyebrow. "Why do you say that?"

"They'd be run out of the neighborhood!" she exclaims. "Wouldn't even need a mob with pitchforks, the gossip and hate mail would do the trick."

"I see." The gears in my head start clicking, piecing together the Baxter family's backstory.

"He wanted to be a filmmaker," she says, looking at her cup. "Always had a camera in his hand. The light show was the finale of some project of his, but after that near-miss, I never saw him recording again."

"What happened to him?"

"No one is sure. He settled down at some point. The younger boy too. Became rather respectable." She glances around as if checking for hidden eavesdroppers before dropping her voice to a whisper. "But then, one day, he disappeared. Nobody knows exactly what happened, if he abandoned the family or died within those walls. Since then, not even a visitor has dared to darken their doorsteps. Except for you and your friend, of course."

I flash her a casual smile, recycling the lie I'd used earlier. "People look alike sometimes."

She narrows her eyes, clearly not convinced by my deflection. "It was dark, and your hair looks much better, but I'm not losing my eyesight just yet."

I spread my hands in mock innocence. "Happens all the time. People see someone and think they recognize them."

She sniffs, tilting her head with a knowing look. "Gossip is currency around here, and I've got expensive tastes. If you see anything..."

I let out a soft chuckle, impressed by her persistence. "Well, there's no gold mine with me, I promise," I reply with a wink. "Rest assured, I'm just a curious outsider trying to piece together the neighborhood's history like a puzzle—minus the missing pieces, of course."

Her lips twitch as if holding back a smile of her own. "Well do tell me if you turn anything else up. Ethel Abernathy down the street has been claiming she saw a real-life vampire out here a few days ago." She shakes her head. "Can you believe it? Here?"

I smile back politely. "Sounds like a real page-turner."

"Even the book club couldn't swallow it," she says, winking. "But I'd still like to one-up her come our meeting next Tuesday. So do visit once you've got your story written, you hear?"

Nodding in false-agreement, I thank her for her time and make my way back down the path, mulling over the morsels of gossip she had shared. Roger being a vengeful ghost after his parents locked him up and then got him shot sounds plausible. Like a B-grade horror film, but still plausible. If Oakheart actually *had* ghosts. Add in magic that looks like fireworks and there's a recipe for a curse right here.

I hoof it back towards the wrought-iron gate, my feet aching. Who knew snooping around could be this painful? So, I do what any sensible gal would do—the minute I breach the gate, I kick off my heels and let them sink into the grass. No point in torturing myself any longer.

Once I'm sure there are no eagle-eyed eavesdroppers lurking about, I start snooping. I circle the manor, my recorder off for once as I let my eyes do the work.

"Talk about gothic charm," I murmur to myself, finally noting the ivy that clings as desperately to the walls as my ambitions do to my career. The house looms, something straight out of a history book, its gray stone walls whispering of bygone eras and a side of supernatural spookiness. It's a place that would make a historian salivate—or a paranormal enthusiast break out into goosebumps.

But I'm not here for aesthetics; I'm hunting clues.

The ground near the manor is soft, the grass a lush carpet that sinks slightly beneath my bare feet. And there, stamped into the earth, are footprints. Not just any prints; these are deliberate, heavy, leading me around the perimeter like breadcrumbs.

"Ghosts still don't have feet," I say with triumph. I follow them with growing anticipation, each step taking me closer to the window inside the first floor's bedroom that is the epicenter of the curse.

"Come on, give me something good," I coax under my breath as if the prints might hear and oblige.

But when I reach the window that marks the heart of the haunting, the footprints vanish, as though whoever—or whatever—made them simply evaporated into the thin air. Or leapt through the window.

But there are no signs of departure, no scuffs or scrapes of a hurried escape. Just an abrupt end and a single flower petal lying next to the sill, crimson against the green.

"Still an odd choice for a so-called ghost," I say, plucking the petal between my fingers and examining it. I tuck the delicate find into my pocket, the edges of another puzzle piece clicking into place—though the big picture's still frustratingly fuzzy. I try the window, yanking the bottom of the frame, but it won't budge. It's locked from the inside and would likely take superhuman strength to break it open.

Something crunches behind me and I whirl around. Alex is in the driver's seat of a town car—one that looks like it's a prop from a black and white movie, rolling up the gravel drive. On a whim, I duck around the corner and watch his arrival. He exits the car with a beautiful bouquet of what looks like red roses.

Roses which Rhett said had an unfortunate meaning for werewolves.

I mutter a note to myself and my tape recorder. Alex stops short before the stairs to the entrance, and I jerk back, hiding from view. All the better not to be seen by him yet, not when the clues are piling up and not necessarily in the elder Baxters' favor. Once I'm sure he's inside, I slip back to the window and peer inside. From the outside, the room looks normal, if dusty, as though someone sprinkled age around the room. Dust that had been kicked up (and ingested by me, yuck) the nights prior.

With a last glance at the manor, I stride back to my car, tossing my purse onto the passenger seat before sliding behind the wheel. As the engine hums to life, I take a moment, letting the silence wrap around me like a lawyer's cloak.

"Okay, Emily, think," I tell myself, pulling away from the curb. The rose, the metal box, the mysterious neighbors, the curse... the lack of *any* actual spectral activity. Maybe I'd been too fixated on the haunted part when I should've been focusing on the magic part. And who's the witch behind it all? Someone out for revenge against the Baxters, whether it's for what they did to Roger or just out of plain old spite.

Whatever it is, I'm *not* scared off. I'll reveal the hidden hands that are playing the Baxter family like pawns. And when I do, it'll be one hell of a billable hour.

Chapter 8

I waltz into Oakheart Estate, the lingering flavors of garlic and rosemary from my dinner still dancing on my taste buds. *Take that, Liz. Fun achieved.* Especially when that fun was a 2-for-1 coupon that gives me lunch tomorrow.

But the moment I step into the formal living room, I'm met with a wall of annoyance that's thicker than the manor's ancient stone walls.

"Ms. Lane." Alex's tone is colder than a vampire's stare in a dark alley. "So much for discretion."

Sylvia stands beside him, arms crossed, eyes like daggers. Looks like they've been practicing their bad cop, mad cop routine.

"I'm not sure—" I start, but the ice in their glares could frost over my words.

"What were you thinking?" Sylvia scoffs, her sharp tone piercing the grand entryway. "Parading around, asking questions of the neighbors. You might as well have lit a beacon!"

"Parading is a bit much," I fire back, trying to keep my cool as I navigate through their accusations. "I was careful. I wore a disguise and everything An eager historian is less alarming than a ghost hunter poking around."

"*Careful*?" Alex's disbelief raises the temperature in the room by a few degrees. "Our entire existence hinges on remaining unnoticed!"

Before I can mount another defense, Trenton saunters into the room with a smirk that could sour milk. "Let's not forget our new favorite headline," he drawls, mischief glinting in his eyes. "Local Vampire Walks Free—Thanks to Attorney Emily Lane."

"Excuse me?" Alex's voice drops to a dangerous growl.

"Murder?" Sylvia turns paler, but fury burns in her eyes. She turns to me, the betrayal written all over her. "You're supposed to be our advocate, not a harbinger of scandal."

"Scandal sounds dramatic," I say, but my heart hammers at their intensity. It's true, Lucian's history is... checkered. And okay, maybe we ended up on the news, but it's not like I planned a prime-time special about it.

"Tell that to the neighbors who now think we harbor criminals," Sylvia snaps.

"Alleged," I correct automatically, lawyer mode kicking in despite the situation. "And he was cleared, remember?"

"Cleared doesn't mean innocent," Alex mutters, his expression darkening.

"It kind of does," I counter, lifting my chin defiantly. "Considering I was his alibi and helped nail the real culprit."

Trenton lets out a low chuckle, crossing his arms "This is getting good. I almost feel like I should pop some popcorn and enjoy the show."

"It's the only entertainment we've got," Amy, the silver-haired teen, chimes in petulantly. "Since you won't let us have a TV."

I shoot Trenton a glare that could freeze hell over, but then I turn back to face Alex and Sylvia, softening my tone. "I get it, you're upset. But trust me, I never meant to bring any harm or unwanted attention to Oakheart Estate. I'm here to help."

"Help?" Sylvia echoes, skepticism lacing her voice. "Or hinder?"

"Definitely not hinder," I say, though their dubious looks suggest they're far from convinced. "I can't break the curse without knowing *why* you're cursed."

"Maybe you should stick to what you know, lawyer lady," Trenton chimes in again, enjoying the tension a little too much. "Leave the ghost hunting to the pros."

"If you find one, be sure to tell me," I say, clenching my jaw. "And your vote of confidence in me is duly noted, Trenton."

"Confidence isn't given, it's earned," Alex chimes in, his gaze unwavering.

I'm about to respond when another voice cuts through the tension from the shadows of the grand entryway. "Enough."

Everyone stops. Even Trenton, who looks good for a snarky remark or two more. Rhett steps in like he's the principal breaking up a schoolyard fight, and suddenly, everyone's pretending they weren't about to claw each other's eyes out.

He moves to stand in front of his fuming parents, basically acting as my human shield against their scorching looks. "Emily was just doing the job I hired her to do." His voice is calm but firm, like he's the king laying down the law. "You handed me this responsibility, remember? When I got back from Missouri."

"When Grandpa dragged you back, you mean," Trenton mutters under his breath.

"Trenton!" Sylvia snaps, shooting him a glare sharp enough to cut glass.

But Rhett and Alex are locked on to each other, ignoring the sideshow.

"The past is just that—past," Rhett says, practically growling. "Isn't that what you said? That we must focus on the present and future if we are to survive. Which means Emily continues her work."

Alex's jaw tightens, and I can almost hear his teeth grinding. "I'm not sure we need her anymore."

"Why not?" I ask.

"There was no haunting last night," Rhett explains, turning to face me.

My eyebrows shoot up, surprise plastered on my face. "No haunting?" I repeat, as if saying it out loud will make it more believable. "Well, that's... unexpected."

"Indeed," Rhett nods, a thoughtful look in his eyes. "Although I'm not convinced our troubles are over, it does mean something has changed. And perhaps it's not a coincidence that it coincided with your arrival, Emily."

"Maybe she's the curse," Trenton says from the sidelines. Somehow, his attempt to pin this on me breaks the tension like a well-timed punchline.

"Right," I say, rolling my eyes. "Because I moonlight as a malevolent spirit on weeknights. It's great cardio."

Rhett doesn't laugh, but I catch a flicker of amusement in his eyes before he turns back to his parents. "Mom, Dad, why don't you go to the east wing? It should be safe there, away from any... potential disturbances."

"East wing, west wing," Sylvia huffs, "might as well lock us in the attic with all this nonsense about safety."

"Better safe than sorry," Rhett insists, arms crossed, clearly not budging.

"Fine," Alex grumbles. Alex and Sylvia are about as pleased with the decision as a pair of vampires at a garlic festival. They shuffle off with the kind of glares that could strip paint, casting wary glances over their shoulders as if they're heading into exile.

Rhett squares his shoulders and turns back to me. "I apologize for my parents," he says. "They're... protective, to put it mildly. And they don't always realize that things they disagree with might actually be the best course. We may not like it, but we'll be better for it in the end."

"You don't have to apologize," I reply. "I understand why they're wary. This... situation is complicated, and I'm an outsider. And," I add with a sigh, "apparently not as subtle as I think I am. But I'm here to help, Rhett. I meant what I said."

Rhett nods slowly, his eyes finally meeting mine. There's a flicker of something there—hope, maybe determination. "And we'll need all the help we can get. Things are shifting, Emily. The hauntings, the curse... I don't think it's over. I think it's just beginning."

He turns, his gaze drifting toward the home's tall windows, where moonlight streams in and casts eerie shadows across the room. The whole place feels like it's holding its breath, waiting for whatever comes next.

Rhett shakes off whatever deep thought was brewing. "Okay, kiddos," he says, turning to address Trenton, Amy, and Noah, who are doing a terrible job of pretending they're not hanging on every word. "You heard the plan. Wrap it up here and find somewhere else to be for the night. No exceptions."

He heads toward the door, throwing one last glance over his shoulder. "Stay out of trouble, Lane. Don't summon anything without me."

And with that, he follows his parents, no hint he's joining us in the epicenter again.

"I'm nineteen," Trenton grumbles, clearly not too thrilled about being lumped in with the younger crew. "Hardly a 'kiddo.'"

"Age is just a number, Trent," I tease, unable to resist. "And right now, yours is apparently synonymous with 'curfew.'"

He gives me a glare that might've been intimidating if it weren't for the dimple giving away his attempt at a serious face. Flopping onto the plush loveseat, he sprawls out, taking up more space than strictly necessary. Amy perches on the armrest beside him, her gaze bouncing between my face and the spot where Rhett disappeared.

"Rhett likes you," she quips with a smirk, her silver hair catching the dim lamplight like some kind of celestial halo.

I roll my eyes. "He hired me, Amy. There's a difference."

She shrugs. "I guess. Maybe it's just nice to have him back."

"Where was he?" I ask. Sylvia's version of the story felt a little too neatly packaged, and I'm itching to see what's in the unedited edition.

Noah, who's been fiddling with a toy car on the floor, pipes up without missing a beat. "Rhett's had a... complicated relationship with the coven," he says in a solemn tone that doesn't match his cherubic face. For a kid, he's got the whole wise-old-man vibe down pat. "After Uncle Roger died, Rhett disappeared. Left us all behind."

"More like ran away," Trenton mutters, slouching deeper into the couch, clearly nursing some old wounds. "Didn't even stick around for the funeral or to help sort out the mess."

"And when he came back, he wasn't the same guy who ditched us," Amy says softly, tossing a quick glance at me, like she's testing how much to reveal. "He got super into the family history and started flexing his leadership skills. He even convinced Grandma to do some construction to update the house."

"But he's not the same guy from before Dad died either," Trenton adds, shrugging. "At least we got something out of this time."

"Oh?" I ask.

Amy smirks. "Yeah, we still don't have cable, but we've got an ethernet connection now."

"I can study the information not in our encyclopedias," Noah adds solemnly.

My eyebrows shoot up so high they nearly disappeared into my hairline. If they go any higher, I'll need a search party to bring them back down. "No internet *or* tv?"

Trenton cracks a smile. "See why you're the most interesting thing to happen to this place in a while? Makes living in this backwater place almost bearable."

"We have the home movies though," Noah adds, like he can't let the misinformation stand.

Amy shoots him a look so sharp it could cut glass. "Noah, hush."

But Trenton, ever the rebel, just shrugs. "Who cares if she knows? It's not like it's a family secret. And if it is, it serves Rhett right for inviting her in."

I blink, curiosity instantly piqued. "Home movies? Of what?"

Amy sighs, clearly resigned now that the cat's out of the bag. "They're my dad's videos—Roger's. He was always messing around with a camera when he was younger."

Mrs. Jennings mentioned Roger's fascination with recording. Seriously, if Roger isn't tangled up in this curse somehow, I'll eat my hat. Once I buy one.

I glance between them, gauging how to push without scaring them off—or getting myself scared off, courtesy of Alex. In the end, I just go for it. "Can I see them?"

Amy hesitates for a beat before nodding. "Sure, why not?" she mutters, standing up. "They're in the attic."

The attic, of course, is as dingy as the rest of the house, an even bigger museum of forgotten things. Dust clings to the air, the floorboards creak with every step, and boxes are piled haphazardly everywhere, like some kind of sad yard sale. There's even a box of unscented cat litter in the corner, which is both random and weirdly unsettling. Because I haven't seen hair or hide of any cat.

Amy gestures to an ancient box TV with a VHS player next to it that looks like it's seen better decades. "It still works... mostly," she says, crouching down to hook it up while Trenton digs through a box labeled *TRASH* and pulls out a VHS marked *CANINE MIDNIGHT* in sloppy handwriting.

"This one's a classic," he says. "Dad and Uncle Rhett's attempt at a horror movie. It's terrible, but hilarious."

The tape clicks into the player, and after a bit of snow and static, the screen jumps to life. A much younger Rhett, maybe twelve years old, appears on screen. He's standing in what I now know is the old study—where the curse is centered. The room's dim light flickers above him, setting the perfect spooky scene, but Rhett's expression doesn't quite sell the horror vibe. Instead, he's biting his lip, trying to stifle a giggle.

"Rhett, be scared!" Roger's voice calls from off-screen, laughing.

"I'm trying," Rhett protests, but his expression is breaking. It's clear he's trying to hold it together, but Roger keeps cracking jokes off-camera, making exaggerated spooky noises.

Eventually, Roger jumps in front of the camera, roaring like a budget horror monster, tackling Rhett in a tangle of limbs and laughter. The video shakes, the camera barely able to keep up with them as they wrestle like a couple of kids pretending to film *The Blair Witch Project*. Rhett looks up, finally letting go of the "scared" act, and breaks into a full grin. It's an expression that lights up his entire face, carefree and completely at odds with the dark, oppressive energy the study holds now.

"Roger, you idiot!" Rhett laughs, shoving his brother away. The tape freezes there for a moment, the image of the two boys suspended in time, untouched by whatever came later.

The video cuts off, and the screen goes to static.

I stare at the blank screen, processing what I just saw. "Rhett seems... lighter," I say, glancing at Amy and Trenton. "Is that what you mean by different?"

Amy has a faint smile playing at the corners of her mouth, the memory clearly hitting her in a softer place. Even Trenton looks a little affected, rubbing at his eyes and muttering about dust.

"Yeah," Amy says with a sigh, leaning against a beam. "He wasn't always so... serious. Back then, he didn't care about responsibilities. Dad was in charge, and it was Uncle Rhett's job to keep things light."

Noah, ever the pensive one, adds, "He's better now though. He even helped me hook up my track with magnets so the cars can drive on their own."

"I guess," Amy concedes. "But when Dad died, it felt like we lost Uncle Rhett too. He just... disappeared."

I chew on that for a moment, glancing at the screen where younger Rhett had been grinning just moments ago. "Thanks for showing me the videos," I say, for lack of anything better to say.

But Trenton, eyes clear of whatever affected him minutes ago, throws me a lifeline. "Guess we'll see if the prodigal son has what it takes to fend off curses and keep nosy lawyers from prying too deep," he says, eyes sparkling with a hint of challenge.

"Well, in my defense, I was hired to figure it out and I don't come across curses every day. It's not the kind of thing you find on LegalZoom," I say, shooting Trenton a playful smile.

He smirks. "Well, then, I hope you make him pay you every cent of his inheritance. Rhett's stubbornness should at least cost him something."

I shrug, playing along. "I'll do my best to get compensated for the frustration." Then I lean in, lowering my voice conspiratorially. "But if you're feeling generous yourself, maybe you could give me a hint or two about the curse's origin. Any witches with a grudge I should know about?"

Trenton straightens up, his expression suddenly serious. "Actually..." He exchanges a quick look with Amy, who nods slowly. "We don't have the best history with witches," he says carefully.

"My mom," she says softly. "She and Dad... well, Grandpa calls it 'wild oats.' They met at a concert."

And there go my eyebrows, vaulting up to the gabled ceiling. Roger had a relationship with a witch, one that resulted in Amy, and *no one* thought to tell me before?

"He snuck out," Noah chimes in solemnly. "We're not allowed to sneak out."

"He was an adult," Trenton says, rolling his eyes. "Anyway, he didn't tell Evelyn he was a wolf, and she didn't admit she was a witch until she got sick. Some problem with the pregnancy."

"She'd tried to use magic, which made Grandma and Grandpa super pissed when they figured it out," Amy adds. "It didn't end up working."

"And then what happened?" I prompt, fully invested in this tableau of family drama and secrets.

Trenton runs a hand through his red hair, a flicker of unease passing over his face. "Well, after Amy was born, Evelyn got even more sick. Said something had gone wrong with the spell, that the magic was tainted. I was only, what, five, I think. But I remember how bad she looked. She couldn't control it anymore, and it was tearing her apart from the inside."

Amy's gaze falls to her hands, her fingers twisting together nervously. "She died about a month after I was born. Her mom, my... grandmother... tried to help, but it didn't work. And Grandma and Grandpa paid her off to leave us alone. But a couple years back, I got a letter..."

I lean forward, trying to convey empathy while keeping my excitement in check as I urge them to continue. "A letter from your grandmother?"

Amy nods. "She said she'd been trying to see me for years. That Grandma and Grandpa used their money to block all access to me, and made her look bad in court. They knew she was a witch and told on her. The judge didn't think a witch should be around a normal person."

Trenton scoffs. "Because turning into a wolf at the full moon is normal."

"Well, no one *knows* that," Amy says bitterly.

"What was your grandmother's name?" I ask gently.

"Amelia," says Amy. "I don't know her last name, but I was named after her." She bites her lip and looks away. "We're not allowed to talk about her."

"*Either* of them," Noah whispers, his eyes darting around the room like saying her name might conjure some dark magic.

This family is just a rabbit hole of secrets waiting to be unraveled. And one of those threads has to lead to a curse break.

Just then, a subtle shift in the atmosphere alerts me to a presence at the doorway. Lucian stands there, his posture relaxed but his eyes sharp as they take in the scene before him. His black hair cascades over his shoulder in a sleek ponytail, and a faint smile tugs at his lips.

"Well, well," he drawls, stepping further into the attic. "Seems I've missed quite the party."

I stand and wipe my hands on my pants. "And that's my cue, 'kiddos.' We're off to check on the curse." I put my hand on Amy's shoulder, a move that feels awkward. "Thank you for sharing that with me."

As the teenagers finally make their exit—Trenton still grumbling about being called "kiddo" like it's a personal affront—I watch them go with a mix of amusement and relief. It's not often that I find myself in the middle of a family drama, not since my family drama fizzled off. But there's something undeniably intriguing about the dynamics in this werewolf household, the layers of tension and loyalty, the unspoken rules simmering just below the surface. It's like watching a live-action soap opera, only with fangs and claws ready to make an appearance at any moment.

Lucian steps closer, a steady, reassuring presence at my side. In the dim light, he looks less like a creature of the night and more like some kind of dark guardian, here to ward off whatever shadows might be lurking.

"I didn't know you were coming tonight," I say.

"Where else would I be but with you?" Lucian's voice is smooth as silk, that damnable half-smile on his lips. He holds my gaze for just a moment too long, and there's a flip in my stomach—one that says 'Danger!' and 'Yes, please!' all at once.

The banter is new, but the interest isn't. Although not to this extent. It had been me pursuing him when we'd first met, looking for a little stress relief. He'd denied me until just before our big blowout but was playing hard to get until we were allies again.

But I've been keeping him at arm's length for a reason. I'd kept everyone at that distance until I finally stopped running from those connections that turned into friendships. And my past romantic relationships? A series of one-night stands and convenient arrangements with zero emotional involvement. Until Matty... and... until Lucian.

How much longer will I be able to resist that damned gorgeous mouth of his?

"Well," I say, trying to keep my voice steady, hoping he can't tell that his choice of words has my insides all tangled up like a cheap cord, "to the epicenter? And I'll catch you up on what I've discovered today."

"Sounds delightful," he says, leaning in just close enough that I can feel the cool brush of his breath against my cheek. And he leads me to the room, one hand pressed low against my back. I tell myself it's the chill of his touch that makes me shiver.

I brush off that jittery feeling that Lucian's touch gave me the minute we cross the threshold of the room and we get to work. We peer behind paintings, check under furnishings, look for anything that seems 'out of place.' But there's nothing. So we wait.

And wait.

Finally, the grandfather clock in the corner strikes one a.m. I'm sprawled on the antique settee, legs draped over one armrest, tape recorder idle by my side. Lucian paces the room like a caged panther, his frustration almost palpable.

"Maybe they're on strike?" I quip, but even as the words leave my lips, we exchange a glance that says we're both baffled. All evening, we've been coiled tight, ready for something—anything—to happen. But the manor remains stubbornly quiet, as if mocking our vigil.

"Could the younger Baxter be right, and your presence is a ghost repellent?" he asks, only half-joking.

"Or yours. They might not be fans of the undead." My attempt at humor wanes as I sit up, stretching limbs stiff from waiting for phantoms that refuse to show. Dust cakes the back of my arms, courtesy of the settee, and I swallow a cough as I attempt to brush it off.

"Do you truly believe this elder Amelia could have cursed the family?" he asks as he comes to my side, helpfully smearing in the dust on my blazer rather than removing any of it.

"It's the best lead we have," I say, wrestling my arm from him and trying not to bemoan the dry cleaning now awaiting me. At least the billables will cover it. "Roger clearly ran with witches," I add. "I'm not sure I'd pony up the cost to curse someone for a grandkid but—"

"But you're not the best source on healthy relationships," Lucian interrupts, his tone dry.

"Hey!" I snap, my offense only partially sincere. "*Familial* relationships, thank you very much. I have quite a few friends now."

"Indeed you do," he says, his gaze lingering on me in a way that makes my pulse quicken just a tad. "Living and dead."

"Well, I've always been drawn to the... unconventional types," I counter with a playful wink. But as I catch his eye, the banter fades, leaving a charged silence between us. An unspoken question hanging in the air, that same expectation from earlier.

I clear my throat. "Let's walk the grounds again," I suggest, grabbing my tape recorder. "Can't hurt to do one last sweep before calling it a night. See if something happened elsewhere instead."

Lucian nods, and we step out of the room. The house feels even grimmer after dark, like it's auditioning for the role of "Creepiest Mansion" in some low-budget horror flick.

Shadows stretch and crawl across the walls, turning hallways I thought I knew into a maze of nope.

"Should we split up now? Cover more ground?" I ask, although the thought of wandering solo down these spooky hallways makes my stomach do a little flip.

"Remain with me," Lucian insists, the protective edge in his voice sending a shiver through me. Not the scared kind either.

"Fine, but only because you asked so nicely," I reply with mock reluctance, earning a smirk from him.

We near the grand staircase, its banisters winding upwards like the coils of a slumbering serpent. Just as I'm wondering if the creaking floorboards are mocking us, something catches my eye—a glint of light bouncing off the foyer wall.

I squint, my heart doing its best impression of a jackhammer as I edge closer. Because in a house like this, a random glint could mean anything—from a harmless piece of antique junk to the start of a full-blown paranormal spectacle.

"Lucian," I call, my voice barely above a whisper. "Look."

He's by my side in an instant, following my pointing finger to where letters scrawl across the wall in what looks suspiciously like blood:

"The truth always finds a way to bleed through."

Fantastic.

The night might have delivered no supernatural theatrics, but it seems the mystery of Oakheart Estate has only deepened, and I'm already bracing myself for the next revelation.

CHAPTER 9

A lawyer-slash-paranormal investigator's work is never done, so here I am, bright and early the next morning, back in action on a Saturday. And by "bright," I mean "bleary-eyed and sleep-deprived," because last night I got approximately zero hours of shut-eye. Not that it had *anything* to do with the creepy, cryptic writing we found scrawled all over Oakheart Estate's walls. And it's definitely not why I asked Lucian to take me home and sneak back to his place through the tunnels.

Nope, totally unrelated.

I flip through the court dockets on my laptop, the dull glow of the screen giving me a headache. The couch—an internet marketplace find that's seen better days—groans in protest as I shift to get comfortable. I've been at this since dawn broke, the coffee has gone cold beside me, and every single document related to the Baxter custody case is sealed tighter than a vampire's coffin at noon. I can't even get a last name for my missing witch.

"Terrific," I mutter. "The rich keep their secrets while the rest of us get a 404 error."

Sifting through the clues leaves a lot of holes. Amelia's my best bet, even if her motives are as murky as a swamp on a foggy night. Maybe she's got a bone to pick with the

Baxters because of Evelyn, or maybe she's just itching for some payback since they outed her to the courts. Roger's the next best, who had his own brush with 'hidden truths,' but there's no witch behind him since ghosts can't hex. Without more to go on, I'm back to square one.

My fingers hover over my phone, thumb poised to text Rhett. My gut tells me to ask him about Amelia, he most *certainly* would know her last name, maybe even her address, but I pause, remembering what Amy and Trenton said—they wouldn't mention Amelia to the family at all. It's a weird family rule, one I don't quite understand, but Lucian's voice echoes in my head, reminding me that I don't exactly have the best instincts when it comes to family dynamics. *Thanks, Lucian,* I think with a touch of bitterness.

Still, he's right, and I'm not about to blow up the family's carefully guarded secrets by charging in and asking about witches. Not unless I have to. Better to tap my other sources first.

I drum my fingers on the scratched table, frustration bubbling up inside me. "Hey, Herle, you know any spells to crack open court records?" I call out, only half expecting a response from the hobgoblin that supposedly lurks in the walls. But as usual, there's nothing but silence.

"Right. You're about as real as my chances of winning a game of hide-and-seek against an invisible man." My laugh is dry, tinted with sarcasm. "Note to self—see if invisibility is real. Could be handy when trying to sneak away from the office for these paranormal capers."

With Herle giving me the usual cold shoulder, I turn to the internet for answers. But it's like trying to find a needle in a haystack, if the needle could cast spells and the haystack was a mess of misinformation.

The cursor blinks mockingly on the webpage of suppositions and bad guesses. *Newsflash, HexHunter666, just because a girl's named 'Celeste' doesn't mean she's automatically a witch.*

I manage to find a 'magical meetup' at a local library, for "witches, warlocks, and other assorted magical beings," according to the description. Which sounds promising, but could also just mean a bunch of teenagers doing card tricks and arguing over the best way to shuffle a tarot deck. Beggars can't be choosers, though, and right now, I'm pretty desperate for a lead. Any lead.

I jot down the time and address, noting that the meetup is this evening. The library's only a few blocks from my place, which is either a lucky coincidence or fate *finally* smiling down on me. I'm going to pretend it's the latter. But, I'm also not keeping all my eggs in one basket, so I'm working the phone, tapping my paranormal contacts.

"Hey, Sara, you seeing Lucian tonight?" I ask, once the line connects.

Sara's voice crackles through the speaker, "Probably. I help him with coven stuff most weekends."

"Will you ask him something for me? I'd do it myself, but I've got... plans." A grin tugs at my lips thinking about the date.

"Plans? As in a date?" Sara's intrigue is almost palpable.

"Don't worry, I've cleared my paranormal schedule. No vampires charged with murder or unicorns fighting off mauling claims."

Sara's chuckle dances through the phone line. "Well, well, Emily, keeping your priorities straight. I hope this one doesn't turn out to be a ghosting werewolf. Get it? *Ghosting?*"

I roll my eyes, even though she can't see it. "Funny you should mention ghosts, as that's actually why I'm after Lucian. Did he tell you about the investigation he's bulldozed his way into?"

"Only enough to make that joke," Sara responds, her voice practically dripping with curiosity.

"Well, can you ask him if he knows any witches?" I say, my tone more serious now. I would've asked Lucian last night, but 'ghost graffiti' tends to be a conversation killer.

So is, apparently, the question now, as there's a weighted pause on the line, the kind that makes you wonder if someone just dropped a cauldron on the other end.

"A witch..." Sara finally says. "Why do you need a witch, Emily?"

I let out a sigh, trying to condense the chaos of the Baxter family curse into a bite-sized explanation while staying 'discreet.' "Long story short, there's a whole mess of drama with my clients, and I'm pretty sure Amelia, no last name, might be the witchy grandma behind it all. Lucian hinted at some magic before, so I figured he knew at least *one* witch so..."

Sara exhales, the tension in her voice dissipating. "I see. Well, witches are... secretive. But I'll talk to him."

"Great. Also, tell him to join the 21st century and get a cell phone, will you?" It rankles slightly that I can't get ahold of him but through another woman. But it isn't her fault. We've come a long way from butting heads over who supported Lucian more.

Sara and I exchange a few more pleasantries before hanging up, leaving me alone with the hum of my laptop and the looming mystery of the Baxter curse.

Just as I'm losing hope, my phone lights up with a new message—a lifeline in the form of Danielle's invitation for lunch.

"Emily, could I convince you to come to mine for lunch in about an hour?" Danielle writes.

A smile splits my face—I could use the break before my next investigative expedition, and Danielle's company is a bonus. Not to mention with her police connections and that werewolf nose for trouble, she might just sniff out a witch for me if Lucian can't come through.

"Looks like we're making progress Herle," I announce, grabbing my purse. Still no response, typical. "Some supernatural buddy you are."

I snag my keys from the hook by the door, my mind already racing with possibilities.

The scent of garlic and thyme hits me the minute the door swings open. Danielle Greene, in a flour-dusted apron, greets me with a warmth that's so genuine it almost feels alien. Our first encounter was through the filter of law enforcement, but she's always been all smiles and homey hospitality. With her hair pinned back by a butterfly clip and in a sunny yellow dress, she looks more like a character from a fairy tale than the big bad wolf I know her to be.

"Emily! I'm so glad you could make it," she beams, pulling me into a hug that's surprisingly strong for someone who spends more time wielding a pen than a barbell. Well, at least, that's what I thought before I knew about the whole werewolf thing.

"Thanks for having me over, Danielle," I say, stepping into the cozy kitchen that smells like something out of a storybook, a far cry from the takeout containers that clutter my own counters. "I was surprised to get your text this morning, but I'm not so far from college that I'll turn down a free meal."

"It's the least I could do after throwing Rhett Baxter into your orbit," Danielle quips, leading me to the breakfast nook where a rustic table is set with an array of mismatched plates and polished silverware. The sight of a home cooked meal spread out before me tugs at something deep inside, a place usually reserved for courtroom victories and the rare moments of quiet solitude.

"This is amazing," I say, sliding into a seat. It does look incredible; hearty and rich and everything my childhood wasn't.

"Thanks! Nothing beats a good meal among friends, right?" Her eyes twinkle with camaraderie.

As we dig in, she fills me in on her world—family dynamics, werewolf pack politics, and things I never imagined talking about over lasagna.

"Jared finally turned twenty, so he's shifting now, and Tony—his younger brother—is feeling left out as the last non-shifter," she says, shaking her head like it's the most relatable family drama.

"Wait, werewolves don't shift until they're twenty?" I ask, fork paused mid-air.

"Nope. Only when we hit formal adulthood," she explains, smiling as she twirls some pasta. "Poor Tony's too young to understand that it just takes time."

So, Trenton's all bark and no bite. The thought makes me smirk as I bite into a piece of buttery garlic bread.

Between bites, I glance up at her. "So, speaking of werewolf politics, what about the dynamics between different supernatural groups? How do werewolves and witches get along?"

"Get along?" Danielle snorts lightly, her eyes crinkling with mirth. "That's an optimistic way to put it. Let's just say we run in different circles—werewolves are pack creatures, fiercely loyal to our own, and witches... well, they have their covens and their own brand of loyalty."

"Is it like rival sports teams or more Montagues and Capulets?" I ask, half-joking.

"Somewhere in between," she says with a wry smile. "There's respect, sometimes grudgingly given, but also a lot of history there. And you know what they say about old habits..."

"Yep, they die hard, just like my cravings for Chinese takeout." I pop a garlic knot into my mouth, pretending it doesn't beat the heck out of cold lo mein.

Danielle laughs, and I think, not for the first time, how refreshing it is to connect with someone who gets the absurdity of life. Not that I'd ever admit it out loud. Keeping things close to the chest is second nature, just like recording every detail that might come in handy later.

I swirl the last of my wine, a rich red that Danielle assured me pairs perfectly with her homemade lasagna. "Okay, so let's say I'm getting the hang of werewolves and witches not exactly being BFFs. Unrelated, but where do vampires fit into this supernatural soap opera?"

Danielle leans back, arms folded as she considers her next words. "You've got the classic love-hate relationship with vampires and werewolves. Think less 'Twilight' and more old-school territorial turf war. Vampires are all about the nightlife, literally, while werewolves have a bit more flexibility with their sunbathing."

"Sounds like a scheduling nightmare," I quip, earning an appreciative chuckle from my host.

"Exactly," she agrees. "And within the werewolf packs themselves? It's like Survivor but with more fur and fewer immunity challenges. Alpha power plays, beta challenges… you get the picture."

"Family dinners must be a hoot," I muse.

"More like a howl," Danielle adds with a smirk.

I lean forward, resting my elbows on the scratched wood of her dining table. Despite our banter, I'm about to broach a serious topic. "And the Baxters' family drama could be straight out of a Shakespearean tragedy," I say. "Turns out there might be a witch pulling the strings. Amelia, Amy's grandmother. You wouldn't know anything about her, would you?" I ask, knowing it's a long shot, but hoping Danielle's connections might give me a lead.

"Amelia, huh?" Danielle raises an eyebrow, considering. "The name doesn't ring any bells. The Baxter coven keeps to themselves. I only knew Rhett through some of the meetings when he returned."

"I still can't believe there are meetings," I say, huffing a laugh. "No witches at these soirees?"

"Witches won't even admit they exist. They're certainly not joining the phone tree," Danielle teases back.

Jokes aside, I'm desperate. "Could you maybe dig around? See what you can find? Maybe in one of your law enforcement databases," I venture, pushing aside the empty plate that held the best lasagna I've ever tasted.

Danielle gives me a pointed look. "Emily, I'm all for supporting friends, but I draw the line at doing their homework

for them. If you hit a wall, call me. We'll brainstorm together."

"Fair enough," I concede with a grin. "And here I thought you'd go all vigilante police officer for me."

"Only on weekdays," she deadpans, taking our plates to the sink.

I lean back in the chair, the warmth from Danielle's kitchen wrapping around me like a well-tailored coat. I've never been one for domesticity, but there's something about the smell of home cooked food and the clink of utensils that makes me wonder what my life could have been. If I hadn't spent my whole existence clawing for independence, making sure I could stand on my own two feet because my parents, in their separate but equally disastrous ways, made it clear I couldn't rely on anyone else. If I hadn't decided success as a lawyer was the only way to prove I could take care of myself.

"Ever think about just... becoming someone else?" I ask, twirling an unused spoon idly between my fingers. "Like a witch, maybe?" I flash her a grin, half-serious.

Danielle chuckles, the sound rich and hearty. "And give up your power suits for robes and pointy hats?" She rests against the counter, her arms crossed as if she's weighing the idea.

"Exactly," I say with mock solemnity. "Imagine the drama. Objections sustained by sheer willpower, or better yet, hexed into oblivion."

"Careful now, counselor," she warns, the amusement in her voice not quite masking the intrigue in her eyes. "Witch-es might walk among us in jeans and tees, but their abilities are no joke. They conjure spells that can heal or harm, see things hidden to others, and sometimes—" she pauses, giv-ing me a pointed look, "—they can sense when someone's trying to dig too deep."

"Sounds handy," I muse. "But I suppose it comes with a whole cauldron of problems."

"More than you'd want to stir," Danielle agrees, pushing away from the counter to refill her coffee mug. "And I technically *get* to be someone else. Every single day at work, I'm playing another character, Officer Greene, regular human."

"Does it bother you?"

Danielle takes a moment, stirring her coffee thoughtfully before meeting my gaze. There's a flicker of something in her expression, a vulnerability that surprises me. "Sometimes," she admits softly. "Being Danielle Greene, the cop, it's... easier. Cleaner, you know? Black and white, right and wrong. But being a werewolf in hiding, that's where it gets complicated. I'm in costume 40 hours a week. But the rest of the time? The werewolf is the real me."

The burden of secrets, of living a dual life in this world of humans and supernatural beings, is something I can't ever understand. "It must be exhausting," I say, my voice gentle.

"It is," Danielle agrees with a weary smile. "But it's the way things are for now. Maybe one day..."

"One day," I echo. "Maybe we'll get lucky and there'll be a change. Something big."

She sets down her mug and regards me thoughtfully. "It won't be luck, Emily. But action. Life's a series of doors, some we open willingly, and others that are thrust upon us. The question is, which one are you willing to step through?"

"You should write greeting cards," I tease, stacking the dishes in the sink with a newfound determination. "Anyway, first things first. I've got a witch to track down, and you've got a city to keep safe."

"Thanks for coming, Em." She walks me to the door, her stride confident. "Good luck with Matty tonight. He doesn't stand a chance against your charms."

"Charms I don't need spells for," I toss back with a wink. The idea still tickles my fancy, but there's something to be said for natural magnetism—something I plan to fully exploit on my date.

"Keep me posted about Amelia," she adds, her tone shifting to a more serious octave. "And remember, witches or not, I've got your back."

"Tell Harold hello," I reply, grinning at the memory of the wall dweller I had the pleasure of meeting during my first visit to her home.

She smirks, not missing a beat. "Tell Herle the same."

With a final wave, I step out into the crisp air, the sharp bite of autumn brushing against my skin.

As I stride down the path to my car, parked under a canopy of golden leaves, I can't shake the feeling that I'm walking a tightrope between two worlds. On one side, the sterile halls of the law firm where ambition is a sharp-edged sword, and on the other, the shadowy realm of the paranormal, where anything seems possible.

"Here's to balancing acts," I mutter to myself, sliding behind the wheel. My reflection in the rearview mirror smirks back at me. Emily Lane, attorney-at-law by day, *witch* hunter by night?

With a newfound sense of purpose, I drive away from Danielle's house, leaving her to her world of badges and justice. I've got my own plans—an afternoon of snooping and an evening that promises romance and secrets. Hopefully not at the same time.

Chapter 10

The meetup is supposed to take place in a room labeled "Community Events," which I'm guessing means it's right between "Tax Prep 101" and "Knitting for Beginners." I wander through the stacks, passing by all the "how-to" books—how to bake bread, how to write a screenplay, how to reinvent your entire life in 30 days. No "How to Find a Witch" book, though. Pity.

As I push open the creaky door to the meeting room, the bright scent of disinfectant immediately hits my nostrils. You'd think a place dedicated to the magical society would smell more like incense and less like lemon, but here we are. It's supposed to be clandestine, a gathering for those with an affinity—or at least a desire—for the arcane. But the room is disappointingly bare, with the only semblance of magic being the flickering fluorescent lights overhead. The walls are lined with drab gray shelves, filled not with ancient tomes or spell books, but with dusty legal binders. A long, mahogany table dominates the center, surrounded by mismatched office chairs. It feels more like I've stumbled into a book club for retired librarians.

A woman with sharp features and a no-nonsense aura sits at the head of the table, her steely gaze boring into me as I enter. She introduces herself as Madame Lorraine, the keeper of this peculiar gathering. Beside her is a man in a tailored suit, his expression unreadable as he observes me with calculating eyes. There's a man with an unruly beard clutching a leather-bound tome like it's a lifeline, and a woman whose scarf has more moons and stars on it than the night sky. At the far end of the table, a young woman taps away at her phone, seemingly disinterested in the surroundings. Another dozen people sit scattered around the room.

Now, Danielle made it clear that witches, like werewolves, can hide in plain sight. But I'm betting my last dollar none of them could conjure a spark if their lives depended on it. They're not witches, but you can tell they wish upon every fallen eyelash to be one.

I make my way to an empty seat, nodding politely at the others already present. The moment I settle into the rickety chair, a low hum of recognition sweeps through the room like an errant spell gone awry. Heads turn, whispers crescendo into chatter, and all at once, I'm thrust into the spotlight without so much as a smoke bomb to mask my entrance.

"Isn't that Emily Lane?" a voice hisses from the back, loud enough to carry.

I wince, realizing my oversight. The red wig that transformed me into 'Emily Smith' is resting on my dresser at home instead of perching atop my head.

Amateur move, Lane, if you want to keep a low profile.

"Excuse me, are you the lawyer from the news? The one who's been defending those... creatures?" A man with spectacles so thick they could double as a magnifying glass leans in, his breath smelling like stale coffee and mint.

"Creatures is a strong word," I say, flashing a smile that's all teeth and no warmth. "And yes, I'm a lawyer, but today, I'm just here to learn, like all of you."

But the floodgates have opened, and I'm swamped by a tidal wave of curiosity. They press in closer, their eagerness palpable, each of them hungry for a brush with the supernatural world I've inadvertently become a part of.

"Have you ever seen a vampire transform?" asks a woman draped in enough amethyst necklaces to start her own crystal shop.

"Well, let's just say my experience with vampires involves more paperwork than transformation," I quip, earning a smattering of chuckles around the table.

A familiar, if unwelcome, face pushes through the throng, his eyes bright with a zeal usually reserved for religious experiences or Black Friday sales. It's a guy I haven't seen in 3 years, when we both hung out at the park in the vampire quarter, the one whose blood apparently didn't pass the vampire taste test.

"Emily!" he exclaims, as though we're old friends and not two strangers linked only by the illicit vampire blood drive. "I knew I recognized you!"

"Seems everyone does today," I mutter under my breath.

"Tell me, why wouldn't the vampires take my blood?" His question hovers between us, laced with disappointment and a hint of accusation.

"Maybe your blood type isn't their... cup of tea," I suggest, shrugging nonchalantly while thinking, *If you weren't so busy fetishizing the entire experience, maybe they'd consider it.* But Lucian runs a tight ship, and he's not about to let his coven be anyone's gothic fantasy league.

"Could I try another coven?" he persists, oblivious to the subtext.

"Good luck with that," I reply, my tone dry as the law books gathering dust on my office shelf. Lucian doesn't tolerate prowlers, and this guy reeks of desperation. There's no way he'll even *find* another coven with a map and personalized directions.

As the questions keep pouring in—from werewolf pack dynamics to the legal ins and outs of ghoul organ donations—a sense of camaraderie builds in the room. These people might not have any real magical abilities, but they're all united by one thing—a fascination with the supernatural. It's like a paranormal fan club, and, somehow, I've found myself right in the middle of it.

"Alright, everyone." I raise my voice, commanding attention with the authority of a courtroom. "Let's dial down the enthusiasm and remember why we're here. Knowledge, right? Not a Q&A with Emily Lane."

A murmur of agreement ripples through the crowd, and they reluctantly take a step back, giving me space to breathe and plot my next move.

"First, let me confirm something," I speak up, my voice slicing through the chatter like a hot knife through butter. "Is anyone a bona fide potions-and-cauldrons witch?"

Madame Lorraine raises an eyebrow, her gaze flickering with a hint of amusement at my question. The man in the tailored suit chuckles softly, a sound that sends shivers down my spine for reasons I can't quite pinpoint. The woman with the celestial scarf leans forward, her eyes sparkling with mischief.

"I try," she says. "I've got the sacrifice part down pat. The reward after? Not so much."

The man clutching the leather tome clears his throat, his beard bristling. "I've been known to mix herbs and try a few incantations too," he admits, his eyes darting around the room as if seeking even a scrap of approval.

I nod, taking in their responses. "Anyone happen to *know* any witches? Say, an older woman named Amelia?"

More head shakes. So, no help and no Witch Academy graduates here to point me in the right direction. Not surprising, but still a letdown. I scan the room, a sea of eager faces all hoping for a spark of connection to a world they only half understand. But still, that's more than a lot of other Chicagoans.

My hunt for witchy wisdom is going to have to wait. The hope that I'd dig up anything useful about Amelia in this crowd is fading faster than an iced coffee on a July afternoon. Instead, I'm smack in the middle of a human curiosity quake, trying to remember why mingling with wannabe witches seemed like a good idea. But hey—maybe I can still turn this fan club meeting into something useful.

"While we're all here sharing our... let's call it 'enthusiasm'... for the supernatural, how about we channel it into something productive?"

Eyebrows raise. Curiosity, the better angel of human nature, peeks through the disappointment.

"I get it. Paranormals are fascinating. But they're not a sideshow attraction." I lean forward, hands on my hips, feeling every inch the lawyer gearing up for a closing argument. "They have limited rights. They face discrimination. And they need advocates, not groupies."

Murmurs turn to nods. It's working. I'm not just throwing spaghetti at the wall; some of it's sticking.

"Let's organize," I continue, warming to the idea myself. "Create a network of support. Educate people. Advocate for policy changes. Show that we're allies, not autograph hounds."

"Are you suggesting we become like... paranormal activists?" someone pipes up, and there's genuine interest in his tone.

"Exactly!" I exclaim, buoyed by the spark of comprehension. "Grassroots, but with less gardening and more civil rights."

There's laughter now, a good sign. A few claps. They're buying what I'm selling, even if it's not the paranormal stories they came for. As the crowd buzzes with the potential of purpose, I allow myself a small, triumphant smirk. This is advocacy in action, and I'll be damned if I don't ride this wave all the way to shore.

"Let's make some noise," I declare, rallying my newfound troops. "And hey, if we shake things up enough, maybe the actual witches will come to us. How's that for a plot twist?"

The trattoria's warm glow wraps around us like a soft blanket, casting a cozy spell over our corner table. Matty's arm skims against mine, sending a jolt of electricity up my spine. Or maybe it's just the early winter static. Hard to say. Either way, it feels nice.

Finally, after months of anticipation, a handful of actual 'dates' with Matty, I can wear the coveted "dress," a sleek and stunning red slip of material that cost more than my entire wardrobe combined. It hugs every curve of my body like it was made for me, and damn, do I feel like a million dollars.

"Is it just me or is the cannoli winking at us from the dessert menu?" Matty asks, his eyes twinkling in that way that makes my heart do a little somersault.

"Flirting with pastry now, are we? Should I be jealous?" I tease back.

"Emily, you wound me," he says, clutching his chest in mock distress. "I only have eyes for the lady who can argue her way out of a paper bag."

"Good answer." I nod approvingly while scanning the menu.

It's comfortable, sitting here with Matty. The way his gaze lingers on me isn't just attraction—it's deeper. Like he's trying to figure me out, or maybe just wishing things were simpler. There's a warmth in it that makes me forget, for just a second, about everything waiting for me outside this cozy bubble.

When he swipes a sip of my wine, his fingers brush mine—warm, inviting, familiar in a way that makes my heart race for reasons I can't chalk up to simple attraction. Matty's my steady rock. He's smart, funny, and easy to be around—once you manage to pry that color-coded calendar out of his hands. Being with him feels like catching my breath after a marathon, a rare, sweet moment of calm in a world that never stops spinning.

He leans back with a satisfied smile after swallowing the stolen sip of wine. "How are things at work, Ms. Partner?"

I let out a pained laugh. "Which part? The usual chaos or my supernatural side hustle?"

His smile falters, concern flickering in those caramel eyes of his. "The werewolf one?" He leans in, voice a little more serious. "Everything okay?"

"It's under control," I reassure him. "Just venturing into some... unconventional territory," I admit with a playful smirk. "Involving witches."

Matty raises an eyebrow, curiosity lighting up his handsome features. "Witches, huh? Like, broomsticks and cauldrons or the lawyer-in-a-power-suit kind?"

"Maybe a bit of both," I admit. "But I can't say much more. Attorney-client privilege and all that jazz. You understand."

"Sure," he nods, his gaze still locked on me, clearly intrigued by the breadcrumb I've tossed him. "Witches in the suburbs," he muses, his voice laced with the warmth of the Chianti and a hint of nostalgia. "My grandma used to tell me stories. Urban legends, you know? Kids would dare each other to go to 'the witch's house' at the end of the cul-de-sac."

"Did you ever take the dare?" I ask, amusement lacing my tone.

"Of course," he chuckles, a boyish gleam in his eyes. "I was a risk taker in my day."

I lean forward, one elbow on the table, trying to imagine him as a tiny rabble-rouser. "Really? You weren't always the guy who schedules bathroom breaks?"

"Hey! I'm not that bad," he protests with a mock scowl.

I grin back. "So was it a witch?"

"Turned out to be just an old lady who enjoyed gardening at night. But there was always that 'what if' hanging in the air."

"Speaking of 'what ifs', and taking risks," I segue, twirling a lock of unbound dark hair around my finger, a move I know doesn't go unnoticed. "You wouldn't know a way to... peek into sealed court records, would you?"

His smile fades a touch, replaced by a sigh and a look that tells me he's already contemplating the maze of moral and legal implications. "Emily," he begins, a serious undertone creeping into his otherwise light demeanor, "you know I can't just pull strings like that. There are rules—"

"Which were made to be bent, not broken," I interject with a wink, hoping to sweeten the proposition. It's a risky dance, asking him to tiptoe the edge of his professional ethics, but it's for a good cause.

Or so I tell myself.

He runs a hand through his hair, clearly torn. "I'll see what I can do," he finally concedes, "*within* the bounds of the law."

"Thank you," I say, my voice soft with gratitude and a touch of guilt. "I owe you one."

"Consider it on your tab," he replies, a small smile playing at the corners of his lips as he reaches across to sweep his fingers against mine. The touch sends a flutter through me, a silent reminder that this isn't just any dinner; it's a date. And despite the supernatural intrigue, it's going rather swimmingly.

"Your grandma would be proud," I tease, nudging his hand with my own. "Braving the witch's lair for a damsel in distress."

"Hey, every good witch needs an ally in the legal system," Matty quips back, the playful banter returning like an old friend.

"Who says I'm the witch?" I tease, arching an eyebrow. "Maybe I'm the unwitting victim of a spell."

"Or maybe," Matty counters, his eyes sparkling with mischief, "you're the enchantress who's got the poor district attorney wrapped around her finger."

"Guilty as charged," I confess, leaning forward, our laughter mingling with the soft sounds of the restaurant.

Just as I'm about to test the PDA policies of the restaurant, the somber ringtone I assigned to Sara Harper—a fittingly Gothic melody—shatters the moment, a harbinger of disruption in our carefully crafted evening. I quickly switch the phone to vibrate, hoping against hope that urgency can wait until after dessert.

Matty arches an eyebrow, a silent question flickering in those warm, honeyed eyes that have been my anchor tonight. Just then, my phone buzzes, and a stream of texts lights up the screen, each one more urgent than the last. Sara's clipped messages flash like distress flares in a dark sea, and the final one hits like a punch: *"Lucian needs you now."*

"Sorry, Matty, I need to take this," I say.

His smile dims a little, but he nods understandingly, the candlelight dancing over his concerned features.

"Of course, no problem," he says, though I catch the shadow of disappointment that crosses his eyes. I step away, pressing the phone to my ear.

"Sara, what's up? Is Lucian okay?" I ask, trying to keep my voice low even as my mind races through a dozen possible problems.

"Emily, it's urgent." Sara's voice slices through the speaker like a chill winter breeze. "Lucian needs you at Oakheart Estate. Now."

"Can't it wait?" I hedge, stealing a longing glance back at the table where Matty feigns interest in the dessert menu.

"No. He says it's critical," she insists, and I can almost see her hazel eyes pleading through the line. Lucian's a busy guy, he wouldn't send Sara unless it was life or death. And for a *vampire*, death is saying something.

"Alright, I'm on my way." I hang up and steel myself for the conversation I'm dreading.

"I'm really sorry, but I have to cut our date short," I start, approaching Matty with apologetic eyes. "But I've got an emergency to deal with."

His expression is kind, but there's a hint of that worry I've been noticing more and more lately. "Everything okay?"

I force a smile, trying to downplay the seriousness. "No new murder charges, promise." I let out a half-hearted laugh. "I'll make it up to you. How about dessert, next time?"

"Rain check accepted," he concedes, standing to his full height, a head taller than me. "But seriously, Emily. Be careful. I know you like to dive into things headfirst, but... just be careful."

Careful disappeared when I started teaming up with the paranormals of Chicago, I think wryly. "Staying safe is my middle name," I fib, though 'trouble' might be a more fitting choice this week. I leave a few bills on the table to cover my share of the meal.

"Take care, Emily," he says, his hand briefly touching mine in a warm, reassuring grip. "And call me, alright? I want to know you're okay."

"Will do, counselor," I assure him, slipping into my professional armor. I throw one last glance over my shoulder as I push through the door, the cozy warmth of the restaurant yielding to the brisk night air.

Chapter 11

The moonlight bathes Oakheart Estate in a moody glow as I roll up. It's one of those nights when even the sky can't decide what's going on—is it purple and blue? Black and yellow? Who knows? Certainly not me with the mood Lucian's abrupt message has plunged me into.

"Did you have plans?" he inquires, materializing from the shadows like a cliché wrapped in an enigma. As usual, he's dressed impeccably in a sleek black suit, accentuating the sharp angles and lean lines of his frame. The soft breeze rustles through the trees, making his long ponytail dance slightly against his back. He looks like he just stepped out of a high-end fashion magazine, effortlessly elegant and captivating.

"Believe it or not, I actually have a life outside of work," I retort, planting a hand on my hip and trying not to notice the way my heart's decided to run a marathon due to his sudden appearance. Despite my irritation at being pulled away from my evening plans, I raced here out of concern for him. But he looks perfectly fine.

"Yes, your friend." Lucian says, raising a brow. "Sara told me of your evening plans. Did you dress this way for him?"

His gaze lingers on me, a warmth spreading across my cheeks that has nothing to do with the cool evening breeze.

Suddenly, I'm a little self-conscious in this dress I picked out to wow Matty. Standing next to Lucian in his fancy suit, we look less like paranormal investigators and more like guests at a posh party.

Heat creeps up my neck, and I clear my throat. "Actually, yes. Until I was summoned here with some supposed urgent need." I dramatically look him up and down. "But you're not on fire, there's no stake poking out of your body. Where's the crisis?"

Lucian leans against the gate like he's got all the time in the world, mischief twinkling in his eyes. "Perhaps Sara misunderstood the urgency of my request."

"Which wouldn't happen if you knew how to use a phone," I mutter, eyeing the ancient vampire who still hasn't mastered the art of texting.

"Phones can be tapped, messages traced," he says dismissively, waving his hand as if swatting away my modern-day concerns.

"Right." I scoff. "Because the world's dying to hear vampire drama."

He brushes off my sarcasm like it's nothing. "I've got a lead," he says, getting down to business.

That piques my interest. "Did your witch friend find Amelia?"

"First, I don't have a 'witch friend'," Lucian corrects me with a pointed look, the moonlight glinting off his gray eyes, reminding me of how hush-hush witches really are. "And second, no, it's someone else."

"Someone else?" I press, curiosity piqued despite my irritation. A new lead in this mess of a case is like a shot of determination. It's what's kept me hustling to make partner, and now it's pulling me deeper into the supernatural rabbit hole.

"Someone who knows the ins and outs of this neighborhood better than any garden club member ever could," he says, a sly grin playing on his lips like he's dangling a juicy secret just out of reach.

"Just what this night needed," I mutter under my breath. "More mystery."

Lucian's smile widens, as if he's heard me—which he probably has. "We can meet with him tonight."

"Must we?" I fiddle with the hem of my dress, remembering the disappointed look in Matty's eyes as I left earlier. "We couldn't do this tomorrow?"

"Are you putting aside work for fun for once?" Lucian asks, raising an eyebrow.

"Well, trying to find some sort of balance in my life," I retort with a playful smile. "Can't be all work and no play."

"Trust me, this will be worth it," he says with a smirk that suggests he's got a trick up his sleeve.

I eye Lucian warily, knowing his idea of 'worthwhile' might not line up with mine. But there's a spark in his eyes that tells me this isn't just another wild goose chase.

With a resigned sigh, I nod. "Lead the way," I say, trying to match his confident tone.

But instead of taking me into Oakheart Estate like I expect, he directs us down the winding road towards the neighboring property.

"We'll be meeting him here," he explains, moving through the shadows like it's his natural habitat.

"Lucian, if we get caught, I swear I'm throwing you under the bus. Or, in your case, under a sunlamp," I grumble, my heels sinking into the manicured lawn as we edge closer to the ostentatious abode next door. Trespassing isn't exactly a new concept to me, but after the frosty reception I received from Alex and Sylvia during my earlier snooping expeditions, I'm not eager to push my luck in this ritzy neighborhood.

"Please, Emily," he scoffs quietly, leading the way with infuriating grace. It's borderline annoying—like he's gliding on invisible skates while the rest of us mere mortals trip over air. "They won't even check. As though anyone would dare cross Mrs. Abernathy's property lines."

We slip past trimmed hedges and beneath low-hanging branches.

"I guess when you're that wealthy, you think your money can protect you from anything," I whisper back, eyeing the lack of security with suspicion. "Either that or her garden gnomes are equipped with laser eyes."

As we slink toward the side garden, Lucian signals for me to duck behind a row of meticulously trimmed bushes. I comply, feeling the damp earth seep through the fabric of my dress. Peering through the leaves, I spy a tall wrought-iron fence encircling what looks like a meticulously tended rose garden.

He murmurs some sort of incantation under his breath. The air seems to shimmer, and I can't help but quip, "I thought you said you didn't have witch friends. Yet here we are, getting cozy with magic."

"Shh," he hushes me, though I catch the flicker of amusement in his eyes. Then, with a pop like a champagne cork, a creature materializes before us.

"Manx at your service," the scaly hobgoblin announces. Like the other hobgoblins I've met recently, he stands at around three feet tall, his body covered in scales that glisten in the moonlight. His head is disproportionate to his small charcoal gray body, with a wide jaw filled with jagged teeth and two small, beady eyes that seem to gleam with mischief.

"Manx, huh?" I eye him skeptically. Business or not, I take my shot at gathering some personal information I'm missing. "You wouldn't happen to know a hobgoblin named Herle, by any chance?"

"Ah, Herle... No, madam," Manx replies.

"Aha!" I shout triumphantly, before being shushed by both Manx and Lucian. "So Herle isn't real."

"Forgive me," Manx interjects, his voice raspy with a touch of annoyance. "I am not acquainted with all hobgoblins in the realm."

"No hobgoblin newsletter or monthly meeting in the Underground?" I ask, brows raised.

"Emily, please," Lucian cuts in, his voice all stern and commanding, though the look in his eyes softens the blow. "Let's stay focused. Manx has information on the witch who used to reside here and her mother."

"There is a price for such knowledge," Manx says, his voice smooth like gravel under a flowing stream. "A delectable trade, if you will."

Internally, I groan. *Here we go again*. Another creature with another quirky request. It's like my life has become a series of side quests in an RPG where I'm perpetually grinding for experience points. But this better not end up like the pixie contract fiasco with Wilkin, where I was supposed to be getting him *out* of a contract and instead had to steal the thing. Not exactly legal work. I'm hiding from the only known supernatural hotspot in town thanks to that little adventure.

"Let me guess," I say, tapping my chin teasingly. "You need a lawyer to... renegotiate your lease by capturing your land-lord. Or you've inherited something and I need to un-hex it."

"Nothing so grandiose," Manx chuckles, sounding less like a villain and more like someone's peculiar uncle. "I simply desire a snack. A particular treat that I can no longer acquire on my own."

"Snacks?" I repeat, my skepticism on full display.

He launches into his predicament with full dramatic flair, practically sighing over the tragic loss of his freedom to hunt down the gourmet truffles he claims to *need*. Apparently, this particular snack is the crème de la crème of hobgoblin delicacies, and without it, life is as dull as a plain rice cake.

"I'll have it delivered," I offer, knowing I can expense it to the Baxters' legal tab.

"No," Manx says. "She discards all packages from strangers."

"What if I drop it off at this spot, then?" I ask.

"I'd prefer it come through a less... clandestine way. She must purchase it herself," he replies, shifting on his feet, his scaly skin rippling.

And there's the catch.

"Fine," I finally relent, the weight of the night pressing down on me. "I'll talk to your snooty lady about her shopping list. But this had better be worth it. If you're sending me on a wild goose chase..."

"Your assistance is most appreciated," Manx interrupts, bowing slightly. "And I assure you, the information I hold is of significant value."

"Great," I say, plastering on a faux smile. "Because nothing screams 'career high' quite like moonlighting as a grocery delivery girl for mystical creatures."

"Ambition comes in many forms," Lucian chimes in, his tone dripping with amusement.

"Right now, my only ambition is to get through this night without any more surprises," I reply, glaring at him before turning back to Manx. "I'll be back when I've cracked the code on your snack situation."

"I look forward to it," Manx nods, the twinkle returning to his eyes. "Good night, Ms. Lane."

"Night, Manx." I sigh, mentally adding 'deliverer of hobgoblin munchies' to my resume. But hey, if it means one step closer to breaking this curse and freeing up my schedule for actual socializing, then I'll play food courier all night long.

The night has stretched on longer than a Monday at the office, and yet here we are, skulking around the edges of a curse like it's our new normal. This time, instead of watching the curse inside the room, we're staking out the exterior. After last night's cryptic message and the nights prior being a total bust, my hopes aren't exactly sky-high.

"Can't believe I'm wearing my good heels for this," I mutter as we huddle beneath the looming shadow of the manor, staring up at the first floor window where the curse likes to put on its spooky light show.

"Comfort over fashion in supernatural sleuthing," Lucian says with a wry smile.

"Easy for you to say," I murmur. "You could make a potato sack look chic."

We fall silent, waiting for midnight to arrive and hopefully bring some answers with it. As the clock chimes twelve, there's a palpable sense of anticipation in the air. The stillness is broken only by the soft, distant hoot of an owl—a sound that feels both eerie and oddly fitting, like the universe is leaning into the drama.

I hold my breath, half expecting the night to slip by without a peep again. If I'm lucky, the curse has moved to writing letters in the steam on a bathroom mirror instead. But just as doubt starts to creep in, a sudden gust of wind kicks up. At first, it's just a faint scratching, but then the sound starts. The haunting has returned, but there's no obvious reason why tonight's any different from the last. The cacophony builds, chaos swirling through the night like a mad whirlwind.

I squint, leaning in closer. "Lucian, look. It's following a pattern. Next up, the bed's going to levitate." My prediction comes true as the bed floats off the floor. "It's the same routine as before. Maybe there's a supernatural remote control hiding somewhere? Like a TV clicker for curses?"

"I'm unsurprised by the repetition." Lucian's voice is a thread of certainty in the dark. "In my experience, the supernatural world is less about convenience and more about tradition. We don't change easily. Vampires and lawyers—we're creatures of habit. Why not curses?"

"Great," I sigh, rolling my eyes. "So, it's just cursed Groundhog Day? Fantastic."

"Your sense of humor remains unscathed, I see," Lucian observes, the corner of his mouth twitching upward in an almost smile.

"Hey, if I don't laugh, I'll cry, and my mascara is too nice for tears," I quip, stepping away from the window. "Last time, we heard something walking around. Let's see if the lawn's turned into a supernatural slip 'n slide."

Lucian chuckles softly as we wander away from the window. The eerie spectacle unfolding before us seems almost melodic, like a twisted lullaby designed to taunt rather than soothe.

I tiptoe around Oakheart Estate's grounds, my gaze glued to the window where the curse is doing its nightly dance. Lucian, the stoic bloodsucker, strides ahead, his focus so intense it's like he's trying to crack a supernatural code with his mind.

"Look at the window now," Lucian instructs, his finger aimed toward the window where the lights flicker in what I've lovingly dubbed 'The Poltergeist Polka.'

"Stunning," I deadpan. "It's like a spooky light show that's trying to Morse code 'go home, Emily, you're out of your league.'" I squint, trying to see past the glare and into the heart of the mystery. But then I notice. Not what's there, but what's *missing*. "No rose."

"Indeed, meaning it isn't a perfect pattern." Lucian murmurs, more to himself than to me.

"Maybe there are other differences," I say. "You should fly around and see if you find anything else from a bird's eye view."

As an ancient vampire, Lucian possesses a unique ability to shapeshift into a raven. It's a skill he hasn't used since his sister was alive, a full two hundred years ago.

Lucian's brow furrows in a deep frown. "I'll remain with you," he replies firmly.

"I'll be fine," I assure him, sensing his hesitation. "I don't need protection."

"It isn't about protection," he responds quietly, his gaze fixed on mine.

"So what's the problem?"

"Recall that you aren't well-versed in familial matters," he says quietly, his voice edged with something dark. "I do not shift anymore."

I flinch at his words, feeling like I've touched a raw nerve. "Right, my mistake," I blurt. "We can both stay firmly planted on the ground then."

Still my eyes wander to the sky, wondering what secrets and answers may lie beyond our reach. With one foot metaphorically stuck in my mouth, I scan the ground for any signs of disturbance, my legal eye *hopefully* catching even the smallest of oddities.

I round the corner alone, Lucian taking his time in the hedges that overlook the Abernathy house, when one of the first floor windows catches my eye. The curtains—the heavy brocade ones that look like they came from a vampire's boudoir—are cracked open. Just a sliver, but enough for me to see inside. The Baxters keep all the back downstairs curtains shut tight like they're afraid of prying eyes. (And yet... all the windows facing the street are fair game, letting anyone see into the cursed room. But having money doesn't always translate to having sense.)

I sneak closer, keeping to the shadows, and peer inside. Alex and Sylvia are there, and they're not having a cozy chat over tea. Alex looks like a coiled spring, his face twisted into something between anger and desperation. His hand grips the back of a chair so hard it looks like he's trying to snap it in half. Sylvia's got her arms up, talking fast, pleading, maybe, but I can't hear a thing. The window's old, the glass thick, and their voices are muffled to nothing. But I don't need sound to see tension when it's practically steaming off them.

Alex says something—no, spits it—and Sylvia flinches like she's been slapped. I bite down on my tongue to keep from gasping out loud. He leans in close, nose to nose, his face tight with something I can't quite place. Anger? Fear? Whatever it is, it makes my stomach flip, like watching a car crash you can't look away from. And then he grabs her arm, not hard but firm, and Sylvia's face pinches like she's holding back tears. Or secrets.

I lean forward, desperate to catch a word, a clue, but Sylvia's eyes flick toward the window, and I duck down behind a bush so fast I nearly eat dirt. I crouch there, heart pounding in my ears, praying they didn't see me. I risk another peek, but Alex is pulling the curtains shut, sealing whatever argument they're having back behind layers of thick, dusty fabric.

I stay there for a beat, trying to avoid touching the ground in my fancy digs, though my knees are a lost cause, and when I finally stand up, my legs are trembling. Whatever that was, it didn't look like a family spat, but something more. Something certainly curse-related.

You aren't well-versed in familial matters, Lucian had just told me. He might be right. Maybe this is just a family trying to keep from falling apart. And Alex, with all his control freak tendencies, might just be doing his best to keep a grip on his wife, his kids, and this mess of a house. But there's something about the look on Sylvia's face, the way Alex grabbed her arm like he was holding on for dear life... it's sticking with me, gnawing at the back of my mind like a dog with a bone.

I take one last glance at the window—curtains shut tight now, like a stage after the show's over—then continue on my search, trying to shake off that creeping feeling in my gut. Lucian joins me, a shake of his head confirming he hasn't found anything.

As we creep around to the opposite side of the house from the cursed room, I spot something strange—a patch of earth that looks like it's been disturbed.

"Lucian, look," I whisper, pointing to the ground. "There are marks here, like something heavy was dragged and buried."

He crouches down, his movements graceful even in the darkness. Moonlight paints his features in an otherworldly glow as he inspects the ground, his expression inscrutable. After a moment, he rises, his gaze sweeping our surroundings with newfound intensity.

"This wasn't here before," Lucian murmurs. "It seems like whatever is causing the curse may have a physical presence outside as well."

He kneels down and traces the ground, deliberate and steady. "You should examine it as well," he says softly, glancing back at me with those piercing gray eyes that seem to see right through my bravado.

I glance down at my already mud-splattered shoes and the designer dress that was definitely not made with dirt in mind. "I'm not exactly dressed for gardening."

Lucian, equally impeccably dressed in his tailored suit, meets my eyes and inclines his head. "I suppose that is my fault, as I brought you here. It's only fair that I do the digging."

The night holds its breath as he digs into the soil. Or, at least, I do. With each scoop, the anticipation grows.

After what feels like an eternity of quiet, broken only by the rustle of leaves and the soft scrape of Lucian's hands in the dirt, he straightens, his expression pensive. "There is nothing," he concludes, his voice soft but certain.

"Of course there isn't," I reply, suppressing the twinge disappointment. Despite my reluctance to get my hands dirty, I still feel a pang of frustration at the lack of answers buried in the earth. It's like chasing shadows in the dark, always one step behind. "It couldn't be that easy, could it?"

Lucian's lips twitch in a half-smile. "Nothing worthwhile ever is, Emily."

"I'll work on getting Manx his truffles," I tell him, determined to crack this case wide open and make the most of my interrupted evening. "Seems like our best bet for now, unless you decide to come clean about your elusive witch friend."

He sidesteps my attempt to pry and edges closer to my side. "Thank you for coming with me tonight and checking," he murmurs, his voice as smooth as silk in the chilly night air. "I know you had other plans."

I glance up at him, the silver moonlight highlighting his sharp features. "The Baxters are my client, you know," I tease.

His chuckle is like music to my ears, deep and rich in the stillness of the night. "Your dedication to your clients is admirable. Almost as admirable as your wit," Lucian replies, his gaze warm and lingering.

A blush tinges my cheeks at his compliment, a flutter of warmth stirring in my chest despite the eerie surroundings. "Right. Well, I'll keep you updated then."

As we reach my car, Lucian gallantly holds open the door for me.

"Oh, and Lucian," I say once I'm settled in and buckled up.

He leans in close, his breath teasing against my skin. "Yes, Emily?" His voice is a soft murmur, filled with unspoken promises.

"Get a phone," I whisper back before driving away with a wide grin on my face.

Chapter 12

"Miranda, you realize that in this instance, Jenna's 'emotional distress' is the legal equivalent of saying, 'it hurt my feelings,' right?" I say into the phone, balancing the receiver between my shoulder and ear while shuffling through the mountain of paperwork on my desk. It's Monday morning and I'm back to the grind.

Miranda scoffs through the speaker, her voice cracking with a dry wit that matches my own. "Jenna's got a flair for the dramatic. Thinks 'Law & Order' reruns count as legal study."

I chuckle, leaning against the mahogany desk that's more polished than my last closing argument. "So you're saying, if melodrama were money, she'd be buying her way onto the Forbes list, huh?"

"Exactly. And after what she did to me... I need to prove her wrong."

"Proving people wrong is my favorite hobby, Miranda." I straighten up. My rebellious streak flares, eager to dive into the fray and stand up for the underdog—or in this case, Rebecca. "How long were you broken up before you and Rebecca started up?"

"Three months, two weeks, and five days. But who's counting?" Miranda's chuckle is warm, a kindred spirit in the chaos of legalese and loopholes.

"Apparently, you are," I tease, scribbling down the timeline. "That's our linchpin. We prove the breakup was clean, and that whatever happened afterwards is just life being life."

"Will do. And Emily? Thanks for not being another suit-wearing vampire," she says, and I can practically hear the smirk in her voice.

"Hey, some of my best friends are bloodsuckers," I answer with feigned indignation. "I'll see you in court, unless I can get it settled."

"Looking forward to it." The line goes dead.

I toss the phone onto the chaos of my desk and scribble a note to myself about Miranda's evidence. With Rebecca unable to testify, now that she's been outed as a paranormal, Miranda is the key to her defense. Jenna should have thought of that before blew up her life. If anyone can help destroy Jenna's case and prove it for the lie it is, it's Miranda.

Before I can move to my next task, Liz steps into my office, holding a manila folder that looks way too official for a Monday morning. I glance up, catching the hint of curiosity in her eyes.

"Got something for you, but I don't know where to save it," she says, wiggling the folder before dropping it onto the edge of my desk. "Lab results on that flower sample you sent in last week."

I straighten up, trying to mask my interest as casual. "Flower sample?"

"Yeah, on the camellia." Liz crosses her arms, smirking. "This risk management gig for the Baxters is getting stranger and stranger."

I freeze mid-reach for the folder. *Camellia?* That can't be right. "Camellia?" I repeat, trying not to sound completely lost. "Are you sure? I thought it was a rose."

Liz tilts her head, giving me that 'you're-kidding-me' look. "Yep. Camellia. They look a little similar, but trust me, they're not the same. I had a fight with the florist for my wedding when they tried to cheap out on my bouquets."

I mentally kick myself for not noticing. "Right. Camellia, not a rose." I plaster on a sardonic smile as I flip the folder open, skimming the results. Benign, non-magical, non-poisonous, non-*anything* but a flower.

"It's kind of important to know the difference, you know?" Liz continues, half-teasing. "Roses have thorns; camellias don't. Also, they bloom differently. Isn't that something a high-profile lawyer should notice?"

I sigh, making a show of rolling my eyes. "Thanks for the botany lesson, Liz. If I ever get trapped in a garden and need to identify flowers to escape, I'll be sure to text you."

She laughs, clearly enjoying my minor humiliation. "Just trying to help. But seriously, camellias? Who even uses those anymore?"

I flip through the lab results with more care now, but my mind is already spinning. *A camellia, not a rose.* I should've noticed, but the realization stirs something else in the back of my mind. Camellia... Amelia. Of course. The flower practically feels like a calling card.

So much for Stardust's claim about witches' stealth and covertness. Might as well have stamped the house with 'Cursed by Lady Amelia' in neon lights.

"Well," I say, leaning back in my chair, "I suppose next time I'll triple-check my flower identification before sending anything to the lab. Wouldn't want another mix-up in my high-stakes floral investigations."

Liz chuckles. "Please do. You don't want to lose a case over a petal mishap." She starts to turn but pauses, glancing at me. "Anything else you need me to handle?"

I wave her off and she sashays back to her desk when my phone buzzes on the desk, Rhett's name flashing on the screen. I hesitate for a second, the tension in my shoulders knotting tighter. With a sigh that feels like it's dragging my soul out, I answer.

"Emily," Rhett's voice rumbles from the other end, anxiety laced with an undercurrent of impatience. "My family's on edge with the curse starting up again. Add in that bloody portent and they're snarling for results."

I pinch the bridge of my nose, wishing for a wand to magically solve this, but alas, I'm just your everyday, non-witchy attorney. "Rhett, you know curses and legalities don't mix well. I'm trying." *I'm trying not to lose my mind,* I want to add, but I figure that wouldn't help either of us.

"Do you have anything?" he prods.

I glance down at my locked cabinet where my notes are, hidden from Liz's well-meaning-but-prying eyes. *Should I mention Amelia?* The thought lingers, but I shove it aside for the moment. "I got the lab results back from the flower—it's just garden variety, literally. And not a rose, either."

"That's it?" His voice hardens, a sharp edge creeping in.

"It's been what, a week? These things take time."

"Time is a luxury we might not have," he growls softly, and I can almost picture his eyes narrowing. "How much grace do you expect?"

"More than what you're giving me now," I retort sharply, but I soften my tone realizing I need him on my side. "I have a lead, okay? Give me until... tomorrow. I should have something more concrete then."

There's a beat of silence, a heavy pause hanging between us. His impatience is palpable, and I know he's not going to let me off the hook easily. I take a breath, mentally running through what Amy and Trenton told me about not mentioning her, and Lucian's warning echoing louder in my head. That I wouldn't know normal family dynamics if they hit me in the face. Still, if I'm going to help, I need to get to the bottom of this—even if it means pushing a little harder.

"The lead in question," I begin carefully, "relates to Amelia."

There's a sharp intake of breath on the other end, and I brace myself, expecting Rhett to snap, to tell me to back off and stay out of his family's business. But he surprises me.

"Amelia?" he echoes, his voice low, but there's no anger. There's something else—something darker. "Good. I've been wondering why no one's said it yet."

I blink, my mind scrambling to catch up. "You... want me to find her?"

"Yes," he growls, this time with a force I didn't expect. "Find her, shout her name from the rooftops if you can manage it. We've been dancing around Amelia for too long, acting like she's not the key to this whole mess."

"I'll do what I can," I say, my voice steady but my mind racing. If Amelia's the key, why force me to find it? What *else* have we been tap-dancing around? "I've already been looking into her, but it's not exactly easy—"

"I don't care how hard it is," Rhett interrupts, his tone firm. "Find her. Dig up whatever you can. If she's the one behind this curse, we need to know how to stop her."

"Okay. I'll find her. Any hints on where to look? Like a last name, a last address?"

"That's what I pay you for," Rhett replies, his voice low and final.

Before I can respond, the line goes dead.

So, Amelia is the likely key, but with nothing from Rhett, there's only one thread to pull. The truffles. Sold in the states by a single distributor, sourced from a mythical sounding location called the Wailing Woods. There was no telling how Manx first got his hands on them, or why they became his Rosebud.

How on earth am I going to persuade Ethel to buy those enchanted morsels? If only they were as easy to gain as cheap takeout.

"Emily?" Liz's voice cuts through my thoughts, sharper than the edge of a subpoena. She's standing at my office doorway, her green eyes wide with concern. Her perfectly coiffed curls seem less bouncy, her usually vibrant posture deflated. She's miles away from the woman who exchanged that floral repartee ten minutes ago. It's like looking at a sad, freckled balloon.

"Spill it, Liz," I say tiredly. "You've got that 'the jury just came back with a question' look."

She bites her lip, a clear sign she's delivering news that could either rock my world or knock it off its axis. "Mr. Lawrence wants to see you. Like, now."

Andrew Lawrence, senior partner. Once separated from me by my supervising partner, but now, I report directly to him. The last time I'd been summoned before him was just before my partner interview, when the news caught wind that I had bailed Lucian out of jail. He wasn't part of the committee that voted me in as partner—those that held their nose because a vamp's money is just as green as a human's. Instead, he nearly canceled my interview, and it was only my quick thinking and insincere smile that kept him from firing me. The lie that I'd done it to attract clients who are sympathetic to paranormals kept me employed, but put me on a short leash. A leash I'd been keeping tight when I'd solved a murder, cleared Lucian's name, and pointed the finger at the then-mayor. And after the promise to myself to be a genuine friend to the paranormal sect, I'd sliced the leash off.

"Did his majesty specify whether I should come bearing gifts or wearing armor?" I ask, my attempts at levity doing little to disguise the thrumming of nerves beneath my skin.

Liz's expression doesn't change, and in that moment, I know this isn't some pat-on-the-back meeting. Lawrence is an attorney who's seen more trials than I've had hot dinners. When he summons you, it's like being called to the principal's office... if the principal could fire you or promote you on a whim.

"Didn't say," she replies. "But the vibe was definitely more guillotine than graduation."

"Great. Nothing like a good beheading before lunch." I push back from my desk, ignoring the twinge of anxiety trying to claw its way up my throat.

"Want me to come with?" Liz offers, already taking a step forward.

"Appreciate it, but unless you're smuggling in a flask of holy water, I think I've got to face this headless horseman solo," I counter with a wry smile. "Keep the fort down, Liz. Either I'll be back to fight another day, or you can swipe the good pens from my desk."

"I've already claimed the pens. And the stapler. If you're not back by lunch, I'm taking your chair too. That thing's way comfier than mine," she says, a sly grin finally breaking through as I stride past her towards whatever fate awaits me in Lawrence's lair.

I march down the corridor with the kind of purpose usually reserved for those about to walk the plank. Pausing before Lawrence's door, I adjust my jacket, taking a deep breath before knocking.

"Come in," his voice rumbles from inside, sounding as welcoming as a tomb.

I push open the door and step into an office that's a perfect marriage of old-world charm and cutting-edge technology—a reflection of Lawrence himself. The polished mahogany desk and leather-bound books practically scream 'I'm better than you,' while the sleek tablet and hidden monitors whisper 'and I know it.' I'd hoped his high-tech-meets-sophistication vibe meant he'd have a modern take on my paranormal ties, but not so much. Instead, it feels like I'm navigating a minefield, and he's the one holding the map.

Lawrence sits behind the desk, fingers steepled like he's plotting world domination, his sharp eyes giving me the kind of once-over that makes you feel both seen and slightly judged. I resist the urge to squirm under his gaze.

"Emily, take a seat," he instructs, gesturing to the chair opposite him. He doesn't rise from his imposing leather chair, and the lack of formality sends a shiver down my spine.

"Mr. Lawrence," I greet, my tone neutral as I comply. "You wanted to see me?"

"Indeed," he begins, his fingers tented like he's masterminding some grand chess game. "It remains *Lane*, correct? Not Mrs. Emily Smith?"

The lie I spun for the Baxters' neighbors comes back to haunt me. I force a chuckle, hoping to brush off his accusation. "Some prefer aliases; adds to the mystery, don't you think?" I try to keep my tone light, but the mirth is hollow.

"Cut the theatrics," he snaps, frosty blue gaze cutting through my facade. "A potential client called, claiming one of our partners was nosing around their neighborhood. Someone who recognized you not as a curious passerby, but as the attorney who's made headlines consorting with... vampires," he says, the words laced with disapproval.

"Consorting is such a medieval term," I quip, unable to help myself. "I prefer 'professional collaboration.'"

"Semantics aside," he continues, unamused, "this individual was quite perturbed. They seemed convinced you were up to no good."

"Up to no good?" I repeat, feigning innocence. "I assure you, my escapades are strictly legal. And for *paying* clients."

He produces a folder and scans its contents. "Yes, your hours this week mention a new client, the Baxter family. What type of legal work involves prowling around wealthy neighborhoods after dark?"

"Risk management," I answer calmly, though my heart thunders in my chest. It's technically the truth, but managing risks of a supernatural nature isn't something Lawrence would understand—or condone.

"Your 'risk management' looks suspiciously like you're acting as muscle for hire, Emily. This firm has a reputation to uphold." Lawrence's stare bores into me.

"Muscle for hire?" I retort, letting a chuckle escape. "You flatter me and my lacking biceps."

"Are the Baxters paranormal clients, Emily?" he asks point-blank, cutting through the banter.

I draw in a sharp breath, locking my response tight behind my lips. Answering him would mean betraying a trust, but refusing would only fuel his suspicions. Lawrence's got me in check, and he knows it. I meet his gaze squarely, my expression carefully blank.

"You know my work is diverse," I finally manage, sidestepping his probe with practiced ambiguity.

"Your 'diversity' could cost us our reputation," he says sternly. "Separate your personal crusades from our business, or you'll find yourself on the wrong side of the courtroom."

As I exit his office, closing the door with a soft click behind me, the tightrope I'm walking feels like it's narrowing. The challenge of maintaining my double life looms larger than ever—ambition and altruism, constantly at odds. As I retreat to my office, the tape recorder in my pocket feels heavy, burdened with secrets and silent pleas for help from those who exist in the shadows. One thing is clear—the line between my two worlds isn't just blurring; it's being erased.***

Liz meets me in the hallway, her green eyes wide with concern. "What happened?" Her curls seem to bristle with curiosity.

"Nothing I can't handle," I start to say, but the words get cut off as my phone buzzes in my pocket like an insistent bumblebee. Frances Montgomery's name flashes on the screen, and suddenly, I feel less like a chewed-out attorney and more like a summoned superhero. Well, minus the cape and spandex.

"Emily Lane," I answer, my voice all business.

"Emily, I need you at a zoning meeting today. It's imperative for my interests," Montgomery dictates, his tone brokering no argument.

"Understood," I reply, a small smile playing on my lips. Despite the earlier friction, this is a reminder that I'm still in the game—still needed. Montgomery was my biggest client, the one that kept me in the running for partner, a whale that forced Johnson & Marcus off my back. Although most of his work appeared legal-adjacent, billables were billable. And a zoning meeting is as close to 'real legal work' as this guy's ever demanded.

"I'll text the details," he finishes.

"What's up?" Liz asks when I hang up.

"Montgomery and a glorious afternoon of debating municipal codes and zoning variances awaits me," I reply, feigning enthusiasm.

Liz lets out an exaggerated sigh, her eyes rolling so far back I'm surprised they don't get stuck. "A zoning meeting? Really? After all the high-stakes excitement you've had with this guy?" She huffs, crossing her arms over her designer blouse. "What about those glamorous political galas from last month? Where's that?"

"Trust me, I remember them well," I muse, my thoughts dancing back to the champagne, the twinkling lights, and Peterson's hands around my neck. A sharp contrast to sterile municipal buildings and endless debates about land use likely awaiting me.

"Wouldn't you rather be rubbing elbows with the city's elite than sitting through another snooze-fest about urban development?" Liz nudges, a hint of longing in her voice.

"Rubbing elbows usually leads to picking pockets, metaphorically speaking." I stare her down, frowning. "You okay?"

She glances up, her green eyes flashing with a mix of frustration and mischief. "Oh, just dreaming of a life less ordinary," she quips, waving her arms with a dramatic flourish. "One where I'm not stuck scheduling depositions and making coffee runs but glamping it up at those galas by your side."

"Ah, the thrilling life of a legal assistant," I say, a smirk playing on my lips. "You know the grass isn't always greener on the high-society side."

"Easy for you to say," she says, frowning. "You get to go to those exclusive things. Even Susan couldn't wrangle an invite to those campaign events. Meaning the rest of us are stuck watching from the outside."

"It's not all that interesting," I reply, trying to cheer her.

"But how do we know that?" She huffs again. "It could be the most boring night in a century, but we'd have no way of knowing. It's special because you're in the know and we're not."

A spark ignites somewhere in the recesses of my brain. An idea begins to appear, nebulous and exciting. I link arms with her as we weave through the maze of cubicles towards my office. We're taking the scenic route to avoid running into Davenport, Haskins, or any *other* partner with a penchant for impromptu grillings. The last thing I need is another round of twenty questions about my nocturnal client relations. That they don't approve is clear, but I'm not asking for permission or forgiveness anymore.

"The next time I get invited to a special event with a potential murderer, I'll be sure to invite you." The corners of my mouth hitch up into a smirk.

"Fine," Liz concedes with a playful pout. "But I'm holding you to that promise of excitement."

"Wouldn't dream of letting you down," I quip, tucking away the bubbling plan for later. For now, the dry world of zoning laws awaits, but who knows what kind of chaos I could stir up between the lines of legalese and ordinance codes.

Chapter 13

The zoning meeting could've been a séance for all the fun it was, and now I'm parked at Moonlit Haven. The place is buzzing with an energy that could rival Times Square on New Year's Eve, a heady mix of holiday spirit and mischief swirling in the air. Stardust, perched on his stool towering over everyone in his glittery platform boots, is too absorbed in the crowd to notice my arrival or my plea for his help in acquiring a basilisk scale.

Liz's claim about exclusivity gave me the idea—if those ladies-who-lunch think the truffles Manx wants are special, they'll be clamoring to purchase them first. I just need to make sure that's Ethel. And how do I get access? I've got an 'in' from the gossip queen down the street, Mrs. Jennings, but there's no way she'll let me tag along unless I had something valuable to offer her in return. Ergo, scale.

"Earth to Major Tom." I wave a hand in front of Stardust's overglittered face teasingly after he'd blown off my first few attempts.

"Darling," he purrs without breaking his gaze. His eyes are glued to Ray, who's diving headfirst into some over-the-top winter costume contest. "Patience is a virtue."

"Virtue won't land me that scale." My voice dips into the realm of pleading. "I'm in a bind here. Please."

"Ah, the urgency of mortals," Stardust sighs dramatically, finally looking at me. "Obtaining a basilic scale... is not for the fainthearted or the pixie-infested, of which you are both."

"Just grab one in the Underground," I beg, a little desperation seeping into my voice. "There was a stall selling them. I'll buy you all the sequins your heart desires."

Stardust just shakes his head, eyes twinkling with amusement. "I have other commitments tonight, darling." And with that, he turns back to the crowd, leaving me with nothing but a rising sense of frustration and eyes blinded from the glitter falling to the floor.

I take a deep breath and let my eyes wander across the room. Moonlit Haven is a hive of supernatural activity, disguised under the guise of an autumn masquerade. Costumed witches mingle with faux-werewolves while various paranormals shamelessly flirt with the humans who think unique looks are just part of a costume.

"Who knew Yetis had such rhythm," I comment dryly, watching a costumed furry behemoth moonwalk across the floor. "Michael Jackson would be proud... or terrified."

"Definitely both," Stardust muses, raising his glass to the creature, who nods in acknowledgment before spinning into a crowd of applauding nymphs.

"Only here would 'Thriller' meet a Charlie Brown Thanksgiving and nobody bats an eye." I shake my head, half-amused, half-wishing I had someone to share the absurdity with.

Danielle waves at me from across the bar, grinning like she's been waiting all night to pounce. She's sitting with a group of five women, all dressed as Bubbles from the Powerpuff Girls. I give her a casual salute back and keep scanning the room.

I spy a few other familiar faces. There's Rebecca, draped across a guy dressed as a woodpecker—because nothing says romance like giant fake feathers. Miranda's right next to them, perched on a barstool and sipping her drink with an air of bored superiority. Her other hand, though, is casually curled around Rebecca's neck, like she's half-claiming her or half-ready to yank her back if the woodpecker gets too bold. Who knew a lawsuit was all it took to bring those two back together?

A couple of donors I recognize from the park are clustered near the bar, and then there's the pair of men in sharp zoot suits, leaning against a corner like they've stepped out of a noir film. They aren't wearing those suits ironically, either—former associates of Frank Mitchell, if I had to guess.

"Emily Lane, cynic with a heart of gold," Stardust teases, nudging me gently. "Why not enjoy the spectacle? After all, isn't life just one grand, bizarre pageant?"

"Easy for you to say. You're practically the master of ceremonies." I smile despite myself, the problem of the Underground and my scale temporarily eclipsed by the twinkling lights and infectious laughter around me. "What is Ray wearing?"

Stardust smirks. "Here he comes, you can ask him."

Ray weaves through the throng of costumed revelers, his unbridled excitement reaching us before the long spindles of his costume do.

"Emily!" he calls out over the din of chatter and music, his grin so infectious it should probably be quarantined. "You're here!"

"Wouldn't miss it," I confirm, eyeing his costume curiously. "And I love the look! But... what exactly are you supposed to be?"

He tosses his striped cape over his shoulder. "Phantom of the Opera meets The Nightmare Before Christmas!"

"Phantom of the Holiday Special, huh?" I say, arching an eyebrow. "That's either genius or a cry for help."

"Genius, without a doubt," Stardust interjects, draping an arm around Ray's shoulder in a show of solidarity. "I stepped aside this year—you know, to give the new talent room to shine." His grin reveals more pride than regret, silent evidence of passing the baton.

"You know you didn't have to do that for me," Ray murmurs, his tan cheeks tinted with a blush that could just be from the excitement—or maybe the bar's heat.

"Of course, I did," Stardust insists as they share a look so tender it could turn *Medusa* to stone. "Besides, I'll be front and center cheering you on. And dying of envy, naturally. Until the next one."

"See, that's true love right there," I say. "Sacrifice and sequins."

"You should do the next one too!" Ray says eagerly. "It's in three weeks! Just before Christmas."

"Sure, why not?" I shrug. "Maybe my law school gang would be up for it."

I tap out a message to the group chat. *"Guys, Moonlit Haven's next costume contest is in three weeks. Think Mardi Gras had a baby with Christmas. Just saying..."*

Almost instantly, Megan fires back, *"OMG yes! Let's do it! Group costume! We can go as the* Legal *Justice League. I'll be Lady Litigator!"*

"She had that one ready to go," I mutter with a smirk. *"If I can go as the Arbitrator, bringing even the most bitter adversaries to their knees... in settlement."*

"What's an arbitrator?" Ray asks, peering over my shoulder.

"A kind of judge meets mediator—never mind, I'll explain later," I reply, just as another message pops up.

Brian chimes in, *"Down for it. As long as I get to wield a gavel."*

Then comes Matty's response, back to being a (handsome) wet blanket in human form—*"Seriously, Em? You know the crowd that place attracts."*

Frank Mitchell and his ilk is probably what he means. But Frank's dead. Although that could be part of Matty's concern...

"Come on, Matty, live a little," I type back, though I can already picture his furrowed brow and the wringing of his ever-worrying hands. *"It's all in good fun. Plus, maybe they'll serving justice-flavored cocktails."*

"Justice-flavored?" Ray asks, puzzled.

"Yep," I confirm with a straight face. "Tastes like righteousness with a twist of lemon."

"Sounds... refreshing?" Ray tries, but even he can't sell it.

"Trust me, it's an acquired taste," I assure him.

"Wait, is that one of those bars?" Megan asks.

I stare at her response for a second. *"If you mean an absolutely awesome one, then yes,"* I reply. But her message stings. Megan doesn't get it. Matty might play along, but he doesn't understand either. Not really. Only Brian, with his hobgoblin in the walls, might keep his eyes open to the paranormal. The other two, they're still living in the human, the *reductionist* world.

"Everything okay?" Ray asks.

"Yeah," I lie, pocketing my phone. "Just the usual."

A gender bent Jack Frost calls Ray's name, and he stands, adjusting his face mask.

"Wish me luck," he says with a deep breath.

"You don't need it," I tell him. Stardust kisses his hand and sends him off.

I turn to Stardust, intent on picking up our conversation where it left off. "Now, about that—"

"Shh!" He cuts me off with a flamboyant wave of his hand, causing glitter to sparkle in the air around us like cosmic dust. "Ray is up next."

"In 10 minutes," I mutter under my breath.

As if summoned by my growing irritation, Lucian and Severin slip through the throng, their vampire grace making it look like they're gliding. Dressed in tailored suits, they're a vampire duo straight out of a Bond film, although I doubt they'd appreciate the comparison. Lucian's black hair is pulled back in a low ponytail, reminiscent of my usual hairstyle, while Severin's blond locks pool around his face ala a well-styled doll. Heads turn as they pass, a few people fanning themselves at the sight of their chiseled looks, but, of course, neither of them seems to notice the attention.

"Emily," Lucian greets with a charming smile. "Enjoying the festivities?"

"Trying to," I say, eyeing the passing parade of costumes. "But I'm also multitasking. Are either of you willing to grab me a basilisk scale the next time you're in the Underground? Preferably within the next day or two?"

Severin squints suspiciously, giving Lucian a silent side-eye before turning back to me. He's Lucian's second-in-command, a stick-in-the-mud rule following type.

Before I'd met him, I thought Lucian was the uptight one, but Severin makes Lucian look like a master of ceremonies at a limbo contest.

"A basilisk scale?" Severin says, caution dripping from every syllable. "Are you planning on brewing a potion, Ms. Lane?"

I raise an eyebrow, smirking at their matching looks of concern. "Nothing so... dramatic. Let's just say it's for work." I flash a grin. "You know, to tip the scales in my favor."

Lucian's forehead wrinkles in a frown. "Emily, if this is some harebrained way to find a witch..."

"I'll have you know I haven't had a harebrained idea in my life," I shoot back, though, let's be real—my idea box is basically full of half-baked plans and sheer luck.

Severin shifts his weight slightly, his icy blue eyes scanning the room before settling back on me. "I'm sorry, Ms. Lane, I cannot do so. After tonight's contest, I'll need to guard the safe as my usual security is indisposed."

"The... safe?" I ask, trying to keep the skepticism out of my voice.

"Yes. As the host of this event, security is my priority," Severin affirms with a curt nod. "Once my team returns, I'll transfer the tender to Lucian's basement vault. But I cannot risk it alone."

I furrow my brow, having never considered how Severin's bar handled cash. "Why don't you deposit it?"

It's a pretty logical question. Then again, human logic's not always a thing with paranormals.

Lucian gives me a look like I'd just suggested he moonlight as an Instagram influencer. "You know why. Think about what we are prohibited from doing."

I remember, at least some, from my research when the firm wanted me to sue Lucian before I stopped that in its tracks. No signing anything under oath, which likely translates to no bank accounts and no contracts in their names. Human laws working against them everywhere they can.

I cross my arms, trying to focus on the conversation and not get distracted by the carnival energy around us. "Right. I forgot bank accounts are no go for you nocturnal types, but maybe there are workarounds?"

"We *have* workarounds," Severin says. "Cash and proxies."

Lucian's expression turns grim. "Cash is not a problem for those of us who've had... centuries to accumulate it. But proxies? Even they're getting more difficult to find. Too many people are fearful of the consequences. And we certainly cannot blame them."

Miranda's job loss is a recent reminder. My own career seems to be teetering on that same edge.

Severin's eyes flash with a hint of annoyance. "Indeed. Bank accounts are the least of our problems."

I realize I'm in the middle of a paranormal problem I rarely considered and guilt rises at how glibly I ignored it. *So much for that new leaf of mine.*

"You're right," I admit. "It's more than just paperwork or access to credit. It's... people understanding that you're not just a monster in the dark. The law won't solve everything, but it can change how you're seen. A shift in perception, little by little."

Severin seems to be weighing his words carefully, his eyes briefly darting to Lucian before fixing back on me. "It's not just about perception, Ms. Lane. It's about survival. For many of us, anonymity is the only protection we have. Drawing attention to ourselves—even for 'good' reasons—can be just as dangerous."

"I get that," I respond, guilt burrowing deeper for oversimplifying things. "But look, every revolution starts with a small step. And maybe that step is as small as being able to deposit your money in a bank."

Lucian's eyes meet mine. "Hope is a dangerous thing to carry, Emily. It burns like the sun when you get too close to it."

I shift, the party's energy buzzing behind me like a radio station I wasn't tuned into. "We know the system is broken," I say. "And if we can fix even one part of it, it's a start. And once there's a crack in the wall, who knows how fast it'll crumble."

There's a silence as the three of us stand there, the revelry of the party feeling strangely muted. I wonder for a moment if I've gone too far, pushing my idealism onto them when the reality they face is much starker. I'm not the one that would get burned.

Lucian finally breaks the silence, raising his glass in a toast. "To crumbling walls," he says, his smile returning, though it's tainted with the edge of something bittersweet.

Severin clinks his glass against Lucian's, then mine, his expression still serious but softer than before. "And to those foolish enough to try."

"To foolishness," I add, and the three of us drink.

I barely have time to bask in the glow of solidarity before Stardust pokes me hard in the shoulder. "Stop flirting with Lucian and pay attention. They're announcing the winners."

"I wasn't flirting," I protest as Lucian and Severin drift off into the party, blending seamlessly with the other creatures of the night. But the commitment I've made won't vanish as easily, I'll make sure of it.

"Sure, sure," Stardust smirks, his glittering eyes fixed on the stage as Jackie Frost takes the mic.

Ray secures second place and Stardust and I cheer wildly for him. He beams with pride, as if he has won the lottery instead of just being a runner-up in a competition full of vampires dressed as accountants and humans dressed as paranormals.

"Second place? I've never placed that high before!" Ray says, his voice riding the wave of ecstatic chatter around us.

The metal medallion dangles from his fingers, catching the light and throwing tiny shapes across his face. It's quite the sight against the backdrop of his meticulously crafted costume.

"Say Star," he says, nudging me with an elbow sharper than a vampire's fang, "let's hit the Underground tonight. Show off my new hardware? What do you say?"

"Because that's exactly what the night scene needs—more shiny things," I say, laughing.

"Darling, you had me at 'show off,'" Stardust drawls, and I swear the air shimmers around him with anticipatory glee.

"Plus," Ray adds, a conspiratorial glint in his eye, "we can snag that scale for Emily."

"Much obliged," I tell them, feeling a warmth spread through my chest that has nothing to do with the crowded room. "You two are the trouble I never knew I needed."

"Only the best kind, love," Stardust winks, and then they're out the door, ready to descend into the pulsing heart of the Underground.

As Ray and Stardust vanish into the night, leaving behind a trail of stardust-like glitter that twinkles in the air, I can't help but feel a surge of gratitude for their friendship. They may be flamboyant and eccentric, but underneath those flashy exteriors, they are fiercely loyal and seem to have my back. I hope I can prove I have theirs.

CHAPTER 14

The midday sun bakes the stamped pavement as I strut down the lane with a little secret tucked in my pocket, feeling every bit the cat about to get the canary. The basilisk scale, iridescent and mesmerizing, is a ticket to this neighborhood's inner circle, and I'm cashing it in.

"Ms. Smith?" Mrs. Jennings' honeyed voice floats across the manicured lawn as she waves from her ivy-covered porch. She's still the picture of suburban sophistication, her large sunglasses hiding eyes that twinkle with a mix of curiosity and mischief. "I hardly recognized you without that fiery red hair."

"Hello, Mrs. Jennings," I say, ascending the steps. "Black is the new black, after all."

She laughs, a perfectly practiced sound. "Did you come by for an introduction to my hairdresser? She could do wonders with those long locks of yours. That bun is dreadful for follicle breakage, you know."

I swallow a sigh. "No, actually, I thought we could do a little... banking together. I have something exclusive I think you might enjoy."

Her eyes light up, a predator scenting a juicy rumor. She ushers me inside, and we settle in the parlor, tea cups chiming gently as they're placed on the table.

I pull out the scale, letting it catch the light and throw prisms across the walls.

Mrs. Jennings' eyes go wide, greed and curiosity battling it out. "What *is* it?"

"A genuine basilisk scale," I confirm with a nod. "Quite the rare commodity. It's said to bring protection *and* a touch of envy from those who lack such treasures."

Envy is her siren song, but she's too shrewd to be taken in without questioning. "How did you come by this?" she asks, raising a perfectly coifed brow.

I lean back, crossing one leg over the other, playing it cool. "Let's just say I've made some rather... unique connections in my line of work."

She hesitates, but I know the hook's baited. Time for the trump card.

"I was playing coy when we last met. You might recall the Peterson murder case?" I say idly. "Solved it. Turns out the supernatural world isn't as cryptic as most think, and those connections come in handy."

Recognition flares in her gaze, and the scale seems to shimmer even brighter in her eyes. "You're that lawyer?"

"Emily Lane, not Smith," I say. "Apologies for the subterfuge but with my reputation, I need to be wary of revealing myself," I say. It's checkmate, as I've just gone from outsider to insider in her social chessboard.

She leans back, eyes gleaming. "You were wrong about being a gold mine. My goodness, and with that scale?"

"Thought you'd say that," I reply, letting the moment stretch. "And I'd love to give it to you, as a token of our newfound friendship. But I'd like to be there when you show it off. How about an invite to today's book club?"

"Consider yourself invited," she says quickly, the words tumbling out in her excitement of hosting someone of my unique social standing. "It would be an honor to have you, Ms. *Lane*."

"Marvelous," I reply, my tone light but my mind already racing ahead to the strategizing I'll need to do in this den of domestic divas. Little do they know, I'm not just here to sip tea—I'm stirring the pot. And I plan to serve it scalding.

The clink of fine China and the murmur of hushed voices greet me as I step into the parlor, which is draped in an opulence that makes my last paycheck look like chump change. The ladies of the neighborhood are perched like exotic birds on floral sofas and high-back chairs, their plumage consisting of cashmere and silk rather than feathers. Each one is a master of the subtle art of one-upmanship, their conversations laced with humble brags about vacation homes and prodigious offspring.

They're deep into discussing some existential novel I haven't read, but bluffing is basically my side hustle at this point. I nod in all the right places, throw in a few vague insights, and soon, they're too busy talking over each other to notice I've got no idea what the book's even about. And it helps that they're more interested in peacocking their interpretations than actually discussing any of the author's motifs.

The atmosphere is electric with social posturing, each member attempting to outshine the last with tales of their children's Ivy League acceptances or the latest European escapade. They brandish their accomplishments like battle-axes, and for a moment, I'm transported back to the courtroom, where every statement is an opening for attack.

"Emily, darling," the hostess coos from across the circle of voracious readers, "do tell us about that Peterson case. It was quite the scandal, wasn't it?"

I take a delicate sip of the tea, its flavor as complex and layered as the social dynamics at play here. There's a tremor of nerves beneath my calm exterior—one of these well-coifed women could be the one who tried to smear my reputation at work—but I quash it down. Spite is a curious motivator, and today it propels me forward.

"Ah, yes, the Mitchell murder," I begin, leaning back in my seat with a nonchalance I don't entirely feel. "Turns out, a keen eye and a bit of supernatural intuition can go a long way."

Fifteen pairs of cultured eyes lock onto mine with a mixture of curiosity and the faintest trace of skepticism. It's almost like being under a spotlight in a courtroom, only this jury is decked out in tweed and twinsets.

"Speaking of supernatural," another pipes up, "weren't you seen in the neighborhood with a rather... unusual man? Ethel claims he was a vampire."

"The one from the news," Ethel Abernathy confirms, her lips curling into a smile that says she's just drawn a royal flush. "Skulking about in the Baxter's garden."

"Sadly, you're mistaken. He's my paralegal," I clarify, voice firm but light. "Trust me, there's nothing otherworldly about his knack for legal research. His talents were necessary on some risk management I'm doing." I let out a small laugh, as if the very idea is preposterous. The steam coming from Ethel's cup seems to have transferred to her ears as I've turned her royal flush into a busted straight.

"I should mention," I continue, leaning in as if sharing a confidential morsel, "my firm handles some of the most exclusive cases in the city. High stakes, high reward. The Baxters, as you mentioned? High-end clients, nothing more. You know how it is; we must keep the affairs of our clientele discreet." I wink at them conspiratorially, even as I plant the seed that the Baxters' weirdness—or my 'skulking' around for them—is merely a figment of overactive imaginations.

After all, in this room where secrets are currency, implying that I'm privy to the most clandestine of deals adds a layer of mystique to my persona. At least, mystique sounds a lot better than peculiarity. As I set the stage for my next move, I can only hope my blend of sardonic charm and calculated revelations has them hanging on every word.

"Although I don't discriminate based on... let's say, unique backgrounds," I say with a casual shrug.

They lean closer, their expressions hungry for more tales of the supernatural. I feel like a high-wire performer, but there's no safety net below, just parquet flooring and a Persian rug worth more than my law degree.

"Ladies," I start, my voice steady despite the flutter in my chest. "I know the idea of paranormals among us can be... a surprise, but they're not the boogeymen, or women, we've been led to believe." There's an uncomfortable shift in the room, chairs creaking, teacups clinking uneasily on saucers. But *this* is the perception shift, one person at a time.

"Think about it," I press on, "they're just trying to make a life for themselves, like anyone else. They hold jobs, pay taxes, *without bank accounts*, I might add, and yes, some even join book clubs." I let that sink in, their expressions morphing from dubious to thoughtful. "I mean, who wouldn't want a vampire's take on 'Dracula,' right?"

There's a ripple of uncomfortable laughter, but I see them thinking, processing. I've cracked open the door, just a bit.

"Being different shouldn't be a crime," I say with more heat than I intend, my hands punctuating the air. "And as someone who has worked closely with them, I promise you, they have stories that would turn our hair white. Stories of survival, resilience... love. Stories you may not *deserve* to learn. Stories you'd be honored to hear at gatherings like this."

A hush falls over the room, the impact of my words hanging heavy. The women seem impressed, their eyes wide, yet I can't tell if it's my conviction or the novelty of the subject that has gripped them.

"Anyway," I segue smoothly, shifting gears before the moment grows too heavy, "speaking of the unique, have you heard of the truffles from the Wailing Woods?" Interest piques, and I know I have them. "They're not your garden variety chocolates. They're incredibly rare. Sourced from a forest that's more legend than reality and crafted by a chocolatier whose skill is surpassed only by his mysterious anonymity."

"Truffles?" Ethel breathes out the word like it's a sacred incantation, her earlier reservations seemingly evaporated in the face of exclusive gastronomy.

"Absolutely," I say with a knowing smile, "and they're said to possess flavors that are... otherworldly." The double entendre isn't lost on me, and judging by the intrigued looks I'm getting, it's not lost on them either.

"Of course," I add, pretending to be hesitant, "they're not exactly easy to come by. It's all about who you know." I let that linger, the allure of exclusivity hanging in the air like the scent of forbidden fruit. "Imagine serving those at your next dinner party," I tease, watching as Ethel's eyes widen, her mind no doubt racing with the social clout she'd rake in. I can practically hear her mental gears spinning, calculating how much social capital she'd earn.

"Will you share your source?" Ethel asks, her eyes gleaming with the thrill of the chase.

"With you, Mrs. Abernathy, gladly." I give them a smile that's all teeth.

As the meeting draws to a close, the conversations buzz with speculations about paranormal encounters and gourmet delicacies. I've thrown the gauntlet down—a challenge to their prejudices—and while I'm not sure if I've changed any deep-seated beliefs today, I've certainly stirred the pot. And with Ethel hooked on the idea of those truffles, I've sown the seeds of my plan neatly within the fertile soil of her competitive nature.

Now, I just need Rhett to give my investigative roots a little more time to grow. And just in time for Tuesday night drinks.

Chapter 15

The city's murmur fades into the background as I stride down the courthouse steps, my heels clicking a steady rhythm against the worn stone. I've just wrapped up another win—a little one, but hey, they all count.

My phone buzzes in my pocket.

"Any update?" Rhett's text is as terse as a judge's ruling.

I suppress the urge to roll my eyes. *"No snack, no chat,"* I type back, knowing full well Rhett's patience is running as thin as one-ply toilet paper. Manx, the only lead in our case and a creature with an appetite for chocolate that rivals my own for sarcasm, has yet to spill the beans—both literally and figuratively. If Ethel doesn't buy those truffles soon, I'll need a Plan B.

"I need something," comes the near-instant reply. Rhett Baxter, werewolf family leader and apparently the king of rush hour, doesn't understand that some things—like supernatural informants—take time. And specially imported chocolates.

'Patience is a virtue, furball,' is what I *want* to say, since the late nights and zero downtime are gnawing at my manners. Before I can fire off a snappy reply, something flickers in my peripheral vision, like heat waves off hot pavement. I whip my head around, and for a heartbeat, I lock eyes with

a hobgoblin I've never seen before. His sharp features melt into a cunning grin, like we shared a private joke. And then, poof. He vanishes like a soap bubble, leaving the air oddly thin and just a little too quiet.

"Give me a sec," is all I manage to send before slipping the phone back into my pocket.

I could keep walking. That'd be the sensible thing, march back to my office, drown myself in paperwork like the good little lawyer Lawrence and the senior partners want me to do. But that's not what I signed up for. My life's turned into a paranormal mystery crossed with a legal drama. And I'm the leading lady, tracking down creatures of myth in high heels and a pencil skirt.

So, I pivot on my heel, scanning the bustling sidewalk for any sign of where the creature might have gone. There—a narrow alleyway between a deli and a faded bookstore calls out to me.

"Real sketchy, Emily," I chide myself, even as I slip into the alley, trading sunlight for shadows. The stench of garbage and damp brick hit me, but it's not enough to turn me back.

"Come out, come out, wherever you are," I whisper, half hoping he'll hear and half praying he won't. If he wanted to speak with me, we could've done this at home, instead of me playing hide-and-seek with dumpsters, listening for any hint of a rustle or a cackle. It's not like hobgoblins don't have a standing invitation there.

I slip the rose-colored glasses onto my nose, and the murky alley transforms into a vibrant canvas. There he is, crouched beside a graffiti-tagged dumpster like he's part of the street art—a hobgoblin with skin the texture and color of overripe plums and eyes like shards of bottle glass.

"Emily Lane," he croaks, his voice a gravelly symphony that somehow fits perfectly in the grimy symphony of the city.

"My reputation precedes me," I quip. "But let's cut to the chase on what you want from me before I lose my patience and my lunch. How can I help?"

His eyes widen, and he slinks out of the shadows, his grin never faltering. "Alright, alright, no need to get snippy. Your efforts have borne fruit. Or rather, snacks."

"Oh?" I arch an eyebrow, leaning against the cool brick wall. This isn't a new problem but an update on an old one. "And here I was worried about the complexities of interdimensional trade laws. So, Manx got his goodies?"

"Indeed," he confirms. "The deal has been fulfilled."

"Fantastic," I say dryly, though a flutter of satisfaction takes wing in my chest. I tuck a stray strand of hair behind my ear and squint at the hobgoblin, still lurking in the shadows. "You guys have a secret handshake or something? Because Manx was pretty adamant about not there not being a hobgoblin phone book."

The hobgoblin tilts his head. "We are merely... acquaintances," he says, the words rolling off his tongue like marbles.

"Right," I snort, "and I'm just casually acquainted with the rule of law." My skepticism must be as clear as my career ambitions because he doesn't press further on his dubious claim.

A passerby glances into the alley, and there's a familiar itch of prying eyes. I can't afford to stick out more than I already do. Lawyer by day, talking-to-herself alley dweller *also* by day isn't a tagline that'll keep Lawrence off my back.

"Listen," I say, lowering my voice and getting straight to business. "Tell Manx to meet me at my place after work. Say, 7:00? We can talk without drawing any attention."

The hobgoblin nods in understanding. "Your dwelling shall receive him."

"Great," I reply. "And no funny business. I've got neighbors who think 'supernatural' is a cable package."

I leave him there, blending back into the shadowy palette of the alley, and stride out onto the sidewalk. My heels click a rhythm of newfound purpose. Another small victory, but even the tallest towers were built brick by brick.

"Got a lead," I send off to Rhett. He sends a thumbs-up emoji that somehow looks impatient.

"Emily Lane," I murmur to myself, "esquire and enigma unraveller." Not bad for a morning's work.

I drum my fingers on the arm of my second-hand sofa, as threadbare as my patience. The clock ticks past our agreed time, and I half expect Manx to materialize with an apology baked in excuses. But maybe punctuality isn't his strong suit.

The apartment air is stale with the day's tension, and the silence is a little too eager for interruption. The walls are thin here; they carry secrets and the occasional thud from next door. I always assumed it was shoddy construction, but the city's hobgoblin population would have me blame the missing Herle.

Needing to stay productive, I flip open my laptop with a gusto usually reserved for a Saturday night and not a Thursday evening laden with legal briefs. My fingers dance across the keys, composing an email to Jenna's lawyer.

"Dear sir," I start, and then pause. Too formal. I hit backspace enough times that it sounds like a metronome. *"Hello!"* I try again, which strikes the right balance between professional and Emily Lane trademark casual. *"We need to chat about Rebecca. You know, the succubus with the lawsuit the size of her... personality."*

My apartment is quiet around me, but the silence doesn't feel empty. It's charged, waiting for me to make my next move. Maybe it's Herle, pushing me on. I smirk and continue typing, arranging a time and place. *"How's Monday at noon? My office, unless you fancy a bit of otherworldly ambiance. I've got a great little cafe in mind. The coffee's strong enough to raise the dead, or at least your spirits."*

I read over the message once, twice, and on the third time, I'm already nodding to myself. *Yes, this will do nicely.* With an exaggerated flourish, I click 'Send' and lean back against the cushion of my thrift store sofa. It groans under my weight, a familiar protest.

"Emily Lane, attorney-at-law, friend to vampires and werewolves, mediator to monsters," I announce to the room, imagining business cards with that title. "Still, wouldn't hurt to add 'Curse Breaker' to the resume." I glance at the clock. "Assuming I do and Manx ever shows up."

A sudden chill sweeps through the room, and goosebumps prickle my arms. I straighten up, eyes scanning the semi-darkness. "Manx, if that's you turning my apartment into a meat locker, it's not appreciated."

"Apologies, Ms. Lane." His voice comes from the corner—a shadow peeling away from shadows. Manx steps into the dim light, still wearing that infuriatingly enigmatic smile. "I didn't mean to give you a frosty reception."

"Ha-ha," I say, flat as day-old soda. None of the other hobgoblins tried to turn me into a popsicle. "Is the freeze-out special to you or do I start blaming Herle for my winter radiator problems too?"

Manx tilts his head, considering. "Herle exists, certainly," he says, but his eyes dart to the side like he's watching a fly do loop-de-loops.

My brows raise. "... That wasn't the question. And you *know* I don't believe you now."

Manx smiles, baring three sets of teeth. "But he sends his regards. Even suggested you might consider a haircut."

My laugh is sharp enough to slice bread. "Right. Tell him I'll chop my locks the day he decides to have a tête-à-tête with me and prove he isn't some longstanding hobgoblin prank. Until then, it stays."

"The message will be conveyed," Manx replies, but there's another twitch in his jaw.

I sink back into the cushions, letting out a sigh that feels like it's been trapped for ages. "Okay, let's cut to the chase. We have business to discuss, and it doesn't involve my hair."

"Very well," Manx agrees, taking the seat opposite me.

I click on my tape recorder and then drum my fingers on the sofa's armrest. "Amelia," I start, steering us onto a course that's more law and less paranormal hairdressing. "I need to know about her."

Manx's eyes narrow like he's reading fine print, and he leans forward just enough to be conspiratorial. "Amelia came around the Baxters more often than you'd think."

"More often than the Baxters knew?" I prod.

"Likely," he murmurs, a lock of dark hair falling across his forehead. "Miss Evelyn got sick and Amelia snuck in through the cellar nearly every night."

The mention of the cellar piques my interest. There's always something captivating about hidden places, secrets tucked away from prying eyes. My mind whirls with possibilities—what could be concealed in that forgotten corner beneath the house, and why was Amelia sneaking in through there?

"The cellar?" I echo, my voice a mix of intrigue and caution. "What was Amelia doing there?"

Manx shakes his head, the light from my creaky fan catching on his scales. "I do not know, miss. But I can tell you what she said on her last visit after Evelyn's death."

I lean forward. "Tell me," I urge, the excitement of unraveling this mystery palpable in my voice.

Manx's gaze meets mine, and he speaks slowly, each word laden with significance. "Her last words were heavy with portent. 'For every action, there is an equal and opposite reaction.' A Newtonian truth that must be a curse."

"Newton didn't have a vengeful witch grandmother." I jot down the quote in my mental notebook, but it fit the 'cost' idea Stardust mentioned. "Did Amelia go all 'eye for an eye' before she checked out?"

"More or less." Manx's lips curl up at the edges, but there's no humor in it. "The Baxters have short memories and even shorter tempers. Witches believe in balance, but her scales tipped towards vengeance."

"Great," I mutter. "A family feud older than my student loan debt." I pause, thinking. "You wouldn't happen to know Amelia's last name, would you? It might help me dig up some dirt."

"Amelia LeFay, of the Monmouth LeFays," he replies smoothly. "But be careful, Emily Lane. Old names can conjure old ghosts."

"Thanks for the tip," I say dryly. "And the pep talk."

"And I thank you for the truffles." He stands, dusting off his scaly legs as though he's been sitting in cobwebs rather than my sofa.

"Of course," I say, standing too. "And if you feel like sharing one of those enchanted morsels, I'm here."

But he's gone, slipping through the crack under the door or whatever it is non-mortals do, leaving me with my thoughts.

"Might have our witch," I text to Rhett. *"Also may want to check out the cellar??"* I add.

"Will leave all investigating to my lawyer," he replies.

At least the ants in his pants demanding progress seem to have slowed. Or maybe they were fleas.

"Equal and opposite reactions... from a bona fide witch," I repeat to myself.

Should I go out and find her alone? The question bounces around my brain like a pinball, each bounce another doubt. I glance around my apartment, at the peeling wallpaper and the stack of case files teetering precariously on my desk. I'm just a human lawyer with an insatiable curiosity that often nudges me toward trouble.

I slide open my messages again and find Sara's name. *"Tell Lucian we have a date with a witch,"* I type.

Her response comes swiftly, a mere few seconds ticking by before the message notification chimes. *"A real witch?"* Sara's text reads, punctuated with a thoughtful emoji. *"I'll pass on the message. When and where?"*

"Tomorrow, sunset. I'll pick him up," I reply. That will give me enough time during work hours to find *something* on Amelia LeFay, or beg Matty and Danielle to get me an address.

There's a new fire kindling in my chest—part determination, part reckless curiosity. Progress, at last. The Baxter curse doesn't stand a chance.

Chapter 16

The engine of my trusty clunker coughs to life like an old man clearing his throat, and I steer us out of the labyrinth of Chicago streets. Lucian slumps in the passenger seat, his long black hair pulled back, making that clean-shaven jawline all too noticeable. He's staring at me with those sharp gray eyes that seem to dissect my thoughts.

"You could have informed me about your rendezvous with Manx last night," he grumbles, shifting to find comfort in the cramped confines of my car.

"Maybe if you embraced the twenty-first century and got a phone, we wouldn't have this problem," I shoot back with a smirk, flicking my gaze from the rearview mirror to his perturbed expression.

He lets out a long, suffering sigh, brushing a hand over his ponytail like it's the source of all his troubles. "And here I thought hobgoblins were reliable. Silly me for not using the supernatural grapevine."

"The woes of ancient vampires in modern times," I quip, steering around a pothole the size of a small crater.

We're heading north, out past the city limits, where the skyscrapers turn into distant jagged teeth on the horizon. Amelia's last known address is beyond the chaos of Chicago, and I hadn't even needed to abuse my friendships to find her location. With her last name in hand and a prior location, the firm's legal database hit pay dirt.

"Seriously though, Lucian," I say, easing the tension as I switch lanes. "You should be accessible. Especially if you're going to play my Guy Friday."

"Point taken, Counselor," he concedes, but there's a playful glint in his eye now. "Next time, send a carrier pigeon."

"Right, because that won't draw any attention," I say with a laugh. This back-and-forth is becoming our thing, and it's dangerously enjoyable.

Lucian's gaze shifts to the passing landscape, his eyes distant, like he's seeing another century flash by, back when horses were the height of speed. "Some things don't need updating," he begins, his voice thick with centuries of knowledge, "humans are always in a hurry to embrace change, to evolve, to adapt. But some things are fine as they already exist. Some methods have worked for centuries for a reason."

I shoot him a sideways glance, his sharp features softened by the glow of the moonlight. "You're talking about more than just communication methods, aren't you?"

His gaze meets mine, intense yet comforting. "Indeed. Creatures like us have endured through time by holding on to traditions that offer stability and strength. The ways of our kind may seem archaic to some, but they provide us with a sense of identity and security."

"You're sounding a little like the Baxters, now," I tell him, my tone sharp but not unkind. "Hiding and holding on to how things used to be."

Lucian's expression darkens slightly at the comparison to the Baxters, his jaw tightening like I hit a nerve. I watch him closely, noting the way his eyes narrow before he shifts in his seat, facing me head-on. "There's a difference between preserving tradition and using it as a shield," he responds tiredly. "The Baxters cling to their ways out of fear and ignorance, closing themselves off from growth and understanding."

I nod, turning back to the road. It stretches ahead full of twists and turns, mirroring the mysteries we're entangled in. "We won't let history repeat itself with them," I say firmly, resolve sparking in my chest.

Lucian gives me a look—half admiring, half something else I can't quite pin down—and for a split second, it feels like the air between us crackles with... yet another *something*. Something he's been broadcasting for the last week. Is it tension? Electricity? I don't know, but whatever it is, it sends my pulse into overdrive.

"Don't look so shocked," I tell him, trying to deflect. "I'm a lawyer—I solve problems for a living."

"It isn't that," Lucian replies, his tone soft but amused. "Your tenacity is quite... attractive, Emily Lane."

"Lucian, flirting with me won't get you a cell phone," I retort, the heat in my cheeks betraying me as much as the smile I can't wipe off my face.

"Who says I'm flirting?" he asks, feigning innocence. "I'm merely stating facts."

"Sure, and I'm just driving Miss Daisy here." I gesture to the road ahead, but my heart is drumming a rapid beat.

"Miss Daisy never had such intriguing blue eyes," he murmurs. His compliment, wrapped in that old-world charm, sends a shiver down my spine.

"Keep it up, and I might start thinking you're smitten with me."

"Would that be so terrible?" His voice is low, a soft growl that somehow finds its way through the noise of the road.

"Depends on who's asking," I reply, my voice steadier than I feel. My tape recorder lies forgotten in my bag; the only record of this moment will be the memory etched in my mind.

"Then consider it a question from someone... intrigued," he says, settling back into his seat as the car hums along.

"Consider it under advisement," I answer, glancing his way. The banter, the teasing—it's starting to feel like more than just a game. But games always end with a winner and a loser. What will this end with?

Gravel crunches under the tires as I steer my trusty hunk of metal off the beaten path, finally bringing it to a stop in front of a cottage that looks like it's been ripped from the pages of a fairy tale. If that fairy tale had a thing for overgrown ivy and the rustic charm of solitude. Hopefully the information we get gives the Baxters some form of happily ever after.

Lucian steps out of the car with a grace that makes me envious, given my exit is more of a struggle, fighting with the seatbelt that's decided now is the perfect time to play clingy.

"Looks like someone hit pause on time here," I comment, stretching my legs and admiring the serene surroundings that feel a world away from the hustle and bustle of Chicago. I steal a glance at Lucian, waiting for his reaction to this quaint little cottage. But of course, his composed demeanor remains unchanged. After living for centuries, I suppose earthly sights must seem trivial to him. Talk about high standards.

"Charming," he remarks dryly, taking in the sight of the secluded dwelling nestled amongst the towering trees.

Before we can soak in too much of the quiet, the creak of a door draws our attention to the figure stepping outside. Her skin is etched with wrinkles, each line a testament to a life fully lived. Her hair, a silvery-white, is pulled into an unruly bun, with a few rebellious strands escaping as if they refuse to be tamed. She's dressed in a simple, earthy green and brown gown that lets her blend seamlessly with the surrounding forest. The lines around her eyes speak of laughter and loss, and there's a weariness in her gaze that isn't from sleepless nights alone. She's probably pushing eighty, but there's a timeless quality about her, making her age feel irrelevant.

"Emily Lane, Lucian Belmont," she greets, her voice a gentle melody, like still waters with hidden currents. "Come inside."

We follow her lead into a living room that's every bit as cozy as the exterior promised. Every nook seems to cradle an artifact or trinket from a life lived on the edges of reality. I sink into an armchair that hugs me like the grandmother I never had, while Lucian perches on the sofa with the casual elegance of a cat claiming its spot in the sun.

"Tea?" Amelia offers, already moving towards the kitchen.

"Please," I accept, shooting Lucian a look that says 'we're out of our league' before turning back to our host. He just nods, his expression unreadable.

She returns, setting down a tray with a China teapot and cups that probably have more history than my entire family tree. With a sigh that seems to pull from the roots of the earth itself, she takes a seat across from us, and the air fills with the scent of herbs and a hint of foreboding.

"I have to admit, I'm impressed you know our names," I say, unable to contain my curiosity any longer. "Is that your magic?"

"Magic," she begins, pouring the tea with hands that don't shake but should, "has always been a part of me. But even the deepest wells run dry." She fixes us with a wry gaze. "Although, even out here, I get cable. Ms. Lane the lawyer and Lucian Belmont the coven leader."

"The wonders of modern technology," Lucian says, eyeing me. I restrain crowing in victory.

"Now, why are you here?" she asks before taking a delicate sip of her tea. The blend must be her own concoction because it's a mix of flavors that I can't quite pinpoint, sweetness with an underlying darkness.

"We need to know about your family," I start, diving right into the heart of it. "And anything you might know about the Baxters..."

Her gaze drifts to the window, lost in memories as she continues. "My daughter, Evelyn, she fell ill after childbirth. I did what any mother would do—I reached into the depths of my power to save her."

Lucian leans forward, his usual mask of control giving way to genuine interest—or is it concern? Hard to tell with him.

"Did it work?" he asks, his voice softer than usual, asking the question even though we know the answer.

"No." The word hangs heavy between us. "I offered all I could, but some demands are too steep. The magic asked for everything, nevertheless, it wasn't enough." Amelia's eyes, shadowed with years of hard-won wisdom, lock onto mine, and I see the finality of loss etched there. "Evelyn passed on, leaving behind a little girl and a gaping hole where my magic used to be."

I sink back into the couch. "Everything comes at a price," I mutter, remembering Stardust's lesson.

"Yes," Amelia confirms, her lips curving into a smile that doesn't quite reach her eyes. It's a smile that's seen things, learned things, and come out the other side knowing the universe keeps a strict ledger.

"Amelia, there's probably a better way to do this, but it's been a *long* week and a half," I say, setting my tea down with a soft clink against the saucer. "Do you know who could have cursed the Baxters?"

Amelia's shifts in her seat, her gaze cutting through the air like a sharpened blade. "The Baxters are cursed?"

"Yes," I confirm, glancing at Lucian.

"No better family for it to happen to," she says, a mischievous grin spreading across her face.

"You must know something," I press gently, letting my inner lawyer off the leash just a bit. "You might not... practice anymore, but maybe a friend? Another coven? Someone willing to punish the Baxters for what they did to you."

"Cursed," she repeats, her gaze drifting to a spot on the wall as if searching for answers in the worn tapestries hanging there. "How?"

I run her through the basics—the single room behaving like a haunted house, the mysterious flower "calling card" (that's possibly a dead end), and, last but not least, the slasher-film-style note scrawled on the wall.

Amelia's eyes light up, intrigued. She leans forward, fingers steepled thoughtfully. "Not exactly typical for most curses or hauntings I've come across," she murmurs, her gaze distant, as if she's flipping through her mental Rolodex of creepy cases.

"And the note?" she prompts, her voice barely above a whisper but brimming with curiosity. "What exactly did it say?"

"It said 'the truth always finds a way to bleed through,' in smeared dark, red letters. I'd say blood, but *I* didn't check..." I trail off, shrugging. Not that blood bothers me. I mean, you don't willingly, *illegally*, donate to vampires if blood freaks you out. But I wasn't about to get close enough to play biohazard bingo.

Amelia tilts her head, a faint smile playing at her lips. "The Baxters have always lived by the code of 'might makes right,' blurring the line between what's lawful and what's just. But true justice," she pauses, her voice soft but firm, "*true* justice has a way of catching up with those who think themselves above it."

Lucian leans forward slightly, his demeanor shifting from passive observer to someone homing in on crucial information. "Are you saying the curse might result from their past actions coming back to haunt them?"

Amelia's gaze sharpens. "Has anyone mentioned strange activity around Rhett specifically? Or... unexpected visitors?"

"Not yet," I admit. "But Rhett's been tense. And the family... they seem ready to burst at the seams with secrets."

She nods. "Rhett Baxter, the current head, may not be the same man as his ancestors, but the sins of the fathers linger on in the choices of their progeny."

"So who could have targeted them with magic?" I ask, frowning.

"The Baxters have a knack for collecting more than just dusty old antiques in their cellar," she says, her tone as dry as desert sand. "You should start there."

I lean back, crossing my arms over my chest with a casual nonchalance. "And here I thought their skeletons were just metaphorical," I quip, but her words land with a weight that sits heavy in my gut.

Amelia's eyes flicker with a knowing gleam, her expression turning solemn. "Curses have a funny way of coming back to bite you, and the Baxters are no exception."

"Karma's a bigger witch than any of us, huh?" I try to smirk, though unease tightens my chest.

Amelia's smile is wry, her gaze flickering with a knowing gleam. "Damn right," she murmurs, her voice a mix of amusement and warning. She stands, signaling the end of story time, and moves to a small, ornate desk tucked away under the window.

"Before you go, Ms. Lane," Amelia says, pulling open a drawer. She retrieves a cream-colored envelope sealed with dark red wax, the kind you'd expect to find in a Victorian romance, not in a suburban cottage. "Could you deliver this to Amy?"

"Sure, but—" I take the envelope, turning it over in my hand. It feels heavier than it looks. "What's in it?"

"Old words needing fresh ears," she replies, cryptic as a sphinx. "Amy will understand."

"Got it. Deliver mysterious letter to a teenager." I tuck the envelope carefully into my bag, feeling its significance weigh against the fabric. "Not ominous at all," I joke, though the chill running down my spine says otherwise.

"Thank you, dear," Amelia says, her gaze holding mine. There's an unspoken urgency there, like she's entrusting me with more than just paper and ink.

"Sure thing." I stand, smoothing out my skirt. "And Amelia, thanks for the... enlightening chat."

"Be careful, Ms. Lane," Amelia says as she walks us to the door. "Not all truths set you free. Some just change the shape of your cage."

Super. Just the pep talk I needed.

I glance over at Lucian, who is already waiting by the door, *now* looking as comfortable as a cat in a bathtub. We shuffle down the cobblestone path, gravel crunching beneath our feet in the twilight silence. The air smells of pine and impending rain, the kind of weather that made you think nature has its own dirty secrets to keep.

"Your chariot awaits," Lucian says, gesturing grandly towards my trusty old clunker like it's a royal carriage.

"Quite the upgrade from pumpkin to rust bucket," I quip, his attempt at lightening the mood a welcome one. The car wheezes in response, as if insulted. "Just don't expect any fairy godmothers or singing woodland creatures."

"We left the godmother behind," he says with a smirk, opening the creaky door for me before sliding into the passenger seat with a grace that no mortal man—and certainly no vehicle of this vintage—should accommodate.

As we drive away, leaving the secluded cottage behind, the weight of Amelia's admission lingers like a ghost in the air.

"Do you believe her?" I ask, breaking the silence that settled between us.

Lucian's brow arches. "Believe which part?"

"That she's really out of magic," I say, glancing over at him. "Did you sense anything?"

He blinks, looking almost offended. "And how would I know?"

"You're practically on a first-name basis with magic, witch friend or no," I point out. "All your hobgoblin dealings, not to mention the wards you were so fond of discussing when you were... staying at my place."

When I tried to close the gap between us, and you politely put up a wall; and now it's me who's keeping a safe distance.

Lucian's lips twitch into a smirk. "I'm surprised you remember all that."

"That's why they pay me the big bucks," I joke with a shrug. "Although *you* never paid me."

Lucian huffs out a laugh, the kind that's more air than sound. "I believe her. If she had any magic left, she would've used it. She certainly would have done whatever it took to see Amy again."

The car falls silent again, the steady hum of the engine filling the void. If Amelia isn't our witch, then who the hell is? And how does that stupid camellia factor in? Because it feels less like a clue and more like a signature for someone who wants to play mind games.

"When do you plan to deliver Amelia's letter?" Lucian asks as we get closer to the city and buildings start growing around us.

I drum my fingers against the steering wheel. "I don't know Lucian. It's not exactly a party invitation, and playing courier for a vengeful witch isn't exactly my idea of a thrilling time."

"Especially given your... tumultuous history with family?" He arches an eyebrow, a corner of his mouth twitching upwards.

"Exactly," I say, letting out a breathy chuckle. "My track record with familial bliss is about as spotless as my car's paint job. And I'd hate to be the delivery girl for a new curse, Amelia's missing magic or not."

Lucian's gaze softens, the dashboard lights giving him this eerie glow that makes him look more concerned than usual. "I understand your hesitation. But there's more at stake here than simply delivering a letter. Family ties and relationships are complex, but they shape us in profound ways. Whatever Amelia's intentions, Amy might hold the key to unraveling the mysteries surrounding the Baxters."

I shoot him a look. "You really think a letter's going to unlock all the Baxter family mysteries? Because I'm betting on 'no.'"

"It's possible," he replies. "Our connections to others can reveal truths we might overlook on our own. We can't afford to discount the importance of family bonds, no matter how strained they may be."

I let out a long, dramatic sigh. "Fine, I'll deliver the letter. But if this backfires, you owe me. Big time."

He laughs, a low, rumbling sound that does all kinds of things to my insides. "I wouldn't have it any other way. Just remember, Emily, sometimes the most unexpected paths lead to the most significant discoveries. And in the journey of unraveling these mysteries, we may also uncover truths about ourselves and our relationships that we never anticipated."

"You supernatural types need to get together and pitch something to American Greetings or Hallmark," I mutter under my breath.

As the city envelops us, the familiar cacophony of urban life creeps back in—the blaring horns, the distant sirens, the rhythmic thumping of nightclub bass. We pull up to his gothic abode in the vampire quarter, the engine going silent as I cut the ignition.

"Tomorrow evening, then? We'll search for the cellar," Lucian suggests as he steps out onto the curb, the night air ruffling his ponytail.

"Tomorrow," I confirm, getting out to say goodbye. "We'll crack this case wide open or die trying."

"Preferably without the dying part," he quips, his smirk flashing in the glow of a nearby streetlamp.

"Speak for yourself," I say, unable to suppress a smile. "Us mere mortals have to live a little dangerously sometimes."

Lucian chuckles as he leans against the car, his eyes dark and intense. "Danger certainly seems to find you, Emily Lane," he remarks, his voice dipping into that sexy vampire tone that would probably melt *anyone* with a pulse.

"Well, what can I say?" I reply, stepping closer with a playful glint in my eye. "Someone needs to keep the adrenaline pumping. Plus, who else would bail you out when your charm gets you into trouble?"

He lifts his hand, his fingers grazing my cheek, and I freeze. His touch is like fire—hotter than you'd expect from someone who's technically undead. His eyes lock onto mine. "You find me charming?"

Anything with and *without a pulse would*, I think. But I stay silent, meeting his smoldering gray eyes with an unflinching gaze, my heart pounding in my chest like a drumbeat. This conversation feels familiar, like we've danced around this before. The memory of my earlier teasing flits to the surface—*charming, infuriatingly cryptic vampire.* Except now, it's not banter. It's heavier, sharper, more serious.

My usual defense mechanism—humor, sarcasm, anything to keep people at arm's length—sputters out like a match in the wind. And it's not because I'm out of clever things to say; it's because I'm not sure I *want* to keep him at arm's length anymore. It's not just the attraction—it's everything else that comes with it. The baggage, the complications, the fact that I *do* find him charming, but that's the least of it. There's something deeper here, something I can't put into words, and maybe that's what scares me most of all. Because if I give in... it means surrendering to something I can't control, and I've spent my entire career building walls around anything I couldn't dominate with logic, strategy, or a well-timed objection.

But here, now, those walls feel more fragile than they've ever been.

As he leans down, the shrill sound of a phone trills from my pocket. The spell breaks, slicing through the moment like a knife.

Lucian steps back, his hand dropping. The connection between us snaps as if it was never there at all.

I let out a slow exhale, the rush of adrenaline beginning to ebb as I retrieve my phone from my pocket. MATTY flashes on the screen. Before I can answer, it diverts to voicemail.

"I should get going," I murmur, the moment gone.

With a final nod, he vanishes into the darkness, leaving me alone with the thrumming pulse of the city and a head full of swirling thoughts. The letter, heavy with secrets; Lucian, with his infuriating charm; and Matty, whose image now seems like a ghost haunting the edges of my mind.

"Get it together, Lane," I mutter as I climb back into the car. But as I drive home, instead of focusing on the curse or letters, all I can think about is how my heart keeps doing that annoying skipping thing every time Lucian looks at me.

And what am I supposed to do about that?

CHAPTER 17

Saturday morning, and here I am at Doyle Electrical Solutions because apparently, a lawyer's work is never done. I push open the door, the little bell overhead chiming a greeting that seems far too cheerful for how early it is. Wires and tools are scattered across the countertops, and there's Rhett Baxter, hunched over a workbench, hands working through a mess of cable. He's less of a snarling beast here, more like a mildly annoyed puppy. That's progress.

"Emily." His voice holds a note of surprise as he stands up straight, wiping his hands on a rag. His fingers fumble slightly as he quickly hides something that looks like a remote under a pile of rags.

I wave the peace offering in my hand—coffee, the universal truce. Werewolf or not, everyone's a little nicer after their caffeine fix. (Though now that I think about it, I should probably ask Danielle if mochas are off limits.) "I come bearing caffeine," I say.

Rhett's eyes light up like I just handed him a winning lottery ticket. He takes the cup, his rough hands curling around it like it's a lifeline. For a guy who can probably tear through steel with those hands, he sure knows how to appreciate a cup of coffee.

"Thanks," he mutters, taking a sip. I might as well have handed him liquid gold.

I take a chance at harnessing some of that gratitude and repairing our rapport after the calls earlier this week. "What are you working on, anyway? Battery operated sailboat?"

He doesn't even blink. "Just some wiring projects."

"Maybe I should hire you to rewire my apartment," I joke, picturing the chaos my electronics often descend into. A testament to my apartment's age or yet another sign of Herle's invisible mischief?

"You solve my curse problem, I'll rewire your entire apartment," he says with a half-smirk that could outshine the moon. "Free of charge."

"I'm working on it," I tell him. Though if I'm being honest, I feel like I've been playing paranormal whack-a-mole and I'm down a hammer.

"About that... I apologize if I've been short with you lately." He shifts, crossing his arms. The muscle in his jaw ticks like it's running on a timer. "Things at home are... complicated."

"Understandable," I say, trying to sound sympathetic despite not really knowing what a 'complicated' family dynamic entails. I'm an orphan with a background check cleaner than a nun's conscience, after all. Minus my past interest in letting vampires suck on my neck.

"My parents are in a state, something about a neighborhood book club Mom never gets invited to," he continues, leaning against the counter. With his arms crossed, he looks every bit the part of a werewolf family leader—albeit one dressed in a flannel shirt and dusty jeans. "Would you know anything about that?" There's a wry twist to his lips, dry as the cereal I had for breakfast.

"Just doing the digging you're paying me for," I reply, shrugging nonchalantly. "As I've told anyone who has asked, my clients are exclusive. They appreciate discretion—and a neighborhood that's open-minded about the supernatural. If that takes some heat off the Baxters…" I let the sentence hang, an unspoken offering of solidarity.

Rhett's expression softens, the sharp scar no longer stark against his skin, a glimmer of warmth shining in his eyes. "Good, good. So, what brings you here today? If not chatting up the neighbors?" he asks.

I shift a bit, mentally preparing for the next part. "An update on Amelia. And, before you freak out—it's not her."

His smile falters. "What do you mean? Amelia's the witch—"

"She's not the witch you're looking for," I cut in, trying to soften the blow. "I talked to her. Whatever magic she might've had, it's gone. She's not behind this. She's about as dangerous as a kitten. Well, maybe a kitten who drank a bowl of resentment, but still harmless."

Rhett's eyebrows shoot up, confusion swirling in his expression. "You're sure?"

I nod. "As sure as a lawyer turned investigator can be. But trust me, this curse, whatever it is, it's someone else."

Rhett stares at me for a moment, processing. His eyes narrow slightly, and then, as if he's made up his mind, he straightens up, his determination flaring. "Then try harder. I don't care who you antagonize, I need to know who's behind this. Louder if you must. I can handle it."

"Don't worry," I say, "loud is kind of my default setting. But you have to give me something to work with. And you've been holding back. I need to find the entrance to that cellar of yours. I figured you wouldn't want me sneaking around today trying to find it."

At that, Rhett's expression shifts again, back to the genial werewolf I thought I knew, and he rubs the back of his neck. "We blocked it off when Evelyn died. Nobody's been down there since."

I arch an eyebrow. "Nobody? I find that hard to believe. Where do I find it?"

He shrugs, his eyes not quite meeting mine. "I can't remember." But that shifty look screams 'dig deeper, Emily.'

"What, someone cast a memory spell on you?" I prod, crossing my arms.

Also something I should probably look into.

"No," he says slowly, his jaw tightening. "It's been fifteen years, you know. It's on the west side of the house, but that's all I can tell you."

I narrow my eyes. "No memory of the entrance, or are you just hoping I don't find it?"

Rhett leans in, lowering his voice. "If I knew, and it helped with this curse, wouldn't I tell you?"

"Guess I'll have to play Nancy Drew then," I murmur. Emily Lane—top-notch attorney, terrible at reading werewolf body language.

He tosses his cup in the trash and stands. "I've got things to take care of. But keep me updated. We need this solved, Emily. And fast."

"Understood. But keep your evenings open, Rhett," I quip, pushing off the wall. "When I crack this case, we'll celebrate at mine with a perfectly wired lamp."

Lucian and I start our evening trudging up the path to the gardens surrounding Oakheart Estate. Gone are the heels and the silken dress that had no place here amongst the thorns and secrets. I'm in my trusty boots and jeans, ready for whatever the night throws at me.

"It's quite surprising to see Emily Lane in something other than courtroom chic," Lucian drawls, a glimmer of appreciation in his sharp gray eyes.

"Hey, I can do casual," I retort, shifting the heavy flashlight in my grip. "Especially when I'm not being yanked from a date."

"Ah, yes. We failed to discuss it last night during our tête-à-tête with Ms. Amelia. The infamous evening with Matty that I cut short." His grin widens, and for a moment, the memory of last night's almost kiss shimmers between us like heat off asphalt.

"Let's focus on the task at hand, shall we?" I snap the words out sharper than I mean to, and a heightened silence falls between us.

The air outside is a crisp slap to my senses, the sky a watercolor wash of twilight blues and bruised purples. With flashlights illuminating our path, we encircle the house, the beams bouncing off the old stone walls. The house creaks ominously, like it's trying to keep its secrets buried.

"Evening, Manx," Lucian says, waving casually to the hedge separating Oakheart Estate from the neighbors.

Lucian's boots crunch on the gravel beside the fence, and I strain to see beyond the reach of my dim flashlight.

"Thought you two were feuding," I say, teasing to keep my nerves from showing. "Since he snubbed you in the Amelia reveal."

"Feuds amongst creatures are more complicated than your human soap operas," Lucian says, his tone light while his eyes scan the darkness.

"More complicated than love triangles?" I ask before I can stop myself, regretting it instantly when Lucian's gaze flicks back to me, piercing and intense.

"Far more," he breathes, and just like that, the playful banter fades into something heavy.

But the mystery of the house calls louder than the tension between us. I clear my throat, trying to break the spell. "Maybe ask Manx where the cellar is."

Lucian's gaze drifts off into the distance. "He's gone," he finally says.

I watch Lucian for a moment longer, unsure if he's telling the truth. "Okay then. Let's keep going."

We move forward, the possibilities hanging over us like a thick, wet blanket.

"Will you deliver Amy's letter tonight?" Lucian asks, breaking the silence.

"Yes, mom," I reply with a roll of my eyes. "I didn't forget my homework."

A faint smile tugs at Lucian's lips. "Good," he says.

We reach the patch of grass where we'd seen markings, but now, it's like the ground erased any trace of it. We scour the area, our boots sinking into the damp earth, but there's nothing. It's as if whatever we saw last time was a figment of our imaginations.

Lucian frowns as he scans the area with his flashlight, the usual confidence in his eyes replaced by frustration.

"Nothing," I mutter, sweeping my flashlight over the ground. The shadows eat up the light, keeping their secrets hidden.

A rustling sound in the bushes startles both of us, and we whip around, flashlights pointed like weapons, but it's just a possum darting off into the night, its eyes glinting in the darkness.

"I don't get it," I mutter, my voice echoing in the stillness. "We saw something here. Rhett confirmed the entrance was on this side of the house. There must be a way to access that damned cellar."

Lucian doesn't respond right away, his attention drifting to the side of the house. He strides over to the wall, his fingers running over the bricks like he's reading an ancient text. And of course, he does it with that vampire grace that screams, 'I've been alive for centuries, and I do everything better than you.'

"Here," he murmurs, pressing on a brick that looks exactly like every other brick on the wall. With a soft click, the section of the wall trembles and swings inward, revealing a narrow stone staircase leading down into the dark.

"Blocked off alright. Guess they don't have building codes for secret rooms?" I say, trying to keep the mood light as we peer into the gaping maw of darkness beyond the wall.

"Or perhaps they had different things to conceal," Lucian replies, his voice filled with an anticipation that should probably worry me more.

We step into the darkness, our flashlights cutting through the dark like twin blades. The stone staircase is like a vertebra, each step a knotted spine leading down into the mysterious depths of the cellar, where secrets and *maybe* even ghosts lurk in the damp. My boots squeak embarrassingly loud, but the darkness nearly swallows the sound. As we descend further, the air grows stale, thick with a musty scent that clings to my throat like the aftertaste of bad coffee. I lick my lips, trying to chase away the dryness that comes with a mix of anticipation and fear.

When we finally reach the bottom, it's like we've stumbled into a time capsule. No skulls or bubbling cauldrons, but the room whispers old money and even older secrets. Shelves sag under the weight of forgotten papers, and ledgers lie in dusty stacks, untouched for years. Heavy, moth-eaten curtains hang from the walls, blocking out any chance of light, assuming there is any underground.

"Looks like the Baxters were hoarders of the less magical variety," I quip, trying to keep the tension at bay. But my joke falls flat, absorbed into the oppressive silence.

We step deeper into the cellar, and it finally starts looking more like a witch's garage sale. My flashlight beam catches on crystals, causing eerie reflections to dance across the walls. Cobwebs cling to the corners and dust collects in the crevices.

Like the seasoned investigator I'm not, I pull out my phone and snap a bunch of pictures. If nothing else, I've got to show Rhett why I deserve hazard pay and maybe get some new wiring in my apartment as a bonus. "Hopefully, taking pictures doesn't provoke any lingering spirits."

Lucian doesn't bite, pun intended. He's scanning the shelves, his expression tight, like he's searching for something and hoping he doesn't find it. "Be careful what you touch. If there *is* anything magical here, it may still have power."

I give him a quick salute, not that he notices in the dark, and turn back to my snooping. My flashlight sweeps over the room, landing on a stack of old documents. They're yellowed with age, corners curling as if trying to hide from the light. The name "Roger Baxter" jumps out at me, scrawled in faded ink on the topmost sheet.

"Well, well, what do we have here?" I mutter, lifting a small stack of papers. They're not curses or ancient spells, but they're definitely something. Deeds to properties, contracts signed by Roger and Alex, and something that looks suspiciously like a will. I flip through quickly, but it's all mundane on the surface.

As I shuffle through the pages, something even more intriguing catches my eye. Tucked between the documents are old photos of Roger and Rhett—Roger holding toddler Amy in his arms, and Rhett, with a grin so wide it's almost painful to look at, balancing a young Trenton on his shoulders. Trenton looks down at Rhett with stars in his eyes. The only expression he's given Rhett lately is a snarl and a pout. I stare at the photos, all four radiating happiness and joy.

Shaking my head, a wry smile tugs at my lips. "Well, at least now I know that expression is a family heirloom." Though I've *yet* to see Alex smile in my presence.

Still no response from Lucian. He's now fixated on a set of tarnished swords hanging on the wall in a star pattern, their tips meeting at a single point. Behind them, crude symbols are etched into the stone, radiating bad vibes like they've been dipped in malevolence. It's both mesmerizing and bone-chillingly eerie, like we've stumbled into the set of a horror movie where things always end badly. But no, this is not Hollywood; it's just a fun evening for Emily Lane, Esq.

Lucian's hand suddenly grips mine, cold and unyielding. His voice slices through the thick air, tight with an edge I almost never hear from him, close to panic. "Emily, we need to leave. Now."

I pull my hand back, resisting the urge to make a crack about being yanked around like a puppet. His urgency, though, it's unsettling. And I don't like unsettling, especially when it's coming from an unflappable vampire who handles surprises like he's ordering coffee.

"Leave? But we just got here," I protest, channeling his normally composed demeanor. "For all we know, we just stumbled into someone's private collection of Halloween props."

Lucian turns, his face a mask of seriousness, eyes locking onto mine. "Trust me, Emily. This is not a place for us to linger. There are powers at play here that we don't understand."

"Lucian," I start, my tone filled with that edge he knows all too well, "you can't just drop a bomb of cryptic drama and expect me to drop everything and follow."

"Please," he says, voice softer, almost vulnerable. "I must go, but it isn't safe for you to remain here."

His words catch me off guard. Lucian—Mr. Cool, Calm, and Centuries-Old—is actually shaken. And if a vampire like him is rattled, then yeah, maybe it's time to listen. But... this is me we're talking about.

"Tell me why." My demand hangs between us, an unyielding force.

His jaw clenches, his composure fraying around the edges. "I'm begging you to simply do as I ask for once. Deliver the letter and then leave."

"Fine," I mutter, relenting. "I'll go. Just give me a minute."

"Promise me," he presses, already retreating to the exit, like a marionette pulled by invisible strings.

I roll my eyes. "Promise," I say, knowing full well my fingers are crossed behind my back.

The moment he's gone, the air shifts, settling around me with a weight that signals I'm alone, properly alone. Alone in the room of mysteries, I'm left with more questions than answers—and a creeping sense of unease that has nothing to do with the chill in the air.

What the hell just happened?

I let out a low breath, half expecting it to fog in the chill of the cellar. But spite is a warm little fire in my chest, and it's got me itching to poke around.

I stride further into the shadows, my eyes scanning the room, hungering for answers. I don't need Lucian to do *my* job, no matter how much I'm getting used to a teammate. I'm here to uncover the truth, to help, to fight for the people caught in the crossfire of secrets and magic.

"Control freak," I mumble under my breath, emboldened by his absence. *So much for 'where else would I be than with you'?*

I return to the swords that so captivated and terrified him.

"Definitely not your run-of-the-mill interior decorating," I quip to the shadows, trying not to let the oddity of it all get to me. Silver blades glint in the weak light, throwing twisted reflections across the room. Are they cursed? Haunted? Or maybe just seriously macabre taste?

As I move closer, something crunches underfoot, and I look down to find a scattering of dried herbs and what looks suspiciously like animal bones. Just what every girl dreams of stepping on in a creepy basement.

It's then that I notice the wires—thick bundles snaking along the baseboard, disappearing into holes drilled into the stone. Some are frayed, their copper veins exposed, hinting at age or neglect. Others seem newer, sheathed in bright plastic insulation.

Recent activity or just Rhett's newfangled electric work? Could this cellar have been some mundane storage space turned ritualistic hub? If these walls could talk...

And that's when I hear it—the howl. Not the distant bay of a neighborhood dog, but a guttural, mournful cry that makes the hairs rise on my arms. It echoes through the cellar, somehow sounding both far away and uncomfortably close.

"Fantastic timing," I mutter, my resolve faltering. Even with the full moon days away, something out there is stirring, and I'm suddenly acutely aware of my own vulnerability. Werewolf clients or not, I know better than to ignore such a warning.

Looks like Lucian wins this round. I'm no fool; I know when it's time to retreat. With one last glance at the swords and their eerie formation, I turn toward the stairs, my ambition momentarily squashed by the realization that I've wandered into something way over my head.

"Next time," I promise the darkness, "bring it on."

Chapter 18

Clutching the letter like a lifeline—or maybe it's a grenade—I stomp out of the cellar. The chill from the underground still clings to me, but I'm fueled by indignation and the need to get this over with.

"Deliver the letter," I mutter to myself, mocking Lucian's baritone. "Sure thing, boss. You're definitely in charge of me. This isn't my client, nope, not at all." Because that's what you do when you're angry; you follow orders. *Hah.*

The tape recorder in my pocket feels like a brick, a constant reminder of the mountain of work still ahead and my lack of answers. The stress of this case—of everything—makes me really wish I could open a vein to a vampire again. Hitting things once a week isn't cutting it when I spend the rest of the week scrambling. A little relief might clear my head.

But no, too complicated, especially with Lucian ghosting out of here like the final girl in a slasher flick.

I finally get inside, my flashlight slicing through the dimness of the house. I enter through the grand foyer where the bloody letters were revealed. It's unsettling how quickly the evidence of dread can be erased, only faint traces of the malevolent message left behind. A grand chandelier hangs precariously above, its crystals dull and dusty, refracting the scant light filtering through the grimy windows.

I head up the staircase, my hand brushing the ornately carved banister. Dust motes swirl in my flashlight's beam like restless spirits. The peeling wallpaper reveals faded floral patterns that were probably all the rage a century ago. A sudden draft sends a chill down my spine, causing me to pull my shirt tighter around me. Every sound—every creak, every rustle—sends my heart racing, ready for whatever might jut out of the darkness. *Thanks, Lucian, for freaking me out.* Now I'm half expecting a zombie or, at the very least, a raccoon with attitude.

I turn yet another corner, one in a maze of identical turns, when I hear a voice drifting from down the hall. It's Trenton, muttering in that low, frustrated tone that practically screams "family drama." I can't catch every word, but I hear enough: "he deserves it," and "never listens to anyone but himself."

Curiosity is my Achilles' heel, so I inch closer, positioning myself behind a half-open door. Through a small gap, I spot Trenton, gesturing like he's on a soap opera. He's got his phone glued to one ear, throwing out phrases like "all his fault" and "ready to hand him the crown, no questions asked," every word dripping with resentment.

I take a step back, my mind spinning. Looks like Trenton's holding onto a grudge the size of Oakheart Estate. But before I can eavesdrop any further, I hear the unmistakable creak of another door opening down the hall. I freeze. Trenton stops talking, and I make a quick exit, sliding down the hall in search of Amy, mentally bookmarking this encounter for later.

Finally, I spot her tucked away in a quiet alcove, looking more like a porcelain doll in some creepy antique store than a member of the coven. My flashlight catches her eyes, and for a moment, all the craziness fades. She's just a girl caught in the middle of this twisted Baxter family mess, waiting for something—anything—to make sense.

"Hey, Amy," I say, offering a smile that feels more genuine than I expect. "I've got something for you." I extend the letter, the paper slightly crumpled from being death-gripped all the way up here. "It's from your grandmother."

Her fingers, delicate but firm, brush mine as she takes the envelope. "Oh, wow. I never... I thought I'd have to wait until I was eighteen to talk to her," she murmurs, her voice laced with a hopefulness that tugs at my heartstrings.

"Yeah, well," I shrug, stepping back to give her some space. "Family's funny like that."

"What was she like?" Amy asks, staring at me from her long lashes.

Cryptic. Magicless. Alone.

"She really loves you," I finally say lamely. "But... just remember, these relationships don't have to be the end all be all of your life. You get to carve out your own path."

Lucian and Danielle's greeting card lingo is rubbing off on me. Although, after all the family talk going on, I'm not sure who I'm really saying that to—her or me. My parents are long gone, a chapter closed so tightly it's as if they were characters from another lifetime. Cousins, aunts, uncles? Might as well be mythical creatures for all the presence they have in my life. But friends? That's unfamiliar territory, one I'm carving out for myself. Six weeks ago, I would've scoffed at the idea—friends were just people you hadn't cross-examined yet. Now, it feels like I'm stitching together a patchwork quilt of companionship, one quirky character witness at a time. Even with Lucian's block ripping out at the seams.

Amy nods, clutching the letter to her chest. "Thanks, Emily."

"Team Mortal Lawyer at your service," I say with a mock salute, the sardonic edge returning to my tone.

"Are you okay? You look... paler than normal." She tilts her head, genuine concern flickering in her eyes.

"Must be the lighting," I deflect with a casual shrug, waving off her observations like cobwebs in an abandoned room. "I'm a night owl, after all. Pale is the new tan."

She doesn't look convinced, but she drops it. "If you ever need backup for your curse-breaking, count me in," she says, a spark of mischief lighting up her eyes. "I am half-witch, after all."

Her gaze drifts down to the letter in her hand, and the playfulness in her expression fades. "They never talk about her, you know—Amelia. It's like she doesn't exist." Her fingers trace the edge of the envelope, hesitant. "I asked about her once when I was real little, and Grandpa flipped out. Uncle Rhett just said to let it go. No magic, no Amelia. It's like a rule."

"Maybe they're just trying to protect you," I suggest, though even I'm not convinced. What do I know about protective families? I'm so far out of my depth that I'm practically underwater.

"Maybe," Amy echoes, but there's no conviction in her voice. She shrugs, a flicker of frustration crossing her face. "But they act like magic is this huge, scary deal we should stay away from. Like if we ignore it, it can't touch us. But, like, hello, we got cursed and still never talked about it."

Her frustration flares, and I can't blame her. This whole family's locked up tighter than a vampire at sunrise, and I'm just the unlucky lawyer caught in the crossfire.

"They think keeping me in the dark will make it all go away," she adds, her grip on the letter tightening. "But I could totally help with the curse if they weren't so secretive! It's just that, thanks to them, I don't know how to cast a proper spell."

I nod, though my curiosity is piqued. Would Evelyn's death alone inspire this level of... stubbornness? "Did anyone ever say why they're all so against magic?"

"Not really. Grandma just says it's dangerous, and that it's taken too much from this family already." She rolls her eyes like she's heard it a thousand times. "She never explains anything, though. Just hits you with that 'I know better' look and says to trust her. Grandpa says the same thing, but he's on a whole other level with it. He gets... weird about it."

"Weird how?" I ask, leaning against the dusty walls like we're having a casual chat about the weather.

"I don't know, he just gets this look—like he's lowkey spooked or something. But he's not scared of much, you know? It's like he's afraid magic is gonna target him or something. Or maybe," she adds, glancing at the letter again, "he's afraid of what it'll do to the rest of us."

I chew over her words before asking, "You said they never talk about magic, but do you ever... feel it? You *are* Evelyn's daughter?"

She bites her lip, looking like she's debating whether to spill the beans. "Lately I've been feeling... I don't know, like something's up. Maybe it's magic or just me being paranoid. But sometimes I get this... buzzing feeling, like static electricity under my skin. I always thought it was just nerves or whatever, but..." She trails off, her grip tightening on the letter.

"But?"

She shrugs, a frustrated sigh escaping her. "I don't know. It's way more intense. And since the... curse, it happens every night at midnight." Her voice drops, as if saying it out loud makes it more real. "Like clockwork. I start feeling that buzz right when the curse starts. And if I'm anywhere near the room, it's a whole different level."

I frown, trying to piece together what she's saying. "So, you're saying the feeling is connected to the curse? Like it triggers something in you?"

Amy nods slowly, her brows knitting together. "Maybe. Or maybe it's just in my head. But every night at midnight, and it's like this... jolt runs through me. It only fades if I get farther away." She glances down at the letter again, her fingers tracing the edge as if searching for answers in the paper. "I don't know. It's probably nothing."

I nod, though my brain's working overtime trying to connect the dots. "Just be careful. Whatever's in that letter... it might not give you the answers you want."

She gives me a determined nod, her fingers curling around the letter. "I guess we'll see, won't we?"

I give her a reassuring smile, though my gut tells me I've just tipped a scale we can't un-tip. "Let me know what you find, okay?" I say. "For now, it's time to regroup and tackle the next mystery," I announce, more to myself than to Amy. "And maybe figure out why my partner in crime-solving decided to turn into the ghost he usually debunks."

With that, I leave her to her thoughts and her letter. As I navigate the maze of hallways, my mind churns with theories and *what ifs*, the reality of what I'm involved sinking in. The old house groans around me like it's struggling under the burden of all its secrets. This family is woven into a web of lies and hidden truths, and every thread seems to loop back to more buried things they're desperate to keep hidden.

But now it's not just their secrets—Lucian's got his own to carry in this investigation.

"Lucian, you infuriating bloodsucker," I mutter under my breath, flipping open my phone's contact list with a practiced flick of my thumb. "You can't just drop a bombshell room of witchcraft and waltz off like Cinderella at midnight."

My thumb hovers over Sara's name, the only lifeline to reach him, but it's not concern that sets my heart pounding, it's irritation. *"Sara,"* I text, *"if you spot Lucian, let him know his disappearing act didn't win him any points."* I attach a handful of photos from the cellar. *"If he's feeling generous after strong-arming his way into this mess, he can find me."*

I wait, but there's only silence. A quick glance at the time confirms I have another two hours before the curse kicks in at midnight. But I'm not sitting through that spectral display without more answers first. Letting annoyance lead the way, I switch to Matty's contact. He's been blissfully unconnected to all this supernatural drama. A nice, normal guy with a normal life.

"Hey, you up?" I text, my thumbs moving with the speed of a caffeinated court reporter.

"Just reading. Why? Want to grab a drink?" His response comes back quick, a digital lifeline tossed into the roiling sea of my bewilderment.

"Always have time for a drink," I reply. *"Location is dealer's choice."*

"How about Moonlit Haven?"

"Really?" I reply, one eyebrow reaching for the sky. He wasn't thrilled about the place when I mentioned it for a law school costume night. He isn't so thrilled about *any* of my supernatural interests.

"Anything for you," his text reads, dripping with sincerity. It sets my heart fluttering like a trapped butterfly.

"Be there in twenty," I type, sealing our impromptu rendezvous with a send button that feels suspiciously like a trigger.

With a last glance at the house that seems to groan with ancient grief, I pull the car out of the gravel lane. The drive to Moonlit Haven passes in a blur of streetlights and contemplation.

"Time to shift gears, Emily," I remind myself, the rearview mirror nodding in agreement. "Tonight, you're just a woman having a drink with a man who likes you. No curses, no creatures, no complications."

Just Matty and a cocktail or two.

Chapter 19

The first rays of morning light slip through the blinds, caressing my face with the promise of a new day. I stretch languidly, a contented yawn escaping me as remnants of last night's date with Matty cling to the edges of my consciousness. It was one for the books, a perfect concoction of laughter and lingering glances. I ended up skipping a second visit to Oakheart, and we closed down Moonlit Haven. I'd gone home without thinking of curses or vampires or *anything* other than Matty's smile.

I reach for my phone, the screen blinking to life under my touch. And there it is—a message from Matty, lighting up my notifications like a beacon of good vibes. *"Had an amazing time yesterday. Night with you > any other place on earth."* The corners of my lips inch upwards into a smile that feels like it could outshine the sun.

"Right back at ya," I type, the keys clicking under my eager thumbs. *"Who knew you were so good at 18th century trivia?"*

Before I can hit send, the cheerful bubble of my morning is punctured by the shrill ring of an incoming call. Sara's name flashes across the screen, a somber reminder that life in the supernatural lane never sticks to office hours.

"Emily, something's come up," Sara's voice is tight, her words clipped. "I need you over here, like, yesterday."

"Okay, slow down, Sara," I say, my brow furrowing. My brain flips into crisis mode, already cataloging worst-case scenarios like a doomsday prepper. "Give me fifteen minutes."

I toss the phone on the bed, already halfway to my closet. Clothes fly off hangers as I search for something that screams 'I'm here to solve your paranormal problems but I also have my life together.' Settling on a pair of black slacks and a crisp white shirt, I wrangle my hair into its trademark messy pony—functional yet stylish, just how I like my litigation strategies.

Coat? Check. Keys? Check. Tape recorder? I grab my trusty sidekick, just in case this little adventure requires more than just my sharp wit and charming personality.

"Hold down the fort, Herle!" I shout as I dart out the door.

As expected, Herle doesn't respond. Emily and Herle—a duo destined for a bad sitcom. But hey, if the shoe fits...

The door to Sara's house swings open with the faintest creak, a sound that wouldn't be out of place in a horror movie. I step over the threshold, immediately hit by the overpowering scent of lavender mixed with something metallic—probably the usual when you work with dead bodies, but today it makes my teeth itch.

"Lucian?" I blurt out, more surprised than I should be. He's slumped in an overstuffed chair that looks like it was plucked straight out of a Victorian novel. Candlelight flickers across his face, casting deep shadows that make him look older, wearier—like someone who's had enough of this century and maybe the last few before it.

"Emily," he says, lifting his head. His voice is gravelly, the usual smooth cadence replaced by fatigue. "I apologize for last night." His sharp gray eyes lock onto mine. It's like he's peering straight into my soul, even though I'm pretty sure it's just sleep deprivation.

"Should I be flattered you ditched me to hang out at a mortician's house?" I quip, trying not to show how much his absence stung. It's petty, but hey, jealousy is a green-eyed monster that doesn't discriminate.

"Believe me, this wasn't my plan either," he says with a sigh, standing up. He's unsteady on his feet, a vampire off-kilter—now there's something you don't see every day.

"Then what was your plan?" I cross my arms, leaning against the doorframe. A candle flickers nearby, its flame reflected in the scratched surface of Sara's dining table. A peek into the interior of the house reveals dozens more candles, covering nearly every surface, giving everything a seance vibe.

"Something in the cellar... it concerned me enough to seek Sara's counsel immediately," Lucian confesses, his gaze dropping to the floor as if the weight of his worries could crack the hardwood.

Lucian isn't one to get rattled easily. With his age and experience, the man's seen more calamities than most history books. But it explains his weird behavior last night.

"What exactly did you find?" I ask, "and where is Sara?"

"Let's just say it's a situation that requires both our expertise," he answers cryptically, running a hand through his disheveled hair.

"Great, nothing says Sunday fun-day like a supernatural crisis." I push away from the doorframe, ready to dive headfirst into whatever mess awaits us. "Alright, let's hear it then. What's got the undead so shaken up before coffee?"

That's when Sara appears. Her usual goth chic look is still in place, but there's something off—her dark brown skin looks paler than usual, and her hazel eyes are dull, like someone turned down the brightness. Even her platinum hair doesn't have the pep it normally does.

"Come, sit," she says, her voice weary as she settles on the worn sofa across from Lucian. The surrounding air seems to hum with tension, a palpable reminder that whatever lurks in the shadows of Sara's home is no laughing matter.

I take a seat opposite them, my gaze flickering between Lucian's stoic facade and Sara's troubled expression. The tension in the room is thick enough it needs a recently sharpened steak knife to cut through it.

"Okay, so it's not just the candlelight making this place feel like a crypt," I mutter to myself, taking in the sea of flickering flames that gives Sara's living room an otherworldly glow. "Spill it, Sara. What's going on? Are you in trouble?"

Sara doesn't laugh. Instead, she leans forward, her eyes locking onto mine with a look that says *brace yourself*. "I understand if this changes things between us, but I need to tell you something."

I lean in too, curiosity turning my spine into a question mark. I consider one of my trademark jokes but something about the seriousness tells me I shouldn't. "What are you talking about, Sara?" I prompt, my voice cautious.

"I'm a witch," she confesses.

I blink. Once. Twice. "A witch?" My voice comes out as a squeak, a mouse surprised in the kitchen at midnight. Not exactly the poised response I aim for in courtrooms.

"Yes," she whispers.

Thousands of thoughts race through my head but they all solidify into a single point: "I knew you had a witch friend!" I crow to Lucian.

Lucian offers a weary chuckle, but the amusement is fleeting. "Yes, Emily. You really know how to keep me on my toes," he quips, though his gaze remains fixed on Sara, a silent acknowledgement passing between them.

Sara's lips twitch into a small half-smile at my outburst, a spark of her usual self breaking through the solemnity that had settled over her just moments ago. "I've been meaning to tell you," she admits, her voice soft but steady. "Recent events just forced my hand."

"Recent events? Do they involve the whole candlelit séance vibe we've got going on here?" I gesture around the room, attempting to lighten the mood despite the gravity of the situation.

Sara's expression turns serious again. "It's more than just ambiance, Emily. It's protection for us in this conversation. Lucian saw something in the cellar..."

"Yeah, he mentioned that. And I sent you those photos," I prompt.

She nods, pulling out her phone and flicking open the snapshot of the swords. Although I hadn't gone for style, the photo looks eerie and like something from a movie. The beam from my flashlight created eerie shadows on the cellar's stone walls behind the swords, illuminating the blades, ancient and ornate, arranged in a circle on the wall.

"This... this configuration," she starts, her eyes fixed on the swords as if they hold the key to a long-forgotten secret. "It mirrors the one used by the rival coven that cursed my family when I was a child."

"Oh, Sara, I'm so sorry," I say. "What happened?"

"We lived in St. Louis, where witches held sway in the shadows. My coven was at the heart of that magic. Respected, powerful, and envied. But there was another coven from the east who couldn't stand that we had what they wanted—influence, strength, unity. Their magic was twisted and fueled by jealousy and a thirst for dominance."

Lucian places a comforting hand on Sara's shoulder, and she covers it with her own. "The night it happened, I was just a kid, barely able to chant the simplest incantations. They cast a curse upon us, something insidious and relentless."

She looks down at the flames between them, her gaze distant again. "It wasn't a flashy spell with lightning bolts and fireworks. It was quiet and creeping. It turned our own magic against us, causing our powers to backfire. Panic spread like wildfire."

Tears pool in her eyes as she finishes her story. "My parents... they fought to save us, but the curse killed them. Killed our coven's magic. And I was left behind."

If my eyebrows climb any higher, they'll merge with my hairline. "I'm so sorry," I repeat. I'm out of my depth here. Sara gives me a small smile through her tears, her eyes shining with unshed emotions I can't fully decipher.

"At least I was lucky enough to find another family," she says softly, her voice trembling slightly. Lucian stands and retrieves a box of tissues, offering it to her with a gentle gesture, which she accepts.

I watch the choreographed dance between them. "Is that how you got connected with Lucian?"

"Actually, it was Severin who found me," Sara replies. "With Lucian's blessing, he took me in and became the older brother I never had. He taught me to control what little magic I had left." Her voice breaks for a moment before she continues. "They both became my family, filling the void that was left when mine was destroyed."

I release a slow breath, guilt tugging at me for ever doubting the depth of their bond. All my inner grumbling about Lucian and Sara feels petty now, almost embarrassingly childish. Even my irritation with Lucian from last night fades, leaving just a trace of shame in its place.

"That is why I was so concerned about you getting involved with a curse," Lucian adds. He rubs at his temples, the dark shadows under his eyes betraying that we're way past his usual bedtime. "Curses are not to be taken lightly. I feared the Baxters' curse could have been as violent as the one that affected Sara's family. We're fortunate it's more mischievous than murderous."

Something warm blooms in my chest at his concern for me. I clear my throat and force the feelings aside. "Fortunate," I echo. "At least having your dirty laundry aired by a metaphysical force isn't lethal."

"Exactly." Lucian flashes a tired smile as he slumps back in his chair. "But I don't know if the arrangement we found means it will escalate to something more dangerous."

I turn to Sara, my mind buzzing with questions. "And so does seeing the configuration of swords mean that coven is... back?" I ask. "That the Baxters are cursed by the same coven that attacked your family?"

Sara's brow furrows in thought. "I don't know," she admits with a sigh. "I did a spell to check if I could sense their magic, but there was nothing there. If it isn't them, it's another coven using their signature curse, which is... unlikely."

"Nice to know this is turning into a supernatural game of Clue." I let out a huff of exasperation. "Do we have any idea who's dealing the cards? Who's this rival coven with a vendetta, and why they're after the Baxters?"

"The details are foggy," Lucian admits, his fingers drumming on the armrest. "We know little of their motives, only that they were powerful and ruthless enough to decimate Sara's lineage."

"Charming bunch." The sarcasm drips from my voice as my mind dissects each piece of information for a clue, an angle, anything. "And there's no old grimoire or witchy Google that can give us a lead?"

Sara and Lucian exchange a glance, both shaking their heads. "Unfortunately, the supernatural world doesn't exactly hand over its secrets," Sara says, a wisp of a smile on her lips despite the grim topic.

I press my fingers to my temples, channeling that stubborn part of me that refuses to back down in a courtroom—or when faced with the supernatural equivalent of a legal puzzle. "If we're going to get to the bottom of this, we need more information."

Sara nods, her eyes reflecting the candlelight like twin beacons of resolve. "Agreed," Sara murmurs. "But where do we start?"

"Start? We dive in headfirst with this one," I say, my confidence inflating like a dollar-store balloon. "We've got to hit up the other covens, shake some trees, and see what falls out."

Lucian leans forward, elbows resting on his knees, a seriousness etched on his haggard features. "Emily," he interjects, "the Baxters—"

"Will have to deal with it," I cut him off, my voice firm. "The sword thing is creepy as a doll collection, and we can't let that slide. Their reputation isn't worth squat if they're dead."

Sara exhales sharply. "It's risky. But you're right."

"Of course, I am." A smirk plays on my lips. "So, we'll need to schedule some meetings. And not just with any old witch or warlock. We want the top hats of the magical community."

"Top hats?" Lucian raises an eyebrow, but there's a twitch of amusement in his voice.

"Figure of speech," I wave him off. "Point is, we're doing this. We're going big." I stand and start pacing. "Lucian, we need a joint coven meeting stat."

"I want to help," Sara says, standing up with a newfound determination that makes her look taller, fiercer.

"Are you willing to check out the blades?" I ask.

She nods.

Lucian stands up, his gaze softening as he looks at Sara. "Sara, the sight of those blades could reopen old wounds best left untouched. I want you to know that you're not alone in this. We will face this together, as a family." His voice carries an uncharacteristic tenderness as he places a hand on her shoulder.

Sara looks up at Lucian. "I can do it," she says.

"I know you can," Lucian replies, his voice calm and steady, cutting through any remaining tension. Then he turns to me. "I'll reach out to the covens to confirm the next meeting."

I watch the exchange between them, feeling a tug at my heart witnessing the bond before me. It's not the charged tension I've come to expect from Lucian; it's a connection rooted in shared history and mutual protection.

"Alright then," I say, my tone resolute. "We each have our tasks cut out for us. Sara, you'll handle checking out those blades. Lucian, get that newsletter ready and set up the meeting. I'll see if there's anything on the internet and do my thing."

Lucian chuckles. His eyes gleam with a mischievous glint as he takes a step closer to me. "Ah, yes, your thing," he muses, a sly smile playing on his lips. "Which is?"

I arch an eyebrow at him playfully, the tension fully replaced with a light and teasing banter. "Oh, you know, Lucian," I retort, "pushing buttons and sticking my nose where it doesn't belong."

"Indeed," he chuckles softly, the sound like velvet over gravel. "A formidable combination, I must admit. And quite the sight to behold."

"Alright team," I say, clapping my hands together, "it's time to get our Scooby-Doo on. Let's unravel this spooky spaghetti and save the day."

And nothing will stand in our way, not even the shadows of old curses and vengeful adversaries lurking in the dark alleys.

CHAPTER 20

The glow of my computer screen is the only light in the office this dreary Monday morning, barely illuminating the legal briefs that seem to whisper accusations about my weekend productivity. Or lack thereof. All this 'risk management' work is wreaking havoc on the rest of my cases. I'm just about to dive into a sea of legalese when my phone buzzes with a text from Sara.

"I'd like to recon the cellar today and check out those blades myself. That okay?"

"Only if there's an invisibility spell you can use," I type back.

"You've watched too many fantasy flicks. That's not how magic works," her response flashes on the screen.

"It needs to. The Neighborhood Watch is more interested in juicy tidbits than any actual crime. You showing up now is asking for a leading role in the next phone chain."

"I guess I'll just have to rely on my stealth skills then," Sara writes.

"Just be careful and don't turn anyone into a toad. Or worse, a mortician," I text, adding a winking emoji for good measure.

"Better a mortician than a lawyer," she quips back. I can almost hear the roll of her eyes, and it warms me more than my neglected cup of coffee ever could. *"BTW, Lucian got*

a coven meeting scheduled for tonight instead of next week. They're using the upcoming holiday season as an excuse."

"Wait, covens celebrate holidays too? I mean, I know Moonlit Haven does a mean holiday party, but do vampires hang mistletoe and wear ugly sweaters?" Suddenly, I'm imagining Lucian in a tacky, Christmas-themed outfit, with Severin wearing reindeer ears. The thought makes me chuckle.

"Maybe not quite like that. But it's a convenient reason to move up the meeting," she types. *"It's in the Underground, so bring your glasses."*

I wince. I've been trying to avoid the Underground. I'll have to find a disguise and hope magical eyes don't recognize me through it. *"Thanks for the heads up. Try not to get caught sneaking around in the shadows."*

Before I forget, I call Rhett again, leaving *another* message for him to call me back ASAP. I could probably text him about the swords I found, but it doesn't seem in good etiquette to drop that bomb on somebody without warning.

As I shut down my computer and gather my things to leave work, I catch Liz's eye and signal that I'm off to another meeting. The coffee shop I'm heading to isn't far, and my meeting with Jenna's lawyer is in less than thirty minutes. The kind of meeting that sounds simple on paper but is bound to come with a headache in a fancy suit.

The bell above the door jingles as I step into the shop, and I spot Jenna's lawyer already parked in a corner booth his face buried in documents. He looks every bit the slick attorney, with his tailored suit and designer leather briefcase. I grab an *Espresso Explosion* from the counter—because I'll need the energy for this—and take a deep breath before making my way over.

"Good afternoon," I say, extending my hand as he rises to greet me. "Emily Lane. Ready to dive in?"

"Of course, Ms. Lane." He shakes my hand firmly before sitting back down, opening his briefcase with a smooth motion. "I must say, your reputation precedes you. I've heard... things about your work in the supernatural field."

"I bet," I reply dryly, attempting to keep my expression neutral. Time to get down to business. "Now, let's talk about this case. You've got a problem that simple prejudice against the paranormals won't fix. If paranormal creatures have limited rights and aren't considered 'people' under the law, how will you prove intent? After all, this is *intentional* infliction of emotional distress. Sure, you might grab a few bigoted jurors, but the entire box?"

He pauses, clearly not expecting me to dive straight into the core of the case. "Well, we'll present evidence that Rebecca recklessly caused harm to Jenna and seek a negligent instruction instead."

"Interesting," I muse, taking a sip of my sugared coffee. "Let's say you do. But you've got to admit that the evidence against Rebecca is thin at best. Miranda has already signed an affidavit stating they were broken up before she started up with Rebecca, which should clear my client of any wrongdoing. No affair, no funny business."

"Jenna's accusations against Miranda are tarnishing her reputation, leaving her credibility suspect. And she's clearly biased," he counters, leaning back in his chair as if he's already won the battle.

"And Jenna isn't?" I say, raising an eyebrow, "Miranda has nothing to lose here, and plenty of time to make things difficult for Jenna. By pursuing this case, Jenna is only exposing herself to more scrutiny and possible backlash."

"And? Jenna isn't after just the money or the revenge. She will go to great lengths to achieve her goals, no matter the cost."

My gaze hardens as I lock eyes with him, a flicker of challenge in my expression. "But is it worth losing everything else in the process? People like Jenna might win battles but lose wars. And unless she wants to keep picking up the broken pieces, you might want to reconsider your strategy, especially when your payday is attached to hers."

He visibly bristles at my words, but I can see the gears turning in his mind. Time to push a little harder.

"Rebecca's on board," I continue, my tone firm and unwavering. "We have leverage, and we're not afraid to use it. This isn't just about winning a case; it's about standing up for those who've been marginalized and discriminated against. Principle is expensive. But we're willing to pay for it. Or... we can negotiate a resolution today, before both sides spend too much more time and money."

"Alright," he concedes with a reluctant nod. "What are you proposing?"

We dive into the negotiations, and I refuse to back down until we reach an agreement that favors Rebecca. In the end, Jenna settles for well under what Rebecca—or her wealthy patron, more like—was willing to pay. As upsetting as it can be, sometimes a little pain in the short term—paying off Jenna—is worth the net positive in the long term.

"Ms. Lane," he says as we shake hands again, "We have a deal. It's been a pleasure working with you."

"Likewise," I reply. "I'll draft up the terms of the settlement and get them to you by the end of the week."

"Next week is fine. I'm sure we'd all rather not work over the holidays." He lets out a light chuckle before continuing,

"My wife and kids would certainly protest if I tried to sneak in any work during our family time."

"The holidays?"

"Thanksgiving," he clarifies with a slight raise of his brow. "This must be why Johnson & Marcus values you so highly. Your dedication is admirable."

Thanksgiving? Right. That's a thing.

I laugh politely. I had forgotten. Even Sara's mention of the holiday season I took to mean general December revelry, not an event in three days. I've never considered it before, after all with no warm gatherings around a festive table to look forward to, no family to come home to, no traditions to uphold. It's just me.

The evening air is crisp as I make my way to the entrance of the Underground, the vibrant and chaotic hub of the supernatural world. The entrance isn't so vibrant, as the Underground is tucked inside Chicago's sewers. Walk long enough—and wear the right headgear—and concrete and asphalt turn into natural stone and the damp, smelly emptiness of the sewers turns into a flamboyant and bustling paranormal marketplace. It's like stepping from one world to another—if you don't mind a little grime on the way.

But my presence isn't the revelation I'm after tonight, not with a ticked-off pixie on my tail and the looming threat of a paranormal police force, warrants and all, potentially coming after me. Once this case is wrapped up, I should definitely do some digging into the trouble I've probably landed myself in.

I quickly don my disguise, more relics of Halloweens' past. A bright green feathered hat perches on my head, covering my signature long hair I've tucked inside, a rainbow boa drapes around my neck and a sparkling tutu wraps around my usual pencil skirt uniform. Finally, I cap the outfit with my rose-colored glasses, functional but still wild. It's absurd, but in the Underground, blending in isn't about subtlety.

As I reach the entrance, Lucian's sharp gaze takes in the entire ensemble, amusement dancing in his gray eyes. "Quite the colorful disguise you've got there," he remarks with a smirk.

"Well, I need to make sure the pixies don't recognize me." I'm risking their ire if they find me. Ire and who knows what else. Looking like a Marti Gras float is a small price to pay.

Lucian nods in agreement but his expression turns serious as he regards me. "Emily, you know how dangerous the Underground can be, especially for humans. Perhaps it would be best if I attended alone, and I can report back on what transpires."

I shake my head, determined. "No way. I'll manage just fine. Remember, I handle more than just legal matters. And I've got a month of self-defense classes under my belt." I look down. "Under my tutu."

Lucian gives me a look that says he wants to argue but knows it won't help. "Very well," he says. "Although if you hadn't decided to visit without me last time, you might not have made an enemy of said pixies."

You wouldn't take me last time, I won't remind him. He'd cried 'danger' about an unbonded human entering the Underground. But *bonded* humans—those who literally bind their souls to paranormal creatures—were fine. And since

Lucian wasn't offering, and I wasn't asking, I went alone. Stardust had my back, though, so it wasn't a total disaster.

"Keep dreaming, Count Charming," I retort. "My past choices are my own, thank you very much. Now let's go. We have a coven meeting to attend."

Together, we splash our way through Chicago's semi-abandoned sewers until stalagmites and stalactites grow around us. With the rose-colored glasses on my head, I just need to wait for the (literal) magic and the dank stone transforms. The grime and filth of the sewers changes into glittering gemstones and lush vegetation, and the quiet hum of life turns into a chaotic symphony of bustling creatures and enchanted goods. The marketplace is a kaleidoscope of colors and shapes, with neon signs advertising potions and spells, and creatures of all sizes and shapes milling about. The stalls are decorated with shimmering fabrics and sparkling jewels. Everywhere I look, there are strange sights and fantastical goods, as various paranormal creatures engage in lively conversations or heated bargaining sessions.

Lucian and I stick close together, his presence a comforting anchor in this sea of supernatural chaos. It's like a psychedelic circus threw up, and I'm front and center.

"Welcome, Mr. Belmont," a gnome merchant calls out, his wrinkled face breaking into a toothy grin as he bows low, his battered blue hat nearly toppling off his head. His skin is leathery, sun-kissed to a shade of deep brown, and his beard—thick and wiry—hangs down to his stomach, speckled with bits of dirt and twigs like he's just rolled out of a garden. "And who might this colorful human be with you tonight?"

Damnit. Not disguised enough. I straighten my posture, adjusting the feathered hat on my head with a self-assured nod. "Emily Lane," I introduce myself, offering a polite smile to the goblin. "Pleasure to be here."

The gnome's black eyes widen in recognition and he takes off his battered green hat. "The lawyer! Heard your name buzzing around the market lately."

"Gossip travels fast in the paranormal world, it seems," I remark with a chuckle, trying to maintain a professional demeanor despite my flamboyant outfit. "The rumors good, at least?"

His grin widens, revealing a mouthful of jagged teeth. "Mostly kudos. Stick around, Ms. Lane. Never a dull moment in the Underground."

"So long as you can make sure a certain pixie doesn't know I'm here?" I ask with a pleading expression.

"You'll owe me if I do," he says, a mischievous glint in his eye.

"Fantastic. Add it to my tab." I'm not even going to think about what that will cost me.

Lucian's hand presses against my back in a silent gesture of support as we navigate further into the vibrant marketplace. He says nothing about my accidental-agreement with the gnome, but I'm sure I'll hear about it later.

Finally, we approach a grand tent at the far edge of the marketplace. He ushers me through the silken entrance, revealing the clandestine grandeur of the coven leader meeting. The interior is only partly fabric, with three stone walls marking the rest of space. The area is illuminated by flickering torches that cast dancing shadows on the walls painted with arcane-looking runes. We slip into the shadowy enclave, filled with beings who would make even Bram Stoker do a double-take. The room buzzes—not with pixies, thank heavens—but with the murmurs of vampires, werewolves, and other entities discussing... well, whatever paranormal bigwigs discuss when they congregate.

"Remember, Emily," Lucian whispers in my ear as we approach a large table filled with coven leaders from various paranormal factions. "You're here to observe, gather information, and only interact if it becomes necessary. I'll coordinate with the leaders who might have knowledge of the curse. Stay nearby, and don't draw attention to yourself."

"Got it," I whisper back, already scanning for a place where I can eavesdrop without drawing too much attention.

I sidestep two sirens on my search for a seat, easily identified by how much I want to remain by their side. There's a magnetic pull to their presence, like gravity has shifted, and I'm suddenly aware that this is how sailors end up walking off cliffs. Even without using their powers on me, I have to drag myself away from them.

"I'm not sure how safe having the meeting tonight is," the first siren says to another, tossing her long, blue hair that sparkles under the torchlight. "It's practically full already!"

"You're such a worrywart," her companion replies, her own silver hair cascading down her back like a glittering waterfall. "It's days away. The wolves are smarter than that."

"If you say so," says the first.

After shaking off the siren-induced haze, I find a secluded spot near the back, close enough to eavesdrop but far enough to avoid unwanted attention. The air is thick with ancient perfume and the undercurrents of power plays. It's like a conference, if conferences were held deep in the earth and the delegates might eat each other.

I scan the crowd, noting the intensity etched on every face as they speak of concerns I can only half-guess. They're oblivious to the fact that I'm recording snippets of their conversation, piecing together a puzzle more complex than last year's tax code.

"Let's hope they're more helpful than a Yelp review for a haunted house," I muse, my sardonic inner monologue keeping me company. There's nothing quite like the scent of a lead, especially when it's buried within layers of supernatural political jargon. If I can unravel who cursed the Baxters and if Sara Harper's family tragedy ties into it, maybe I'll get to walk out of here with more than just a sparkling tutu and a story. And if I can persuade this motley crew to aid in lifting the curse? Well, that'll be one for the books—my book, specifically. The one where ambition meets the arcane and I somehow end up as the heroine.

Chapter 21

The conference table is a battleground, and the generals are an eclectic mix of fanged, furred, and fabulously arcane. I sit back in the shadows listening as they launch into the meat of the meeting—territory disputes that could make the Hatfields and McCoys look like a mild family disagreement. A dozen paranormals stand in a line behind the podium while the coven leaders at the table listen with *surprisingly* rapt attention.

"Borderlines must be respected," a gravel-voiced werewolf growls, his words sending ripples through the room. The vampires nod sagely at this; after all, territorial pissing contests aren't exclusive to the canine crowd. "There cannot be overlaps."

"Overlaps by whom?" another paranormal rasps. A ghoul this time, if I'm identifying her right.

Her skin has a pale, almost sickly grayish hue, pulled tight over her bones, giving her a gaunt appearance. It's as if her face was sculpted from ash, her cheeks sunken in, and her lips—well, if you could call them lips—are a thin, cracked line of bluish-gray. Her eyes are what really stand out though, glowing faintly like dull embers in a dying fire, set deep in shadowed sockets. Her hair hangs limp, stringy, and black, framing her skeletal face in loose, unruly strands. I duck down in my seat, wrapping the boa tighter around my neck, hoping her forced diet of fake-flesh is filling enough that she won't feel inclined to take a bite out of me.

"The territories were given to us by the humans," she continues, her voice as dry and cracked as the dead leaves outside. "You and your wolves divvy it up how you like. But my people will maintain what little we've been given."

A handful of paranormals hiss, others bare their teeth.

Lucian stands. "Relations between our covens are paramount," Lucian says, his voice smooth as aged whiskey. "We can ill afford to turn on one another when the world above remains intolerant to our existence." He looks relaxed, but there's a tension in his jaw, a reminder of the time he was more defendant than diplomat, when they all blamed him for their human troubles.

"Lucian's right," a siren sings out, her voice weaving through the air, making even the most stoic shifter sway. "We cannot let old grudges cloud our judgment."

"But what if we can no longer ignore the threat looming over us?" A voice interjects, the tone oddly familiar. I swivel to find Rhett Baxter leaning against a wall, his face set in a firm scowl. Beside him is Alex, looking like he's about ready to leash his son to a post. They're both towering over everyone, their werewolf heritage impossible to miss in their steely gazes. Although, the *reason* for that hard expression appears to differ.

Murmurs start up, most sounding irritated that he skipped the line, but some more focused on what he's just said.

"What threat?" one of the coven leaders presses, leaning forward with interest.

"Of the humans," Rhett replies. "Perhaps if they knew how well-connected we truly were, they would have to respect us."

I press the record button a little harder, a frown creasing my brow. My hand itches to jot down notes, but the tape recorder will have to do. Rhett's words feel loaded, but I can't quite put my finger on the trigger. His eyes meet mine for a fleeting second, with no recognition, but there's a depth there I can't read. Alex's glare, though, speaks volumes.

"Our people are police, politicians, we work the markets even if we can't legally invest. If we let some of those families' skeletons out of the proverbial closet, we could shift power dynamics," Rhett adds, cryptic as a fortune cookie.

"Interesting theory for one who has the ability to blend in," Lucian comments, giving Rhett a long look that has volumes written in the silence.

But Rhett's right to some extent. If you'd asked me two months ago how the many paranormals govern themselves, I couldn't tell you. Most people still can't name more than three species. If humans *knew* what was beneath their feet, would they do better? Wasn't that partly my pitch to Lucian and Severin—changing the perception with an information overload?

"Moving on," the siren cuts through the tension, redirecting the focus to the next topic on the agenda, something benign about crop prices.

A break is called, and I stretch my legs, feeling like a minnow among the sharks. I need more than vague insinuations and mystical musings. I need hard facts, something concrete I can sink my teeth into.

"Think they'll serve cookies at the next break?" I quip to Lucian as we head towards the refreshment table. "Maybe some blood type O-negative macarons for our fanged friends?"

He chuckles, shaking his head. "Keep your day job, Emily. Comedy isn't your strong suit."

"Everyone's a critic," I retort, grabbing a bottle of water. "Did you learn anything?"

"Not much," he admits, his expression darkening slightly. "The coven leaders seem more interested in posturing than providing useful information. If anyone knows anything about the curse, they're not sharing it."

I raise an eyebrow. "Do I need to start shaking people down? I mean, I've got the sarcasm, the leather boots, and the general air of someone who's not here to play nice."

Lucian smirks faintly. "Tempting, but I doubt intimidation would work. They'd likely just get even more cryptic. The open forum is next—perhaps someone will come forward willingly."

I take a sip of water and nod. "Well, here's hoping someone spills the beans before I have to resort to my latest interrogation technique—annoying them into submission."

I spot Rhett and Alex across the room, locked in what looks like a heated exchange. Rhett's leaning against the wall, arms crossed, scanning the room with a look that could turn granite into dust. Alex, on the other hand, is practically spitting with frustration, his voice sharp enough to cut glass.

Excusing myself from Lucian, I make my way across the room, carefully sidestepping a brooding vampire who looks like he's contemplating his centuries-old feud with daylight. I give him a wide berth—no need to become collateral damage in his eternal sulk.

As I approach, Alex's voice cuts through the hum of conversation, sharp and unmistakable.

"What you're suggesting is reckless!" His voice is sharp, each word like a shot. "Exposing ourselves to humans—parading our power around like some kind of spectacle—will put a target on our backs."

"Or it'll make them think twice about doing us harm," Rhett fires back, defiant. "Don't you get it? They already know we exist, but they don't know what we're capable of. If they fear us, they'll respect us."

"They won't respect us—they'll hunt us!" Alex hisses, voice low but seething. "They'll bring their silver bullets, their stakes, and all the other tools they've invented to control us. You really think this will make us safer? You think revealing ourselves is going to fix anything?"

"I think we can't keep hiding forever." Rhett's voice drops lower, and I have to strain to hear him. "This curse, this—whatever's happening in this house—it's just a symptom. A symptom of us pretending we're something we're not."

"Or maybe it's a symptom of poor leadership," someone says. Trenton stands just off to the side, arms crossed, glaring daggers at Rhett. I hadn't even realized he was here. He looks every bit the outsider at a family reunion he wasn't invited to. "Sure, let them see what we're capable of. Or rather... what Rhett's leadership has led us to."

Rhett's eyes narrow. "What's that supposed to mean, Trenton?"

Trenton shrugs, a glint of something unreadable in his gaze. "I'm just saying, if the curse is real, maybe it's a warning—one that wouldn't be necessary if you'd made some different choices."

Alex's jaw tightens, and I can almost see the steam rising from his ears. "Enough. This isn't a game. This is our family's safety."

But Rhett ignores him, focusing on Trenton with a hard look. "You think I'm the reason we're cursed?"

Trenton's smile doesn't quite reach his eyes. "I think the curse is a convenient excuse. Maybe if people start questioning your ability to lead, they'll finally see why you're not the right person for the job."

It hits me then—could Trenton actually be behind this curse? Setting Rhett up to fail, to embarrass him publicly? If people think the curse is linked to Rhett's leadership, it'd be a fast track to eroding his authority. But why hurt his family to do it? Both Rhett and Trenton are acting suspiciously tonight, but would either go so far as to bring a curse that could kill their entire family line?

I step forward, clearing my throat. "Sorry to interrupt the family feud," I say, keeping my tone light. "But from what I overheard, I think I've got some information that might be relevant."

Alex whips around, eyes narrowing at me like I'm the last person he wanted to see. "What did you hear?" he demands, stepping toward me as if he thinks he can intimidate me into silence.

Rhett looks surprised to see me. His eyes flick over my disguise. "Emily? Is that you?" He frowns, his earlier anger melting into confusion. "What are you wearing?"

"Long story," I say, glancing around the room to make sure no one else is listening. "I needed to stay under the radar. But listen—I've been digging, literally at one point, and finally found the cellar."

Rhett straightens, shooting a glance at Alex. "Will I be checking your wiring sometime soon?"

"Maybe, and you're going to want to hear this." I drop my voice lower. "There were artifacts, symbols... things that point to a much bigger problem. And I'm telling you, this isn't just a little family haunting. It's something older, darker. It mimics a curse from years ago, out of St. Louis, one that destroyed an entire coven."

"The Harper curse?" Rhett's answer is quick, and I can see the wheels turning in his head.

I blink. "You know about it?"

Rhett shrugs. "A good coven leader knows the risks to their people."

Trenton lets out a low chuckle, crossing his arms. "A 'good leader' also makes sure his people don't end up cursed in the first place. Funny how *that* detail slipped by you, Uncle."

Rhett's jaw clenches, and I swear he's seconds away from swinging at his nephew. But he takes a breath, forcing himself to stay calm. "Are you suggesting I brought this on us?"

Trenton just shrugs, looking every bit the smug kid enjoying a moment of superiority. "I'm just saying, maybe the curse is exactly what this family needs to see how things really are."

Rhett turns to me, dismissing Trenton's jab. "Go on, Emily. Tell us everything you've found."

I glance at Alex, who's glaring daggers, his jaw set so tight I'm surprised it doesn't snap. "There's evidence the curse that took out the Harper family has been repeated. Now, I know it's risky, but I'd like to share it with the group. Get their insight," I continue. "I know you wanted it kept under wraps, but we don't have a lot of time, and if this curse is what I think it is, keeping yourselves hidden might not be an option anymore. It might not even work."

"No," Alex snaps. "No more risks. No more gambles. We stick to the plan—"

"What plan?" I cut in, frustration bubbling to the surface. "The one where you keep everything a secret and hope it'll just go away on its own? Or the one where you pretend that keeping me out of the loop is going to magically solve your problems?"

Rhett lets out a slow breath and addresses Alex. "You put me in charge for a reason. If Emily's uncovered something that can help, we need to know. *Everyone* needs to know."

Alex's expression doesn't change—he's still furious, still pacing like a caged wolf—but Rhett turns from him to give me a nod. "Keep going Emily."

"You'd better be right about this," Alex says lowly, and it isn't clear if he's talking to me or Rhett. "Because if this goes sideways, we'll all have bigger problems than a curse."

"I'm not wrong," I reply, meeting his gaze. "This is bigger than all of us. But I'll figure it out."

I click off the recorder, stash it away, and brace for the second half of this otherworldly summit.

"Lucian, will I start another territory war if I add my name to the speaker's list?" I ask, tapping his arm as the murmurs around us signify the meeting is about to reconvene. "I mean, this is just like a city council meeting, right? Only with more fangs and fur involved."

I'll be like those people that show up to school board meetings who don't have any kids in the district. At least, I *hope* I'll be more useful.

"It's an open forum," Lucian says, raising a brow. "But should you put yourself forward?"

I catch the subtle concern in Lucian's gaze—a flicker of protectiveness that somehow warms my insides, even with the weight of the situation pressing down on us. "I need to, Lucian. This isn't just about one coven or one faction. First, it's a witch coven, then a werewolf's. What's next? If there's a threat looming over all supernatural beings, I want to do my part in unraveling it, even if it's messy. Especially if it's messy."

"Very well," he says, his gaze sweeping the room. "Although I must say, if you're to speak, I am sure your presence will be much more... enlivening than the usual disputes."

"Thrilled to be your source of entertainment," I quip as I make my way to the sign-up sheet, scrawling my name with a flourish, ready to contribute what I've uncovered about the hidden chamber and its potential dangers.

When it's my turn, I stride to the podium with a confidence I partly have to fake. The room falls silent, every paranormal leader present fixes their gaze on me—some curious, some calculating.

"Good evening," I begin, surveying the room. "I'm Emily Lane, and I bring news that affects those of us in this room. It's about the Baxters." A collective rustle sweeps through the crowd. "And it's not just them. There's a curse—similar to the one that struck Sara Harper's coven in St. Louis. Surprised? So was I. Worried? You should be. Because if we don't come together to address this, who knows which family, which coven will be next?"

"Who is Sara?" a werewolf asks.

"Severin's girl," a siren answers. The werewolf frowns, like that didn't answer her question.

"Many of you know Sara, or know of her plight," I continue.

"What plight?" the siren from earlier asks.

"The mortician is a witch?" asks another in the audience.

My eyes flick to Lucian for help, as I can feel the room's interest pivot, focusing more on Sara than the curse. *Was this not common knowledge?* Will Sara mind that I aired her dirty—and rather violent—laundry to the room?

Lucian stands abruptly, cutting through the whispers. "I will address that," he says, his voice firm, though I can see the tension in the way he holds himself. "Sara Harper is, indeed, a witch—something many of you may not have known. Her coven in St. Louis was decimated by a powerful curse years ago."

The room goes silent. My stomach tightens; I should've known better than to drop Sara's name so casually. But now it's out there, and there's no taking it back.

Lucian finishes his explanation, leaving the revelation hanging in the air like a fog. I send an apology to the universe, already planning to make it up to Sara with something extravagant. Maybe diamonds. Definitely wine.

"Anyway," I say, trying to steer the conversation back. "As I mentioned, this has happened before. And now, the Baxters are facing a similar curse. It's been relatively benign so far. Annoying, but nothing major. But it's changing. Chicago could be facing a threat that's more widespread, more dangerous than we initially thought."

Murmurs swell into clamor as concern creases the faces before me. Though the Baxters haven't always been the darlings of the supernatural community, no one can deny the gravity of the situation.

"I know the Baxters aren't winning any popularity contests," I continue, aiming for a lighter tone to break the tension. Trenton's eye roll is nearly audible. "But this is bigger than old grudges."

The room shifts, the gravity of my words sinking in. It's not just about the Baxters anymore, this is about the future of everyone here.

"Please come find me if you have any information on this matter. We must find the hexer and nullify this curse. Thank you for your attention," I finish, stepping away from the microphone.

I step back from the podium, but the room's collective gaze clings to me, a wave of hushed whispers following my every move. I slide into an empty seat beside Lucian, stealing a glance at him for a bit of reassurance. But his face is set, his expression hard, and there's an unmistakable tension between his brows.

"Sara's past was kept private for a reason," he nearly hisses. "Now you've exposed her to a room full of paranormals who will no doubt spread it beyond this meeting." He leans closer, eyes darkening. "Do you understand what you've done?"

I swallow hard, the weight of my mistake settling in. "I'm sorry, Lucian. I didn't mean to—"

"It's done," he says, his voice cold. "But don't think for a moment this won't have consequences."

I nod, the heat of embarrassment creeping up my neck. "I'll make it right with her."

He doesn't respond, just turns his attention back to the room, but I can feel the strain between us, the disappointment radiating from him like a cloud.

My stomach twists as I sit back in my chair. I've stirred up more than I intended tonight. The room might be buzzing about the curse, but all I can think about is the look on Lucian's face—and what it might cost to fix this.

CHAPTER 22

I pace the length of my tiny kitchen, the click of the recorder in my hand a steady pulse against the silence. "Hexer leads—zero. Coven input—zilch," I mutter into the device, my voice tinged with frustration. Not a single coven leader had any clue about our hexer or curse. It's like trying to catch smoke with a net.

But I'm not giving up yet. It's only been—I glance at the clock—ten hours since I left the coven meeting. Ten hours since I exposed Sara as a witch. I may be new to this friendship thing, but I know I'm not winning "Best Friend of the Year" for this.

I grab my phone and dial Sara's number for the seventh time, guilt tugging at me for possibly putting her in harm's way by unintentionally revealing her secret. The phone rings, once, twice, three times, then straight to voicemail. Anxiety gnaws at me like a stray on day-old pizza. She must be upset with me, betrayed, even. I mean, who wouldn't be? You trust someone to keep your secret, and what do they do? Spill it.

Sighing heavily, I abandon the call. *"I'm so sorry about last night,"* I text, another in a long line of unanswered apologies. I know she must have a good reason for not picking up, even if it's just 'fed up with Emily Lane today,' but the nagging guilt persists.

Nagging guilt and a lack of sleep. After the coven meeting, my brain treated me to another round of sleeplessness. I run a hand through my tangled hair, grimacing at my reflection in the dark kitchen window. Bloodshot eyes, dark circles that look like I haven't slept since the invention of the printing press—the classic insomnia look.

Sleep has been elusive since the whole curse debacle started ramping up, and the constant mental merry-go-round isn't doing me any favors. Every time I close my eyes, my brain kicks into overdrive, running through a checklist of every possible thing I could have done differently. Could've found a better lead on the hexer. Could've kept Sara's secret.

With a resolve to try again with Sara later, I grab my bag and head out into the brisk morning air.

I make my way to the firm, the hubbub of city life swirling around me like a chaotic dance. The morning rush is in full swing, with people hurrying to their destinations like pieces on a chessboard. The glass doors of the building slide open, welcoming me with that cold, sterile air of corporate doom.

Liz greets me with her usual sunny smile, but there's an underlying tension in her eyes that mirrors my own feelings. "Tough morning?" she asks, following me into my office, her curly red locks bouncing.

"You could say that," I mutter, shrugging off my coat and tossing it over the back of my chair. My brain is still half in witch/curse territory, and I really don't have time for firm drama today.

Liz perches herself on the edge of my desk, her emerald eyes wide, serious. "Do you want to talk about it?"

I consider it for a moment, wondering if unloading all the recent chaos onto Liz would make me feel better or worse. Liz isn't a fan of anything paranormal. I won't find support in her corner.

"No, I'm fine." I shake off the feeling. "Any messages?"

She hesitates for a beat before delivering the blow. "Actually yes," she says. "The senior partners want to see you. They've set up a 9:00 a.m. in the big conference room."

My stomach drops like I'm on a roller coaster, but one that won't leave me smiling at the end. "Any idea what this is about?" I ask, knowing Liz usually has the inside scoop before anyone else does.

Liz shakes her head, but there's a flicker of something in her eyes—foreboding. "No spoilers," she says with a small, forced smile.

"Great," I mutter, making my way to the ominous double doors of the main conference room. With my recent luck, I have a sinking feeling that this meeting won't be a 'congrats, you're amazing' kind of meeting.

Inside, the senior partners are seated like a lineup of stone-faced gargoyles come to life. Haskins, Davenport, Lawrence, and Hargrove—names that strike fear into the hearts of many junior associates, and apparently, me too, even if I'm a partner.

"Emily," Davenport begins, his voice solemn, "we've been made aware of your... affiliations with certain... entities."

"Supernatural beings, you mean?" I cut in, unable to help myself. Why dance around the elephant in the room when you can tango with it? "I thought we had this conversation when I made partner. It wasn't a secret."

"Exactly," Haskins says sharply. "But then you promised you were only courting their allies, not the creatures themselves."

"And here I thought you'd be happy that we're expanding our client base," I shoot back, unable to help myself. Yeah, because sarcasm always helps in high-stakes situations.

"Accounting briefed us on the Rebecca Marquise case," Davenport says, flipping open a file. "And her... status."

"It's a wonder she could even pay," Hargrove mutters down the table.

"Yes, it's a pity the paranormal citizens of our society don't have bank accounts and have to rely on humans as go betweens," I say, sounding snippy.

Hargrove clears his throat. "And let us not forget the complaint from a potential client last week—"

"And I bet if you talk to any of them now," I interject, flashing a sharp smile, "they'd have glowing reports."

After all, they ended up *loving* me at the book club.

"That remains to be seen," Hargrove says, clearly unimpressed. "But your involvement has raised concerns about your judgment and ability to maintain professional objectivity."

"Which means?" I prompt, even though I can already feel the guillotine's blade hovering above my neck.

"Effective immediately, you're being removed from the Sanderson fire matter," Lawrence delivers the blow with clinical detachment.

"I see," I manage, my voice tight. "That's a high-profile case."

"Indeed," Hargrove adds, "but we cannot risk the firm's reputation."

"Understood." I nod, schooling my face into neutrality while my insides churn with frustration. There's a twisted irony in being punished for doing too much good.

"Dismissed," Haskins waves me off, and I exit, their disapproval hanging like an albatross around my neck.

"Hey," Liz whispers as I pass by her desk, "you okay?"

"Never better," I lie, flashing her a grin that feels more like a grimace. "Who needs a career, anyway?"

"Emily..."

"It's fine, Liz," I interrupt, not ready to dissect my emotions. "I've got work to do, for the cases I have left, I mean."

Alone, I take a deep breath and look at my framed law degree. "Well, diploma, it's just you and me against the world." I let out a sigh. Today, the world feels particularly large—and I feel especially small.

After an afternoon of 'legitimate' business (and a lot of pretending I wasn't about to combust from stress), I decide to reach out to the law school crew. It's Tuesday night, and Megan usually plans something fun to unwind after the day's chaos. If anyone can pull me out of this funk, it's her.

My phone feels like a lead weight in my hand as I tap out a message. *"Guess who just got sidelined from the case of the century for fraternizing with the fanged and furry?"* I type, my thumbs moving with the speed of someone trying to outrun their own shadow.

"Tonight's drinks are on me," I add before hitting send, a flicker of anticipation warming the cold pit in my stomach.

I rest my cheek against the cool surface of my desk, giving myself a moment of self-pity. The mahogany wood, once a symbol of my ambition, now feels more like a plank on a sinking ship, and I'm clinging to it for dear life.

The buzz of my phone jolts me upright, and I snatch it up, expecting the usual barrage of emojis and sympathy. Instead, Megan's name flashes on the screen, her message concise and apologetic. *"Can't make it tonight, Em. Family flew in for Thanksgiving. Raincheck?"*

But... it's a Tuesday.

Then Brian chimes in— *"Same here, family stuff."*

And Matty right behind him— *"Next week?"*

Megan *never* bails on a Tuesday. She's the glue, the one who never flakes, the queen of 'we'll make it happen.' Her absence hits harder than the rest because if Megan can't prioritize our little reunions, what does that say about my place in their lives? About all the choices I've made?

"Sure thing," I reply, the words tasting as flat as they look on the screen. I drop the phone back on the desk, staring at it as if it might spontaneously combust and take all my troubles with it.

It buzzes again, not a group text but a lifeline from Matty. *"Hey,"* the text reads, *"remember that night we closed down O'Malley's after Brian killed that oil case? Almost as fatal as Moonlit Haven last week. I'm still paying for those extra rounds. How about we relive that once this holiday madness is over? Just the two of us this time."*

A smile tugs at my lips despite the dumpster fire my life is becoming. It's impossible to forget that night. We'd all laughed until our sides ached, and the air between Matty and I hummed with something electric, something promising. But what did I do with that spark? I shoved it aside for work and... well, for getting bitten by vampires when I needed to blow off steam. Brilliant priorities.

My thumb hovers over the keyboard. I type, then delete, then type again. *"Looking forward to it. O'Malley's won't know what hit it... again,"* I text back, hiding behind humor like it's my personal shield. *"Enjoy family time and eat some turkey for me."*

"Always. Keep your head up, Lane. Whatever's happening, you've got it. You're the greatest non-government lawyer I know."

I laugh to myself, the tight knot in my chest loosening just a little. *"Only because I learned from the best. And by that, I mean watching reruns of 'The Practice.'"* I shove the phone back into my purse before I can overthink the interaction, but not before his message leaves me feeling a *little* less alone in the universe.

"Family first, Lane," I mutter, parroting the advice I see in the media. But who's left when your own 'family' is AWOL, an encyclopedia of the supernatural is screening your calls, and your only non-paranormal friends have to bail? Your career, you'd hope. But mine is floundering.

I lean back in my chair, letting out a long breath, and rake my fingers through my hair, pulling it from its bun. Strands spill around my face, a dark curtain to hide behind.

"Who needs a high-profile case, anyway?" I scoff, trying to convince myself more than anyone else. After all, who wouldn't trade courtroom drama for battling the curses and supernatural politics? It's a no-brainer... if your brain's been pickled in brine.

"Pull it together, Emily," I chide myself. My voice is a mix of pep talk and self-deprecation, a cocktail I've grown rather fond of over the years. One that—the last day has proved—won't be leaving me any time soon. Not when I'm the only one offering up words of encouragement lately. "You can handle a little career turbulence."

But it's not just the career turbulence. It's the radio silence from my friends, the gnawing guilt over Sara, and the sinking feeling that the only person I can rely on right now can be found staring back at me from the mirror. And, lately, she's been making some bad calls.

"Okay, so no drinks with the crew," I say, forcing myself to stand. It's just me, my diploma, and a growing suspicion that my destiny lies somewhere off the beaten path, away from the well-trodden road to partner at a prestigious firm.

"But there's still work to be done, cases to crack, curses to lift," I finish. I sound like a trailer for a B-movie, but it's enough to get my feet moving. Because if there's one thing Emily Lane doesn't do, it's wallow.

"Chin up, Lane. There's a mystery afoot, and you're just the lawyer to solve it."

But first, I could use *someone* in my corner.

I shove the heavy door to Moonlit Haven open, the familiar creak barely registering over the sound of my own exasperation. I'm expecting the usual buzz of paranormal clientele, but tonight, the bar is as lifeless as a mausoleum at midnight.

No customers at the bar, no lively conversations floating in the air. Just the faint hum of the overhead lights and the steady drip of what I assume is the world's slowest leaky tap. Even the usual mafiosos are nowhere to be seen, and the shifters? Vanished like they have better things to do than hang out with a lawyer who just got benched from her biggest case.

"Could've at least let a girl know there's a supernatural conference going on somewhere," I mutter under my breath, sidling up to the bar with the grace of a zombie after a marathon.

The bartender—Noah, I remember—offers me a nod that's more of an involuntary twitch than a greeting. "Whiskey, Emily?"

"Make it a double," I reply, hoisting myself onto a stool and unceremoniously dropping my tape recorder and bag beside me. It clunks against the wood, echoing in the empty space.

I'd tried to salvage the night by swinging by the vampire quarter, having an open invitation to appear on any night there wasn't a 'special coven only' meeting, thinking at least there would be some semblance of life—or well, you know—but the cobblestone streets had been deserted. Not a fang or flutter in sight.

"Should've brought a book," I mutter, swirling the ice in my glass. It clinks mockingly as if to say, 'Well, at least you have us for company.'

The silence is suffocating, so I reach for my phone, hitting Sara's number for the umpteenth time. Straight to voicemail. Again. The digital beep mocks me like an unanswered question in a quiet courtroom.

I shift, the cool leather of the barstool failing to chill the sting of isolation gnawing at my insides. Everyone has their tribe—a family, a coven, a pack. But me? I'm about as solo as a witch without a broomstick.

"Who needs 'em, anyway? Any of 'em?" I declare to no one in particular, the words bouncing off the walls and back at me like an echo of denial.

Thing is, lying to yourself gets a whole lot harder when you're running on fumes. It's like your brain's too tired to keep up with the mental acrobatics, so everything just blurs together until you can't tell whether you're hiding the truth, denying it, or just plain avoiding it. And right now, I'm doing all three. Badly.

A gust of wind heralds the door swinging open, and Rebecca strides in like she owns the place. Her white hair is a stark contrast to the interior of the bar, her presence a sudden burst of life in a sea of stillness.

"Emily Lane," she announces with that signature smirk of hers. Noah drops a glass of something black and bubbly in front of an empty stool beside me.

"Rebecca," I acknowledge, not quite keeping the relief out of my voice. "Didn't think I'd see another soul tonight."

"Couldn't miss thanking my favorite lawyer and this was the first place I knew to check," she says, sliding into a seat. "You did wonders with my case."

"Miranda must be thrilled too," I reply.

"Thrilled enough to give it another shot," Rebecca confirms, waggling her eyebrows. "We're playing it by ear this time. Open relationship and all that jazz."

"Modern love," I quip, raising my glass in a silent toast.

She tilts her head, fixing me with a sharp look. "Are you looking for your own love story, Emily? Because this place?" She gestures to the empty bar. "Not the best venue. And with that expression on your face, you're not exactly selling it."

I laugh, a short, bitter sound. "Yeah, well, getting sidelined from a major case will give anyone a few extra wrinkles."

Rebecca's smirk deepens. "You shouldn't let them push you around like that. You've got options and power, Emily. More than you realize."

"Power?" I repeat, unable to keep the disbelief out of my voice. "I can't even get a return phone call half the time."

Rebecca waves a hand dismissively. "Power isn't about what's in your contact list. It's about how you use what you've got. You got me out of a nasty bind situation, and you barely broke a sweat."

"I'm just glad we got it settled," I say, tipping my drink in her direction.

"You know, word is getting around," she says, leaning in conspiratorially. "Emily Lane, exclusive attorney for the preternaturally afflicted. There will likely be many more people calling you."

"Ha. Sounds like a tagline for a bad TV show." I shake my head, though the idea of filling my docket with paranormal cases isn't without its appeal, especially after today's slap on the wrist.

"I'm quite serious," Rebecca presses, her gaze intense. "You could have a career in this. You have the brains, the guts, the tape recorder..." She nods towards my trusty sidekick sitting on the bar. "What have you got to lose?"

"Sanity, stability, a regular paycheck..." I trail off, but the seed is planted, and it's rooting into my frustration, spreading tendrils in every little crack of dissatisfaction with work. With being 'partner.' If I went out on my own, no Johnson & Marcus holding me back, I could do what I promised, do what I want, without worrying about a pink slip.

Except you doing what you want is why you're here alone tonight.

Rebecca grins, and I have to remind myself to breathe. "Just think about it, would you?" She pushes her empty glass toward Noah. "Put her drinks on my tab," she tells him with a wink. "Consider it a thank you." With that, she slides off her stool, gives me a last, meaningful glance, and saunters out the door.

I stare at my whiskey, swirling the last bit of liquid around in a glass that's seen more lip prints tonight than a mistletoe at a Christmas party. Noah fills it a second time. I drain the glass and tap it on the bar for another. Noah watches me with a careful eye, and I can sense the question before it even leaves his mouth.

"Emily," he says gently, "is there anyone I can call for you?"

I shake my head, a tired smile playing on my lips. Because who would answer? "Nah, just a ride."

The night presses in, heavy and thick, and with a last glance at the empty bar, I slide off the stool. My heels click against the floor, echoing the steady beat of loneliness following me tonight. Everyone else has somewhere to be, someone to turn to. But me? I've got a curse to solve, work to do, and no one to help me do it.

"*Someone's* going to jail for magical misconduct," I declare to no one in particular, my voice bouncing back to me with all the reassurance of a boomerang. "As soon as I figure out if that's a real thing."

Chapter 23

Dying sunlight filters through the blinds, casting long stripes across my desk, and I feel more like a shadow than a person. Everyone else left the office by noon for the holiday weekend, but not me. I've been sitting here, sifting through notes scrawled on legal pads, scribbles that now seem more like desperate pleas than leads, trying to make sense of Rhett's case... and the few cases the firm thinks I should focus on. But each note, each scribble, seems less like a lead and more like a desperate plea for answers that just won't come.

I glance at the clock. Two fifteen. No messages, no breakthroughs, just silence and a growing sense of futility.

But then, the shrill ring of my phone pierces the quiet space. Caller ID flashes Sara's name. My stomach tightens. *Finally.* After 24 hours of silence, she must still be livid after Monday's unintentional revelation of her witchy lineage to the entire supernatural council.

"Hey, Sara," I answer, bracing for impact.

"Can you come over?" Her voice is flat, and it sends a tremor of worry down my spine. That's not anger. That's something worse—disappointment.

"Sure thing. Give me fifteen minutes."

The office is deserted. The clacking of keyboards and murmured phone calls that usually fill the air have been replaced by eerie silence, like the world forgot about me and moved on.

"Happy holiday weekend," I mutter to myself as I head towards the elevators. Only Paige is there, reading a glossy magazine, waiting for calls from all those people who *don't* leave early for Thanksgiving.

For once, I'm one of the early-birds, but my fluttery stomach tells me Sara won't be sharing any turkey and cranberry sauce with me.

The drive to her house is a blur of red lights, honking horns, and rehearsed apologies, but finally, I'm standing on Sara's porch. Before I can knock, the door swings open. There he stands—Lucian, in all his undead glory, standing in the dimly lit hallway. His long black hair is tied back as usual, his face more solemn than a judge delivering a sentence.

"Lucian, wow, didn't expect to see you skulking around in daylight *again*. What's the occasion? Garlic sale at the farmer's market?" I quip, trying to defuse my nerves with humor.

No smile. He's not even humoring me. Instead, his voice is low, like it's weighed down with something heavy. "Emily."

A chill pricks at my resolve. If Lucian's this annoyed, things are worse than I thought. And suddenly, I'm not just worried about Sara being upset with me, I'm scared for what comes next.

I shuffle past Lucian into Sara's living room, my apology already tumbling out. "Sara, about Monday night—I never meant to—"

"Expose me?" Sara finishes flatly, her arms crossed over her chest as she leans against the fireplace mantel. She looks more like a statue than my friend, frozen in a place I'm not sure if I can reach.

I perch on the edge of Sara's well-worn sofa, hands twisted together in my lap. "I never meant to, Sara. I thought... I assumed some people already knew." I'm grasping at straws, and it sounds just as weak as I feel.

"Assumed?" Her hazel eyes narrow, cutting into me. "Emily, I've been careful. I've kept it under wraps so tightly, I even ditched my old name." The calm in her voice is worse than shouting, like she's given up.

My heart sinks a little more with each word. *Great job, Em.* Not only did you stir the pot, but you also splashed it all over someone trying to stay clean.

Lucian clears his throat, and the tension in the room ratchets up another notch. "It's typical Emily, isn't it? Charging forward, leaving wreckage in your wake without thinking about the consequences. It's the Widow Mitchell repeated."

The Widow Mitchell—when I'd been so sure she was the culprit, I pointed the finger before we had confirmation. In response, Peterson put the paranormals on a harsh lockdown, ones that didn't end until I finally exposed him.

"Hey," I bristle, guilt and anger flaring. "This is nothing like that. You all were on board with me going to the coven leaders for information. The curse is a ticking time bomb, remember?"

He stares me down, his steely eyes cutting through me. "Subtlety, Emily. Subtlety is an art. And what you did was no Rembrandt."

"Subtlety doesn't get answers, Lucian," I fire back. "Time isn't exactly on our side here."

Sara sighs, a sound like wind through autumn leaves, and straightens up. "What's done is done." She waves a dismissive hand, though her eyes don't quite meet mine. Her calmness is unnerving. There's no anger, no fire, just a cold resignation that makes my stomach sink. "Let's just focus on what we do next, okay?"

"Agreed," Lucian mutters, though his eyes linger on me, heavy with disapproval. I can almost hear the 'I told you so' hanging unspoken between us.

And I realize *why* I'd been keeping him at arm's length. Everything's snapped back into focus, like a cold slap to the face. His subtle overtures, the banter, the charm. It all had me reconsidering things. But now? His disapproval stings like an open wound. He sees me as reckless, impulsive Emily, the one who charges in without thinking, and I can't shake the feeling that maybe that's all he'll ever see. I hate it. I hate how his gaze makes me feel like I've let him down, like I'm the problem to be fixed, like I'm not enough. And that realization? It pisses me off.

Because who is Lucian to judge me? Sure, he's got his centuries-old wisdom and vampire grace, but I'm the one out here dealing with cursed families, werewolves, and ticking time bombs. I'm the one *trying* while he stands on the sidelines, critiquing my every move like some ancient art critic.

I bite back the urge to say something snarky, something that would cut. Sara is who matters right now.

"I am sorry," I say, forcing myself to look at Sara instead of Lucian, whose silent judgment is making my skin crawl. "I wasn't trying to expose you. I just thought—I didn't realize how tightly you'd kept it under wraps." My voice wavers, and I grit my teeth, trying to keep it steady. "I don't know if it helps at all, but if there's anything you need me to do to fix this, just say the word."

Sara shakes her head, her expression distant. "There's nothing you can fix," she replies, rubbing her temples as if trying to smooth away the tension in the room. "It's just... damage control, as usual. I'll have to explain things to a few people, and some of those conversations will be more complicated than others. But I'll deal with it." The resignation in her voice hits me like a punch. "I appreciate the apology, Emily. And I believe you mean it. But..." She trails off, her gaze drifting off somewhere I can't follow. "I need some time to figure out how I feel about it."

The room falls into a thick silence, and for a moment, I'm standing on the edge of something—something that feels like the end of whatever shaky friendship we managed to cobble together. I'm not sure I can fix this, and no amount of apologies will change that.

"What did you want to see me about?" I finally ask, desperate to change the subject before the impact of my mistake crushes me.

Sara motions for us to follow her into the kitchen. The sunlight streaming in through the windows feels at odds with the conversation we've just had. She leans against the counter, her arms folded tightly. "I checked out Oakheart Estate yesterday." There's a flicker of irritation in her eyes. "I was careful, and I made sure no one saw me."

I wince, pushing back a stray lock of hair that's escaped my bun. Unsaid is the understanding that *she* didn't out *my* investigation to the neighborhood. "Thanks for that."

"It's a joke," she says flatly. "No magic anywhere in that cellar. It was less 'ancient curse' and more... amateur hour at a yard sale."

"Excuse me?" My eyebrows shoot up. "Are you saying..."

"It wasn't magic. Not even close." Sara chuckles dryly, shaking her head. "All your Scooby-Doo jokes were apparently prophetic. This is guy-in-a-sheet levels of mundane. You need to find your curse elsewhere."

"Wait, no magic at all?" The pieces start falling into place, but they're not fitting the puzzle I thought I was solving. Rhett needs to hear this—stat. I'm already mentally composing the text message in my head. No supernatural shenanigans, just plain old human deceit. Classic.

"Looks like it." Sara shrugs, but there's a sharpness in her hazel eyes. "I couldn't get inside the house to check the room, so I can't rule out magic inside. But the cellar—those swords—are nothing, an old-fashioned trick to stir up fear."

"So, it might still come down to exposure," I say, the realization settling over me like a dark cloud. "That's what my initial clues pointed to. Whoever's behind this wanted to make enough noise to scare the neighbors and force the Baxters out into the open. The swords were just another tactic."

"Who benefits from that?" Sara asks.

I chew over the question, the cogs in my mind turning as I piece together the motives behind this elaborate ruse. "Someone who doesn't want the werewolves hiding in plain sight anymore," I say, a knot of worry forming in my stomach. "Someone who wants to force their hand."

Rhett had almost said as much nights ago. Would he. .. haunt himself? Does he have a witch friend of his own pulling the strings he threaded together?

"Someone who wants chaos," Sara adds, her voice flat but pointed. "And it worked. At least, they got to me."

"We still need to figure out who's behind this," I say, rubbing at my temples. "Someone went to a lot of trouble to make us think it was magic. We're missing something, something crucial. And I need to find out why."

Lucian finally speaks from his spot in the doorway, hiding from the sunlight. "Or maybe you just want to play hero, Emily," he says, his voice cutting through the room like a knife. "Again."

His accusation stings, and I fire back without thinking. "Playing hero is your job, Mr. Coven Leader. I'm just trying to solve a mystery."

"By trampling over everyone else's peace?" His gray eyes flash dangerously.

"Enough!" Sara steps between us, hands raised like a referee calling time-out. "Arguing solves nothing. If you want to solve this, you need to be delicate. Someone will realize we know the swords are faked. If they are a witch, they could escalate in another way. Something worse than exposure."

I give a quick nod in agreement. We're no closer to breaking the curse, and now there's the added tension of the damage I've done to Sara's trust. But Lucian? He can be disappointed. I've got bigger things to worry about.

"I can do quiet," I reply, though I'm not sure who I'm trying to convince. "We can go to Oakheart tonight and I'll stay as far under the radar as you need me to."

"We can't," Lucian says curtly. "The coven has business that needs attention."

I swallow hard, my chest tight. I glance at Sara, hoping for some kind of reassurance, but her gaze drifts away again, distant. She'll be there, she's part of the coven, after all.

"Of course." I force a smile. "I understand. The coven comes first."

Without waiting for their responses, I turn and head for the door. There's nothing left to say.

I drive aimlessly for what feels like hours, watching the city blur past through the windshield. People are out there laughing, meeting friends, grabbing drinks with people who actually text back. But me? I'm just... driving. Nowhere to go, no one to see.

I pull over to the side of the road, gripping the steering wheel until my knuckles turn white. The car is silent except for the ticking of the cooling engine, the city sounds muffled behind the windows. My phone is silent in the passenger seat, not a single message from anyone. Not Sara. Not Danielle. Not Matty. No one.

The isolation hits me harder than it ever has. My human friends bailed on me, leaving me to drown in my own mess. They barely understand the world I'm navigating now. And the supernatural side? Turns out, I'm just the clueless lawyer meddling in things I don't understand. An outsider. The one no one trusts. Not when all I seem to do is make things worse.

I blink back tears, but one slips out anyway. Great. *Just what I need, Emily Lane crying alone in her car like a scene from a bad rom-com.*

I swipe it away, furious with myself for feeling this way, for letting it get this bad. I thought I was helping people. I thought I was making a difference. But all I've done is push everyone away. Sara's disappointed, Lucian's angry, and I'm just... tired.

Work's all I've got left. But even there, the firm's benched me on the big cases. I'm stuck chasing down curses and paranormal drama, while my career slips through my fingers.

I let out a shaky breath and reach for my phone. *No more wallowing, Lane, remember? You don't give up. Ever.* I scroll through my contacts until Rhett's name comes up. If he's behind this mess, I need to figure it out. If not... well, he's the only one still taking my calls.

I hit "call," and the phone rings in the silence of my car, each ring louder and more accusing than the last.

"Emily?" His voice is clipped, like he's already regretting answering. "This better be good."

I almost hang up. I have nothing groundbreaking to report, just more proof I'm drowning in a sea of confusion. But I press on, swallowing down that sticky feeling of failure. "Turns out there's no magic in the cellar. It's just... trickery. Something mundane."

There's a long pause, the kind that makes me think I've made a huge mistake. "What do the cops say about that?" he asks, voice like sandpaper against my already-raw nerves.

"The cops?" I hesitate, feeling like I've made a misstep somewhere. "They aren't... involved."

Another heavy silence, and then Rhett's voice sharpens. "You said you were handling it, Emily. Getting those needed involved. Monday night you were going to sing it from the rooftops. How is that happening without the authorities?"

I swallow the urge to snap at him. He's irritated. I'm irritated. Not a great combination. "Rhett, the last thing you need is cops sniffing around Oakheart. They'll start asking questions you don't want to answer." I take a breath, trying to keep my voice steady. Alex and Sylvia looked ready to vivisect me when I was just chatting up the neighbors. If I go to the police, I'll be a skeleton in the Baxters' cellar. "The place is already tangled up in rumors," I say. "You don't want to add police reports to that."

"I'm not worried about a few rumors, Emily," he snaps. "I'm worried about whoever's behind this. We've got kids in the house, for Hades' sake. If that Harper curse—"

"It's not," I'm quick to interrupt. "It isn't the same curse. It's nothing. Not even magic."

He growls, the sound both irritated and long-suffering. "The cops should at least know that someone's been trespassing."

"I get it," I say, trying to sound calm when really, I'm just exhausted. "But bringing the police into this will only make it messier. They wouldn't know what to do with half of what's in that house. Besides," I soften my tone, hoping to ease the tension, "we don't even know what we're dealing with yet. Better to keep things quiet until we have something concrete."

Rhett's silence is thick with irritation. "So, what's your plan then, Emily? Because right now, it sounds like a lot of nothing."

I grit my teeth. "I'm following another lead," I say, faking confidence like I'm arguing in front of a jury. The truth is, my lead is more like a vague hope that I'll trip over something useful. And then, I should stop, but I can't hold it in. "Rhett, you said something Monday night at the coven meeting. Could you... are you holding something back on this?"

More silence. I hold my breath, waiting for the shoe to drop. He'd talked about exposure, about forcing the family out into the open. The curse, real or otherwise, gives him that, gift-wrapped with a bow.

When Rhett finally speaks, his voice is cold and sharp. "What are you saying?"

"The curse, mundane or not, would get you what you wanted at the meeting," I say, the accusation hanging in the air like an unpleasant smell.

"You think *I'm* behind this?" His voice drops, cold and sharp. "Emily, if I wanted to expose the family, I wouldn't be playing these stupid games. You think I'd waste time dressing up some basement like a haunted house? I have better things to do."

"It was just a thought. One of many."

"Well, that's the wrong one," he snaps, and there's a long, tense pause before he speaks again, calmer now. "But you may be on the right track that we should be looking even closer to home. Someone who wouldn't mind me being blamed."

"Trenton," I reply, following his train of thought. Trenton's resentment had been palpable—if anyone would set up a theatrical curse to make Rhett look bad, it'd be him. Unless Rhett wronged a stage magician in his past, Trenton is as good a guess as any. He was already angling for change. "Maybe he thinks it'll force everyone's hand, make people see how things are being run under your watch."

"It's not a bad lead," he says, sounding oddly subdued. "He's been so... angry. As though nothing I do is good enough. He hasn't been the same since I returned," he adds, unknowingly echoing what Trenton had said about him.

"I'll dig into the cellar again," I decide, my resolve firming. "See if I can find something to him, or anyone else."

His irritation resurfaces, sharp and clear. "You'd better. It's been weeks. You need to get it done."

I nod, even though he can't see me. "I'll get it done."

"I look forward to seeing you tonight," he says, though there's no sincerity in his tone. "Because this is your last chance or we'll be taking our money elsewhere."

My last chance? The words hit like a sucker punch. I swallow the lump in my throat, gripping the steering wheel so tight my knuckles ache. "You won't regret it," I say, though I'm pretty sure he already does. He hangs up before I can say more.

"Great start to the long weekend, Lane." I mutter to myself as I spin the wheel back towards the suburbs. "Of course, he hired a *lawyer* for a private investigator matter but sure, my fault for not figuring it out yet."

I hit the gas, heading out of the city, the lights fading behind me as the streets give way to open fields and dark, twisting trees. Oakheart's waiting, but somehow, the weight of what's really waiting for me—this mess, this isolation—it's heavier than anything I can face with just a flashlight and a tape recorder.

"Guess it's up to you, Emily," I say out loud, as if the empty car is going to give me the pep talk I need. "Oakheart isn't going to save itself."

CHAPTER 24

The sun's nearly down when I arrive at the threshold of Oakheart Estate's hidden cellar again, where the air is thick with the musky scent of secrets and mildew. It feels like stepping into the mouth of a beast that hasn't seen a dentist in a century. I take a deep breath—half expecting to inhale a cobweb—and flick on the flashlight app on my phone.

Every step down the creaky stairs is like the house itself voicing its protest, as if it knows what I'm about to uncover and isn't too happy about it. The beam from my phone cuts through the darkness, throwing exaggerated shadows against the walls. Because what this situation needs is more dramatic lighting.

At the bottom, I'm greeted by the swords. The supposed 'artifacts' that helped kick-start the chaos of this week. Not last week's mess, of course. Can't blame them for everything. But I would if I could.

I run my fingers along the cold stone walls, feeling for anomalies, dragging my nails across surfaces in search of hollow sounds. It's all very 'Shawshank Redemption,' except I'm hopefully not crawling through a river of *ahem* at the end of this. A loose brick or a draft would be super helpful right about now. My tape recorder clicks softly as I note down observations, knowing full well the eerie ambiance it adds to the entire scene.

I push aside a moth-eaten curtain to reveal... another wall. Because of course. The wall stares back at me, a mocking challenge in the sea of dust and cobwebs. Stubborn as I am, I don't back down from a staring contest, especially with an inanimate object that's likely hiding more than just dead spiders. My fingers trace the edges, searching for a catch or lever—a secret handshake with this old house.

"Where are you hiding?" I ask the room, half hoping it will answer back. It would give me a solid lead, at least. If I'm lucky, ghosts are touchy with their personal space and will come out to greet me. But no, the only thing talking back in this cellar is me.

My determination hardens like day-old gum on a shoe. I *will* find something down here even if I have to turn into a human dowsing rod. There's no other option. I tap, press, and knock on everything within arm's reach, enduring the symphony of echoes my actions inspire. If there's a hidden compartment playing hard to get, I'm about to turn into its worst nightmare.

I go onto my knees, wishing I'd changed out of my pencil skirt, and drag my fingers against the hole the wires vanish through. Wires mean there's something there. Even if it's just a crawl space.

And then... a click, soft as a whisper but as satisfying as a gavel striking wood, echoes in the cramped space. A section of stone gives way, no bigger than a breadbox, but still something.

"Ah-ha!" The exclamation leaps from my lips as I reach into the darkness like I'm about to pull a rabbit out of a hat—or, knowing my luck, a dead animal.

It unveils a false panel, and I tug at the edges until it swings open like the door to Narnia, if Narnia were less 'majestic lion and winter wonderland' and more 'potential tetanus risk.' But behind it lies a tiny passage, a narrow tunnel carved into the very bones of the estate, a few feet tall and wide. The air tastes of earth and mold, and I suppress the urge to sneeze. No need to bless the antisocial ghosts.

I get down on all fours, cursing my pencil skirt again for its lack of adventure readiness. I should've worn the pantsuit. As I crawl through the tight space, the claustrophobia is instant, the walls closing in like they want a piece of the legal action. It's so dark my eyes might as well be closed, and I half expect to bump heads with a skeleton. Instead, my hand encounters a spider web, and I do a silent scream because now is not the time for arachnophobia to make its grand entrance.

"Next time," I promise myself through gritted teeth, "I'm sending in a drone."

But then, the space widens, and the promise of discovery propels me forward. I can almost taste the truth. It's not sweet—it never is—but it's necessary. And I didn't claw my way up the legal ladder to balk at a little dirt under my nails, or fear in my throat.

"Almost there," I whisper, my voice steady despite the pounding of my heart. "This better be worth it."

The space widens further, and I wriggle out like a reluctant debutante from a limousine, emerging into a room with the charm of an interrogation cell. Blinking away the dust in my eyes, I take in the stark reality of wires snaking across the floor and walls lined with video cameras that stare back at me with unblinking, electronic eyes.

"Okay, this is less 'haunted mansion' and more 'Big Brother's creepy cousin,'" I quip to myself, trying to keep the edge off the chill creeping up my spine.

I step over a tangle of cables, my shoes clicking against the concrete floor, which feels too solid after the give of the earthen tunnel. The cameras are everywhere, their lenses trained on various angles, likely capturing every nook and cranny of Oakheart Estate.

It's strange, sure, but in a place like this, odd is practically the house specialty. There's no other entrance I can see, meaning there's another hidden panel in one of those walls, or whoever uses this room enjoys crawling through the dust. I barely fit in the space, though, so unless Noah dabbles in surveillance, there must be another entrance.

I step closer to the control panel, eyes narrowing as I notice a smaller set of screens positioned off to the side. They're all zeroed in on the cursed room, each monitor fixed on a different angle, like it's waiting for a grand performance.

And there, beside the screens, is a wooden box, with an intricately carved pattern around the edges, almost identical to the one I'd stumbled on that first night. The familiar curiosity tickles the back of my mind. I open it cautiously, and inside, nestled like a treasure, is a remote. I pick it up, turning it over, and that's when I spot it—one of the screws on the back is missing.

A little mental bell dings in my head. The box I found that first night—the one lined in iron—had a loose screw stuck in a corner. My brain starts connecting dots faster than I can process, and before I know it, I'm pressing the button on the remote.

The screens light up, and on them, the cursed room explodes in chaos. Furniture flies across the room as if yanked by invisible hands, curtains thrash wildly, and the entire scene looks like a storm hit it straight out of a horror movie. There's wind howling, lights flickering; all perfectly choreographed, all identical to every other night I've witnessed. Dust whips through the air, clearly meticulously reapplied for tonight's show. I swallow hard. I'm on the brink of a breakthrough or a breakdown, and I haven't decided which. Someone has been playing puppet master with *all* the alleged ghosts here, not just those blasted swords, and I'm betting it isn't Casper.

Static electricity prickles along my skin, buzzing up my arms and through my fingers, and my hair rises with it. The air is thick with the charge from whatever high-voltage magic wired into this room. It's like standing too close to a generator, the buzzing charge making my teeth hum. I realize just how much power it must take to pull this off, night after night, and the answer is clear as a spotlight.

None of this is supernatural. Not the swords, not the basement. And not the clearly fake curse. It's all mechanical, electric, a staged show that's all smoke and mirrors, powered by who knows what kind of tech.

All the clues narrow down to a single suspect, peeling away every other red herring tossed in my path.

The Baxters have their own personal electrician, someone who can wire anything from lamps to boats. The same guy who rewired the house for ethernet could just as easily slide something else into those walls. He's the one who plays with Tesla coils and causally mentions how they can transmit power wirelessly. The man who stopped his grouchy routine to help rig up Noah's cars with magnets and electricity so they can run on their own. Every one of those "little" hints—the convenient timing of each 'haunting'—it all screamed inside job.

The signs were all there, blinking at me like the neon lights of Moonlit Haven. Amy's 'buzzing' feeling when she was near the room, the static electricity. The screw I ignored. The unscented cat litter in a home without a cat—perfect for dust creation—that I didn't even question. Rhett's near-admission on Monday night I let him explain away. Even his denial today, which I should've pressed harder on instead of letting him steer me toward Trenton. It was all there, pointing to him. The realization settles, heavy and sharp.

How did I miss this?

"Rhett," I say, his name practically a curse. The pieces fit together with a sickening click. "You sly dog."

I don't have time to process anything else because I feel a presence just behind me, and I freeze.

"One of my proudest achievements," Rhett says, his voice as smooth and smug as a politician at a press conference. The reminder of my last dealings with a politician isn't a comfortable one.

I swallow hard and turn slowly, forcing myself to keep my face calm, even though my heart's racing like it's late for its own appointment. Rhett stands there, smirking, his eyes glinting in a way that makes my stomach twist.

"You deserve an Oscar nomination," I say, mustering all the bravado I can scrape together while my mind tries to figure out his angle now. "Truly. Creating an in-home haunted house that's more Amityville than reality TV takes talent."

His face doesn't change, not a flicker. "You have no idea."

"Bravo," I say, inching backward, giving him my best *I'm totally calm* grin. "But if you wanted this to have a prime-time audience, why hire someone who'd end up debunking it?" I watch his face, and suddenly it clicks. His family.

"Never mind. Now you get to keep your hands clean and your family's trust. I find out it's a ruse, but then we can blame someone else for it? Another coven? Magicless Amelia? Then good ol' dad will listen to your pleas about exposing the family for your 'safety,' the kids will keep idolizing you, and Trenton will have no basis to complain."

He lets out a dry laugh, a sound as hollow as crawlspace I came through. "Oakheart Estate has always been the talk of the neighborhood," he explains. "The 'weird Baxter place,' they call it, with the disappearing son. I told you before, it was our secrecy that let Roger die," he growls. "When I came back from St. Louis, I knew things needed to change, but my parents were determined to keep everything in the shadows. So, I gave them a curse," he says, making air quotes. "Something simple, a surefire way to get the curious masses knocking."

I glance around the room, gesturing to the cameras and cables. "Nothing about this is simple."

His smile is unnerving, like he's savoring the moment. "True. And yet, the neighbors kept brushing it off, looking away. So, I had to escalate." He takes a step closer, his gaze sharper than ever. "And that's where you came in."

His smirk deepens. "I needed someone who'd walk in here with a lot of noise and not much caution. Someone who'd kick up a fuss and make people *look*. I mean, look at you—*really* look at you." He crosses his arms, satisfaction oozing from every pore. "Dani sung your praises and that had me curious. Who was this human she thought was so special? And, damn, you're practically a one-woman spotlight. You're loud, *bold*, remember?"

"Not in *everything*," I mutter, but he's on a roll.

"Look at how you handled Peterson—headlines all over town. Then our city council meeting. You're unforgettable, even in a bad wig, chattering to yourself in the corner. Or your fake stint as the neighborhood historian. And let's not even start on your *activism*." He sneers. "Get Emily Lane here, and she'll make waves. Big, messy waves. I even figured you'd do something extra-judicial once you got a taste of Amelia's history. Breaking and entering didn't phase you with the Belmont case. What wouldn't you do this time? Give you a little leeway, and the neighbors would be dying to know what the Baxter family was hiding."

"But I didn't," I fill in for him. "I just forced you to change your plans. I didn't catch that the flower was a rose, hence the bunny trail about loss and relationships. And then I took the remote, which is why the 'curse' stopped for a few nights, isn't it?"

He nods, looking momentarily irritated before pride takes over again. "The iron box kept the remote's signal contained, free from interference. When you took it, I had to retool things, get the frequency working from a distance."

"And the message, yet another hint towards Amelia, right? About family and truth, all things hidden after Evelyn and Roger."

His hands tighten into fists. "It was a hint toward *anything*. A bloody message on the wall would surely loosen your lips. I needed you louder, and you weren't doing it right. Even when you started moving in the right direction, you knocked out Amelia as a suspect without making a peep. So, I had to escalate again."

"The swords," I say, my throat tight. The 'curse' Lucian would recognize because of Sara. "And since I debunked that, you're trying to push me toward Trenton? Can't imagine what other 'escalation' I interrupted this time."

He shrugs, almost casually. "I just needed a reason to get you here."

"Well, here I am. With no wild exposé, no media circus. Sorry to disappoint." I force a wobbly grin, keeping my voice steady as I swallow down the panic at being played. "Tell you what, I'll go to the press if that's what you're after. Maggie Hart from the news liked me. Or with a few whispers, I could make you the topic de jour of next week's book club. Whatever you want, client's choice."

Rhett's smile widens, an expression that makes my skin crawl. "Oh, Emily," he says, voice dripping with false sympathy. "It's too late for that."

A chill spreads through me as he steps closer, letting the silence hang in the air, enjoying every second of my unease. "Tonight's a full moon," he continues, almost casually. "And a dead lawyer found here in Oakheart, surrounded by a family of werewolves? *That* would get people talking."

I should have realized he would suggest something extraordinary. Someone who builds a haunted house studio just for kicks would want a grand finale. But murder? I have a strange urge to kick myself for ignoring Lucian's warning when we started on this job; I never predicted these consequences.

"Rhett," I say, trying to keep my tone light, like this is all just a bad idea we can laugh about later. "Let's skip the 'murder at the full moon' routine and brainstorm over breakfast tomorrow. I'll swing by first thing—I'll even bring a casserole. A little lawyer-client-thanksgiving. Assuming the stores are open, but—"

He raises a finger, shushing me with a smirk that's more terrifying than any of the 'hauntings' he rigged. "No need for speeches. You've already done your part. Now it's time for you to finish it."

My few weeks of self-defense classes will be no match against a brick wall in human form. I glance around, looking for any escape route, but the shadows seem to close in. There's probably a door somewhere behind him, but my only real exit is the crawlspace I came through.

And here I thought this case wouldn't end with me running for my life *again*.

CHAPTER 25

"You're forgetting something," I tell Rhett, my voice steady even though my pulse is going haywire.

Rhett stares at me, that cold smile spreading wider across his face. It's the kind of smile that says *game on.* He's calm, too calm.

"Is that so?" he asks, voice dripping with smug certainty.

"Your plan hinges on getting caught, right? We both know the city's trigger-happy when it comes to jailing paranormals," I say, channeling my best 'closing argument' tone. "They'll lock you up and throw away the key. You'll be puppy chow in no time, worse off than me."

He smirks, unfazed. "It's worth it."

I wilt like a snowman in a Chicago summer. Didn't that silly lawsuit against Rebecca show what lengths people will go to?

"Okay, but what about your family?" I ask, scrambling for a new angle. "They'll be dragged down with you. And... I know many people just as strong as you and they might not take kindly to this being my—" I gulp, "—my murder scene."

His smirk deepens, sinister as a Halloween mask. "You mean the people you threw under the bus Monday night?

Or your vampire partner?" He sneers. "If he cared, he'd have warned you not to come here alone on the full moon."

There's something deeper in his eyes, something far more twisted than I realized. My stomach drops as I recognize how far gone he really is. But just as I'm about to come up with another argument, footsteps echo through the hallway.

"Uncle Rhett?" Trenton's voice cuts through the tension, sounding a little confused. "I saw Emily's car outside. Great Granny is in one of her moods again. She'll probably go after Emily's calves if she's out. Do we need to lock the east wing?"

The footsteps grow louder, and I shuffle back toward the crawlspace. Rhett bares his teeth at me, and with the way the scar cuts across his face, he looks downright dangerous.

"Is this some kind of secret room?" Trenton's voice floats in from somewhere behind me, getting closer with every word. And then, as if on cue, a panel in the wall slides open, depositing him into the room like some kind of bewildered delivery. He stumbles forward, glancing back as the wall swings shut seamlessly, blending right back into place.

If I weren't, you know, about to die in here, I might actually be impressed with the craftsmanship.

Trenton stares at us like he's stepped into an alternate universe. "What... what is this?"

Rhett's expression hardens. "Trenton," he drawls, "excellent timing. Emily's going to help me with a task tonight. You can help too."

Trenton's gaze flicks between us, confusion twisting his face. "What are you talking about?"

I force a smile, barely holding my fear at bay. "Oh, you know. Just a little family bonding time in the creepy horror show Rhett's got going here. Nothing says love like plotting a good murder, right?"

Trenton's brows furrow, his eyes darting from me to Rhett. "Uncle Rhett... what are you doing?"

Rhett stands tall, his face cold and sharp. "What our family's always done, Trenton. Making hard choices. Leading the coven when things get tough. You've wanted leadership, you've wanted to prove yourself. This is your opportunity, Trenton. We must take necessary steps to bring our pack into the future. That's all you've wanted, right?"

"I wanted... like, fewer curfews and cable, maybe knock you down a peg," Trenton mumbles, his frown deepening. "Not—"

"Not exposure?" Rhett interrupts. "Of course you do. You want out of the dark, then take this step with me into the light. We let the world know who we are and what we're capable of. We won't be paranormals with 'fewer rights' anymore. We'll be powerful. Feared."

"More like imprisoned," I cut in, giving Trenton a desperate look. "You want responsibility? Freedom? This isn't the way. Take a few online courses in leadership, introduce yourselves to the neighbors, start fresh. Move out, go public. But don't kill someone."

Rhett's confidence doesn't waver, and for a terrifying moment, I see how absolutely certain he is. "Trenton will help, Emily," he says with a smugness that makes my skin crawl. "He understands loyalty. *He* understands family," he finishes with a look that says I don't.

But Trenton's face isn't a sure thing—he's skeptical, hesitant. There's a flicker of doubt there that has me thinking, for just a moment, that maybe he's on my side. Trenton's been angry, pushing back against Rhett since I met him. Just maybe, he's about to do it again.

Then I remember what Sylvia revealed, how Trenton had idolized Rhett as a kid, that photo of them with Rhett as his hero, larger than life. Rhett's words settle in the silence, and I can see Trenton's doubt fading, his shoulders loosening as if the pull of loyalty is outweighing his anger.

"Trenton," I press, desperation creeping into my voice. "You don't have to do this. You don't have to follow Rhett down this path. You have your own mind, your own choice here."

"Trenton," Rhett growls, "it's time you stepped up for this family. Be the man Roger raised you to be."

Rhett's body starts to tremble, his muscles twitching and his shoulders hunching forward. It's horrifying watching the change start. Rhett's face contorts, bones shifting beneath his skin as his eyes go feral. He snarls, half at me, half at Trenton, who looks as horrified as I feel.

"Trenton, you're part of this," Rhett says, his voice a low growl as his body bends and reshapes itself. He's turning, and it's the most terrifying thing I've ever seen. "Do what's right for the family!"

The sight of Rhett's transformation is so grotesque I nearly freeze. His body contorts, bones cracking and shifting like they're made of rubber. His face warps, teeth sharpening, eyes turning wild. It's like watching a horror movie without the safety of the 'it's only a screen' buffer. And that's when I realize I have a small window now, also known as the crawlspace, and I'm not sticking around for Act Two.

I don't think. I dive, scrambling on hands and knees, the rough stone floor scraping my palms and knees raw, but right now, I'd take scrapes over claws any day. Behind me, Rhett's voice drops into a deep, guttural growl, and that snarl echoes down the tunnel, bouncing off the walls and making my hair stand on end.

I squeeze myself deeper into the crawlspace, shoving forward as fast as I can, feeling every jagged edge and dirt clump under my hands. The snarls grow louder, closer, echoing like I'm being chased by a freight train with teeth. I don't dare look back, because looking back could mean slowing down, and I can't die here.

A howl so close it nearly knocks the scream out of me makes me shove myself forward even harder, my heart slamming in my chest like it's trying to break free and run for it. Darkness presses in, dirt clings to my hands, and I keep clawing forward, desperate to reach the other side.

I burst out of the crawlspace and into the cellar, practically tripping over myself as I scramble to my feet, lungs burning and legs shaking. But I can't stop, not with Rhett behind me, so I sprint through the cluttered cellar, dodging dusty shelves, boxes, old furniture. The stairs are just ahead of me, promising freedom, and I can hear him snarling and scratching his way closer.

My feet hit the stairs, and I'm half-running, half-crawling up them, one hand clinging to the stone wall while I drag myself up, praying that no unhinged werewolves are waiting on the other side. My lungs are on fire, but I don't stop. I burst out the door like a cannonball shot from a cannon that's decided it's had enough of this world, gasping and gulping in the frigid night air. But there's no time to savor the relief of freedom, so I keep running, racing across the grounds like the devil himself is nipping at my heels. Which, let's be honest, he sort of is.

Now would be a great time for a hobgoblin to pop out of a bush or something, I think wildly, absurdly, as I tear across the grass. Because if there's ever a moment for supernatural backup, it's right now.

My heels sink into the wet grass, slowing me down, and I can practically feel Rhett getting closer, breathing down my neck. In one frantic, desperate move, I kick them off, stumbling forward in bare feet, the cold, damp earth squishing under my toes. My skirt tugs at my thighs, twisting and pulling with every step, but I grit my teeth and keep going, ignoring the sting of every snag, every tear.

Behind me are heavy thuds—big, lumbering, and getting faster. I don't look back. I can't. My legs are burning, my lungs feel like they're about to explode, and yet I just keep running, pushing harder, because the alternative is stopping, and that's not an option.

And then, just to make this sprint even more dramatic, my life flashes before my eyes in little snapshots. Missed lunches with friends, nights at work that stretched on too long, phone calls I ignored because I was "busy." My mind flickers to Sara, to Lucian, to Stardust and Ray, Megan and Matty, even Danielle. All people with a network, a family, a coven. And Rhett, willing to commit horrific acts in some twisted desire to help his family. They have something I've never had—people who'd rally behind them, people who'd share their burdens.

Six weeks. That's all I had, really. And maybe if I'd tried harder, there'd have been more. Regret mixes with the terror in my gut, and I think, *Maybe if I'd spent less time at work, less time putting my desires first, and more time with people who actually care, I wouldn't be here right now, running for my life in bare feet on a lawn.*

It's stupid, of course—no amount of heartfelt dinners would change the fact that I'm being chased by a murderous werewolf—but the thought still stings. I could be at a coven meeting, or a 'Friendsgiving,' or *anywhere* but alone at a werewolf's house on the full moon.

Then, just as I think I might actually make it, when the front gates are looming before me, something hot and sharp slices across my calf. It's quick, fiery, a tearing pain that lights up my nerves like a warning siren, and I know instantly—*claws.* That one word flashes through my mind, terror crackling right behind it. My legs buckle, and I stumble forward, my balance gone as I crash down. The ground rushes up to meet me, the world tilting and spinning like a nightmare carnival ride I never signed up for. My thoughts scatter, tumbling one over the other, and I think again of all the things I never did, all the people I didn't appreciate enough, all the goals that never mattered.

The regret is so bitter it sticks in my throat, and the last thing I feel is that gnawing, aching sense of everything I'll never get to fix.

And then, just like that, the world goes black.

CHAPTER 26

The first thing I notice is the ceiling. Sterile white, dotted with little holes that could be hiding a hundred years' worth of dust and germs, and possibly a small family of spiders. I blink, adjusting to the sharp lights and an antiseptic smell so sharp it could scrub memories from my brain. The second thing I notice is the throbbing in my leg, which feels like it's been tenderized by a mallet, and a dull ache that stretches from my head down to my toes. My mouth feels like I swallowed a cactus, and my head's pounding like it's doing a drum solo.

So... not dead. That's a start.

I shift a little, taking in the room. There's an IV drip stuck in my arm and a monitor humming softly beside me. I've seen hospital rooms enough times to recognize it, but waking up in one is a novel experience. My vision clears, and I spot someone beside me, dressed in all white, with a scrunched-up halo of silver hair covering their face.

My first thought is ridiculous, my second no better. *Is this an angel? Or the paranormal welcome committee here to tell me I didn't make it?* Because if I'm actually dead and stuck in some post-life waiting room, I'm going to need to have a word with management.

Then the "angel" turns toward me, and it's Amy, looking half-dead herself. She's also in a hospital gown, hair a tangled mess, and dark circles under her eyes that look like she's auditioning for *Night of the Living Dead.*

"Amy," I croak out, my voice scratchy. "Did I miss the memo about the hospital pajama party?"

She gives me a weak smile, and there's a look of relief in her eyes that makes me think maybe things were worse than I thought. "You're awake," she says, like there was a decent chance I wouldn't be.

"Barely," I mutter, shifting again and feeling a sharp twinge in my leg. "So... not to gloss over the very appreciated bedside vigil and all, but what happened? Last thing I remember, I was trying not to trip over my own feet and become werewolf food."

Amy sighs, leaning back in her chair as though the effort of sitting up is almost too much. "It was rough for a minute." She frowns, like she's mentally arranging the bullet points. "While you were crawling out of the cellar, Trenton found me and told me everything. We both ran outside to cut off Rhett before he got you."

I blink at her. "Trenton?" So glad being an accessory to murder wasn't on his to-do list, because I remember it being a little touch-and-go. "Okay. And then you both just... reasoned with Rhett?"

Because the man/monster I left didn't look like he had a single reasonable hair left anywhere on his hairy body.

She lets out a laugh, low and dry. "No. I... I had to flex my magic skills."

"Skills?" I say, brows rising, which just makes my head hurt more. "You could cast a spell?" After all, wasn't she telling me only a few nights ago she knew as much magic as a rock?

"Yeah," she says, almost shyly. "It was always there, like I thought. But last night, I don't know. I really, *really* wanted it, wanted to stop him. And, well, it worked. I zapped him in the back."

"Hold on," I say, raising a finger. "If you knocked him out, why am *I* here?"

Amy glances down at my leg. "Rhett got a solid bite on your calf before I could stop him. And you... fell. You were knocked out, and they were freaking out about a concussion."

Of course. I escape a werewolf attack only to get taken down by gravity.

"Figures," I mutter, sinking back against the pillow. "So let me get this straight: you saved me from becoming Rhett's midnight snack by tapping into a magic power you've never used before?"

"Basically," she says, managing a little smile, which looks a bit proud. As she should be.

"Alright, so why are *you* here?" I ask, gesturing to her gown and the general "about to collapse" vibe she's giving off.

"Magical exhaustion," she says with a sheepish little shrug, like it's no big deal. Her gaze shifts down, and she twirls a loose thread on her hospital gown. "I... well, I sacrificed some of my energy to knock him out. Turns out, magic isn't big on freebies."

I let out a low whistle, feeling a newfound respect. "Guess I owe you double thanks—and sorry for not mentioning the whole 'magic requires sacrifice' part earlier. I probably could have offered that up when we were talking about Amelia."

Amy lets out a little laugh, waving her hand dismissively. "No big deal."

"Wait," I say, waving my hands, which I can now see are covered in tiny bandages and iodine. My mind is clearly racing as fast as a snail. "The hospital is treating you for magical exhaustion? Your grandparents *let* you come to a regular hospital?"

"No," she says. "The hospital thinks its regular exhaustion. And Dani kind of forced them to take me when they brought you in."

"Dani?" I feel like a parrot with all these echoes.

"She came after the paranormal police took Rhett."

I stare at her, processing. "The paranormal police?"

Honestly, I can't keep doing this. I'm past shock at this point, but even I have limits.

Amy grins, looking equally exhausted but satisfied. "For real. Great Granny called them. Turns out the attempted murder didn't faze them, but the 'honor' crimes against the coven were a no go."

"I knew it," I mutter, shaking my head and regretting it instantly. "I *knew* there had to be some kind of paranormal law enforcement out there." Although knowing that *attempted murder* is fine, but betraying your coven isn't makes me a little leery of trying to practice in any of *their* courts.

I sink back against the pillow, letting it all sink in. I'm alive, saved by Amy's last-minute magic, and Rhett's cooling his paws with the paranormal police. If I hadn't just bashed my head on the ground, I'd think this whole thing was some fever dream.

A knock on the door is another clue that this is reality. But it's the people who walk in that give it away—two faces I'd never expect to see together outside the courthouse or maybe a sitcom: Danielle and Megan.

They look oddly right standing next to each other. Megan's box braids fall loose around a bright pink bustier, a bold contrast to her smooth, deep brown skin. Meanwhile, Danielle, in her usual style-defying logic, is rocking a lime-green sundress dotted with tiny strawberries, ignoring the fact that it's practically winter outside. Together, they look like some kind of fashion mash-up—a bold, spring-themed duo in the middle of my sterile, fluorescent hospital room.

Amy stands up, still looking woozy, and gives Danielle a quick hug. "Morning visiting hours must have started," she says to the room. "Gotta get back before Grandma and Grandpa show up."

And then she leaves me with people I thought could be my two biggest cheerleaders, even if they were rooting for different teams.

Until Tuesday night, that is.

Concussed or not, I still have my pride, and I raise an eyebrow at Megan. "Don't you have family to get to? It's a holiday."

Megan rolls her eyes, her expression softening. "Visiting a friend who was almost murdered kind of trumps dinner with relatives I see every year. Besides," she smirks, "Matty was here for the first near-death experience. It's my turn."

I let out a snort. "Guess that means Brian's got dibs for the next one," I say, a little too flippantly. Megan doesn't find it funny.

"Emily, that's not—" Megan stops, clearly not in the mood for jokes. "Let's just keep it at two near-misses, okay?"

Danielle clears her throat and steps in, looking from Megan to me with a gentle patience I can't quite believe I deserve. "Don't worry, Emily," she says with a small wink, "now that I know how much trouble you are, I've got the network engaged." Her eyes slide to the walls. Without my glasses, I can't see any hobgoblins lurking there, but I get the meaning.

I glance between them, my heart doing an odd little flutter. "Right, so...Danielle, Megan. Megan, this is Danielle. Cop meet defense lawyer, I guess."

The two of them exchange a smile, Megan extending a hand. "Nice to meet you, Danielle. Any friend of Emily's, etcetera, etcetera."

Danielle laughs, shaking her hand. "Good to meet you too, Megan."

"How'd you two meet?" Megan asks, tipping up her glasses. "Girl here hasn't been much for socializing until recently."

I open my mouth to shoot back something witty, but I can't quite find the energy. She's not wrong, after all.

Danielle jumps in. "I was tangentially involved in her work with Lucian's case."

Megan's smile tightens, and she glances at me, her brows raised. "You got caught in that supernatural drama?"

"I'm part of it actually," Danielle says, in her usual warm tone. "I'm a werewolf."

The room freezes. Danielle keeps her gentle smile while Megan's face runs through a dozen expressions. My mind races back to the casual remarks Megan made right before I took Rhett's case, her hesitation when I suggested a night at Moonlit Haven. My two worlds colliding, and I don't know how Megan's going to take it.

Megan finally manages a shaky smile. "Nice to meet you. I'm... a Gemini."

For a beat, the room hangs in awkward silence, like we're all holding our breath. Then Danielle lets out a laugh, and even Megan's lips twitch into a smirk.

"Don't worry, Megan," Danielle says, her voice kind but amused. "You're safe here. It's not a full moon or anything." She shoots me a look, one that's scolding and a little mischievous at the same time. "Besides, I only bite if I'm asked nicely."

That breaks the remaining tension, and I manage a snort-laugh, wincing as my head throbs. When white spots stop dancing in my eyes, I glance at Megan, whose grin is a little more genuine, but she still looks like she's got a hundred questions.

"Good to know," she says, aiming for light, though her voice betrays just a bit of wariness. "I guess I've just got some catching up to do on Emily's... circle."

"You and me both," I mutter, rubbing a hand over my face, still groggy. My leg aches, a gentle reminder that I'm not exactly bouncing back after the ordeal. I can feel both of them watching me, concern practically radiating off them, and it makes me pause. The memory of my sprint across the Baxter lawn flickers in my mind. The regrets that piled up as I ran for my life.

Danielle's gentle smile fades, replaced with something softer. "What's going on?"

"You mean besides the aftermath of a werewolf mauling?" I let out another laugh, less painful this time, but it sounds hollow, even to me. Neither of them bites, and I feel my shoulders slump, the weight of everything settling over me. "Yeah, I... well, just before I blacked out, I had one of those 'life flashing before my eyes' moments." I try to keep my tone light, but my voice cracks slightly. "I thought about... well, my life and... all the people in my life. You all have people—friends, family, whole networks. You've got support systems, people to lean on. I'm no good at that."

Danielle sits down beside me, holding my hand in hers. Her expression is soft, and I prepare myself for some kind of gentle greeting card wisdom. Instead, she snaps, "What is wrong with you?"

I blink, thrown completely off balance. I turn to Megan for support, but she's nodding, her chin set in a way that says she agrees with Danielle's opinion, whatever it may be.

"Excuse me?" I manage.

Danielle raises an eyebrow, giving me a look that makes me feel about three inches tall. "You heard me. What's wrong with you, thinking you're all alone in this? Do you see where we are right now?"

Megan leans forward, her arms crossed, looking at me with that unyielding stare she usually saves for overpaid expert witnesses. "You're not alone, Emily. But you seem to have this little... habit of deciding you are."

I stare at them, half offended, half speechless. "Look, I wasn't trying to be a martyr or anything," I say defensively. "I'm just saying that for a long time, I didn't have... well, this." I gesture around at the hospital room, at them both. "People who would actually drop everything to check on me. I was all about work, you know that. And I've been trying, with Tuesday night drinks, with dinners. But whatever I've been doing to build those 'connections' isn't working. Because my roots with you all are shallow." I cross my arms, feeling a little mulish. "It's not like I got any invitations this week. So, yeah, the 'me, myself, and I' routine isn't something I made up."

Danielle narrows her eyes, unimpressed. "And whose fault is that, Emily?" She gives me a gentle shake. "You don't exactly put yourself out there. You're trying, but are you really? You've never asked to spend time with me, it's always me reaching out. And even when I do, when I welcome you into my home, it's like you're expecting it to be the last time. I mean, half the time I see you with anyone, it's like you're holding your breath, waiting for people to let you down."

Megan nods. "Exactly. You could have, I don't know, *told me* you were bummed about Tuesday night. You could have invited us over for Friendsgiving or something."

"I mentioned my youngest cousin was being a handful," Danielle adds, rolling her eyes. "I could have used an escape today. Spending it with you *outside a hospital room.*"

"It's like you're expecting us to disappear or bail at the first sign of trouble," Megan says, "and then you can feel depressingly vindicated when we do, at poor lonely Emily." She pauses, looking pointedly at me. "But we're still here, aren't we?"

Embarrassment wants to rise, so I cling to my defenses. "Well, excuse me for not knowing I had a fan club," I mumble, the sarcasm weak even to my own ears. But Megan's right: I haven't put myself out there. What Sara'd told me when I decided to do this 'paranormal thing' had me open the doors to not just paranormals but to others. But I wasn't knocking on any doors myself.

I have this habit of waiting for people to reach out first, of keeping everyone at arm's length, so if they leave, it'll sting just a little less. That's why Tuesday night hurt so much, I felt like I tried and got shot down. Same with Lucian, I'd finally warmed to his flirtations, and he did an about-face too.

Megan softens, but only a little. "I'm going to let some of this *literal stupidity* slide, seeing as you're still recovering from a werewolf attack and all. And because I overheard one of the nurses say you're experiencing pretty severe sleep deprivation," she says.

That might explain some of the choices I've made recently.

I sit there, letting their words sink in, trying to ignore the uncomfortable prickling behind my eyes. "Okay," I finally say. "So—" I clear my throat, "—who's up for celebrating this non-death of mine? Once I'm out of this hospital bed—"

"And slept for at least a full night," Danielle interjects mildly.

"—I'll invite you out somewhere," I finish.

"Good," Megan says, patting my arm. "And maybe next time, you'll realize we're here for you before you have to get mauled to believe it."

I nod, the weight in my chest lifting. It's not some sweeping revelation or a sappy epiphany. It's just... nice. Simple. Like the warmth you feel coming back inside after a bitter cold.

"Deal," I say. "Now let me tell you all about this so-called curse."

"I know your type," the doctor is saying on her rounds after Danielle and Megan left, "because I'm the same. You want to jump right back into things."

The doctor's voice drones on about sleep and stress management, and I try to focus. I do. But it's hard when she's talking about life as if it's some neat package of hours and healthy habits I can stack up in a row, one right after the other.

"Aim for seven to nine hours of sleep," she says, and I nearly laugh. When's the last time I clocked anything close to that? I can't remember the last time I slept for more than five. And since meeting Rhett, I think I got a solid two. Lawyers, like doctors, don't just sleep and relax—we refuel on coffee, power through days, and schedule recovery time between cases. When did I last take a real vacation? When did I last not check my email at 3 a.m.?

"Chronic stress can weaken your immune system. You should find a regular outlet," she's saying, the words slipping in and out as my mind wanders.

Sure, doc. Self-defense class has its benefits, but my most effective stress reliever is both illegal and super awkward, thanks to the Lucian fiasco.

And, 'stressed' is the life I chose. Fourteen years ago, I stepped onto this path—the one that has me chasing deadlines, swimming in paperwork, and, occasionally, running from werewolves. It's not exactly a "wellness retreat" kind of gig. I went into law for stability, validation, security. After Lucian's case, I told myself there was more to it, that it could be about connection and standing up for those who don't have anyone. But I couldn't shake the safety net I'd built. I wanted to have it all. Instead, I'm floundering at work and, clearly, not excelling at being a friend. I'm on my way to fixing that last part, once I make amends with Sara and put myself out there. But the job? That's something entirely different.

And my mind catches on a thought, as sharp as a paper cut.

Why am I doing this to myself?

I've poured everything into this career because I'm supposed to. It's how I keep myself safe. But here I am, exhausted, stretched thin, barely treading water. When I try to live up to the promises I've made—to Danielle, to Sara, to Stardust—I'm drowning. Or more like, Johnson & Marcus holds my head under water.

The doctor's talking about immune systems and meditation, but the words aren't sinking in. Because deep down, I know the truth: my job isn't making me healthier, and it isn't making me happy. Maybe—no, definitely—it's time for a change.

If I were to quit, I could do the paranormal thing full-time. Actually help people who need it, who exist outside the protection of any court. Maybe even dip my toe in that whole 'paranormal police' thing. The Baxter case was a disaster, but Rebecca's wasn't. Lucian's wasn't. Those were something. I could fight real battles without dealing with Haskins, Lawrence, and Davenport breathing down my neck. It'd be messy, for sure. But it'd be mine.

"Emily?" The doctor's looking at me expectantly, snapping me back to reality.

"Right," I say, nodding, pretending I caught every word. "Seven to nine hours of sleep. Stress management. Got it." But in my mind, the wheels are turning.

I think I already know what I need to do.

CHAPTER 27

Saturday evening, and my living room is a chaotic mess of takeout containers and abandoned mugs—a fitting backdrop for my new life as a soon-to-be ex-bigshot-lawyer. A few weeks of non-stop work and even my usual half-hearted attempts at cleaning have fallen by the wayside.

"Herle," I call to the walls, mostly out of habit now, "if you'd ever like to tidy up while I'm gone, I wouldn't mind. I'll even buy you those fancy truffles, the ones hobgoblins supposedly love." I pause, waiting for a sign, a single scratch in the walls that might tell me he's more than just a figment of paranormal gossip. But there's only silence.

If Herle were real, maybe he'd wonder where I've been the last two nights. If only the answer was something better than "recovering from a werewolf mauling."

Fresh from my hospital release, I wasted no time messaging Sara to schedule lunch. It went surprisingly well, all things considered. She gave me a harsh lecture, as if my ears hadn't already been boxed in by Megan and Danielle. But the worry told me she still cared and that our friendship still has a chance. She also passed on well wishes from Stardust and the others. Afternoon visiting hours aren't exactly vampire-friendly, even with sunset at 4:30 nowadays. And apparently getting to the hospital without being redirected to the blood bank is a hassle. Just another thing to add to my list, now that I'll have all this free time.

I turn back to the laptop on my coffee table, where my resignation email to Johnson & Marcus waits for my final blessing. My mind wanders to all the angles I've worked through, but ultimately, it's a no-brainer. My savings account has been growing dust-free thanks to my frugal ways, and Danielle's meeting me tomorrow to talk through potential new clients. Paranormal clients. *Genuine cases*, vetted this time.

The letter on the coffee table is another push forward. Mrs. Jennings' husband is on the board of some fancy-pants bank, and she apparently repeated my book club spiel to him. After what I can only imagine were *very* polite but relentless demands from her, the bank is planning to revise their account requirements to include paranormals. It's sort of like how immigrants and non-citizens can get accounts—definitely not perfect, but it's a start, and infinitely better than stuffing cash under a mattress.

With a deep breath, I hit *Send*. It's done. I'm out. Free to dive headfirst into work that doesn't come with memo reminders and bonus evaluations. Free to tackle whatever the paranormal world throws my way next. For better or worse.

The doorbell rings, pulling me from my victory lap in front of the screen. I kick a pile of takeout boxes into the trash and stack the mugs precariously in the sink. After smoothing down my long hair and trying not to look too much like someone whose last snooze was medicated—the oversized law school t-shirt and sweatpants surely not helping—I swing open the door.

Lucian stands there, looking annoyingly perfect, his dark eyes taking me in with that almost smile he loves to employ.

"Emily," he says, voice a low rumble.

"Lucian," I reply, trying for nonchalance but probably landing somewhere between a smirk and a gawk. A few days away have softened the sting of our last conversation, and Megan's blunt observations have given me a little clarity. Maybe I *was* just waiting for him to criticize me—so I could push him away without feeling guilty or worrying about things getting close to serious.

He steps closer, studying me with a look that's warm an d... concerned? "Sara let me know you were discharged this morning. I thought I'd come by to check on you."

"Yeah, you know how it is," I say, aiming for breezy. "Some people curl up with a good book. I thought I'd spend my evening in the woods with a werewolf."

He shakes his head. "Had I known that's where you were going after you left Sara's place that night, I'd—"

"Don't worry about it," I interrupt, brushing off the concern. "Bad choices are on me. Blame exhaustion, stress—whatever makes it sound less stupid."

His smile dims, his gaze flicking to my leg. "I heard you were hurt."

Without thinking, I bend down and pull up the leg of my sweats, revealing the four stitched gouges running across my calf. He drops to one knee, examining the stitches closely, his face unreadable.

"How long until you heal?" he asks softly, his fingers hovering close, almost brushing my skin.

Flushing, I tug the fabric back down. "A few weeks, maybe a month."

He stands, clasping his hands behind him, his expression unreadable. "I'm glad there wasn't more damage."

"You and me both," I say with a sigh. "Now I just need to find a stress reliever that doesn't involve full moons or sharp claws."

He raises an eyebrow. "Stress relief? I seem to remember you had a few... unconventional methods for that. Except one, which stuck." His gaze dips to my neck, a spark of mischief in his eyes.

I smirk, crossing my arms, the ease of talking to him returning easily. "Funny. Turns out TV marathons and wine aren't doctor-recommended coping mechanisms. And as for the other... I think I've moved on from vices. Just looking for good things now."

He's quiet for a moment, his expression softer than before. Just as I wonder if I've said too much, someone clears their throat behind him.

"Matty!" I say, ducking around Lucian to greet him. He stands there, holding two six-packs of beer, his expression softening as he looks at me. He lifts the six-packs a bit, as if to say, *Look, I come bearing gifts.* Lucian steps back slightly, giving us space as I squeeze Matty's arm in greeting.

"Matty, have you met Lucian?" I gesture between them.

"Not formally, but I certainly remember him," Matty says, giving Lucian a polite nod. "Good to see you again."

"Likewise," Lucian replies, a knowing look in his eyes. "You're one of Ms. Sinclair's finest, as I recall." Ms. Sinclair, the district attorney who charged Lucian with murder.

Before things can get too awkward, Megan and Brian show up, chattering as they approach.

I grin and wave them in. "Guys, this is Lucian. Lucian, meet Megan and Brian. Welcome to the law school post-hospital recovery party I'm hosting." Calling it a 'party' might be overstating it, considering the chips are still in the bag and the wine came from a gas station clearance shelf. But it's the first time I'm having people over who weren't here for a one-night stand. Or in hopes of *becoming* one.

"OMG I cannot *wait* to raid your closets," Megan says with a smirk. "We can finally give up the pencil skirts and get you into something fashionable."

"Do you think Herle knows Pietre?" Brian asks, following Megan through the entry and into the apartment. Matty eyes Lucian for another long second before trailing in behind him.

Lucian hovers on the threshold, glancing over his shoulder like he's ready to make a graceful exit. "Well," he says with a soft smile, "I should let you get back to your evening."

Before he can step away, I'm somehow calling after him. "Lucian?"

He stops, looking back with a slight tilt to his head.

"Maybe we could... do dinner sometime?"

His gaze shifts to my neckline, that familiar glimmer of amusement lighting his eyes.

I wave my hands, trying to clarify. "Not my neck! I mean dinner like dinner, not your kind of dinner. I'm trying to put myself out there." My cheeks heat. This isn't getting easier. "Just, you know, as friends. A casual outing," I finish.

His lips curve into a genuine smile, and he nods. "I'd like that, Emily. As friends." With one last look, he turns and heads down the steps, disappearing into the early evening.

The door closes, and I turn to find Megan watching me with a grin that's somewhere between impressed and mischievous.

"Damn, he's gorgeous in person," she says, shaking her head. "I wouldn't mind letting him suck on my neck."

I roll my eyes, suppressing a smile. "Trust me. It's more trouble than it's worth."

Everyone laughs, and the warmth of it fills the room. As I look around, something settles in me, a quiet sense that maybe I'm exactly where I'm meant to be.

AUTHOR'S NOTE

Thank you for reading COVENS AND CURSES, book 2 in my Emily Lane Paranormal Mysteries series.

If you're interested in more of my writing, check out my website (**kmalady.com**). You can find other fun information there about my other projects, like *The Ascend Trials* (a romantic YA portal fantasy all about subverting tropes), *Threads of Fate* (an NA romantic fantasy series adapted from greek myths), and more!

EMILY LANE WILL RETURN

After another nap.

www.ingramcontent.com/pod-product-compliance
Lightning Source LLC
Chambersburg PA
CBHW061642190726
48289CB00006B/1711